"Fire!"

"One tube fired." Howarth looked up, horror-struck at what had just been done, but Henderson gave him no time for guilt.

"Shut the bow tube doors."

"Bow tube doors shut."

Henderson stared around at the officers and men in the control room, challenging anyone to question his last action. Nobody dared, realizing that there had been no alternative.

"Soviet torpedoes four thousand yards and still latched on to decoys," Lt. Crooke called out from sonar. "Our own torpedo.... fifty seconds to impact."

Fifty seconds. Seconds when the Soviets might try their own decoys. It was the first offensive weapon used by *Saturn*, designed to clear a path as well as intimidate.

"Fifteen seconds to impact, track good.... Five seconds to impact...."

They heard the explosion...

THE SATURN EXPERIMENT

THE SATURN EXPERIMENT

Peter Shepherd

WARNER BOOKS

A Warner Communications Company

This Warner Books Edition was originally published in England by
WH Allen & Co., 44 Hill Street, London W1X 8LB

Cover art by Marc Eriksen
Cover design by Mike Stromberg

Warner Books, Inc.
666 Fifth Avenue
New York, N.Y. 10103

Ⓦ A Warner Communications Company

Printed in the United States of America

First Warner Books Printing: June, 1989

10 9 8 7 6 5 4 3 2 1

— FOREWORD —

During 1982, a Soviet submarine was beached outside Stockholm. In early 1983 a suspected Soviet submarine was located in the Hardangersfjord, Norway. Because the Soviets denied any responsibility for the vessel, the Norwegians fired ASROCs (Anti-Submarine Rockets) at her, in an attempt to force her to the surface.

It is equally possible that NATO submarines are being sent into Communist waters, and *The Saturn Experiment* is about this eventuality. Except that in this case, news of the mission reaches the Soviets before the submarine *Saturn* arrives.

The story is the brainchild of John Pearson, himself an ex-Royal Navy Submariner. I am particularly indebted to him for his attention to detail, his comprehensive knowledge of both submarines and surface vessels, and above all his determination to see this book both written and published.

It goes without saying that all the characters portrayed are products of our imagination: should any of these bear a similarity to anyone living or dead, this is purely coincidental and never intended.

Peter Shepherd

— CHAPTER 1 —

Murmansk, 23rd April

It was still bitterly cold. The dry polar wind made eyes water and cracked lips. It forced the ten-man delegation who were picking their way along the busy narrow walkway in the dry dock to hold the collars of their coats tightly round their faces. They all wore hats.

They were dwarfed by the towering hull of the *Kharkov* on their left. The huge expanse of steel plate was bedecked with lamps, scaffolding, chain hoists and ropes. Men in blue overalls swarmed over it, some with arc welders whose brilliant sapphire lightning flashed in counterpoint to the din of hammers, drills, compressors, fork-lift trucks, winches and cranes. All around the ship men were calling, shouting and running. Pop music was blaring from obscured loud-speakers, adding to the cacophony.

The man leading the group was Viktor Nikolev, the director of the shipyard, the only one not in uniform, the only one who felt completely at home in the Dante-esque scene around them. He strode forward, almost oblivious to those behind him, pausing only to caution them to mind a piece of loose flex or watch out for some projecting object they might bump into. He came to a stairwell and waited for the others to catch up before disappearing down it. They followed, still clutching their collars. Halfway down, the stairs led onto a balcony which was level with the base of the *Kharkov*'s keel. They gathered there in a group, waiting

1

for Nikolev to explain. Almost opposite them was a large nacelle, a metal pod about fifty feet long and twenty feet wide, jutting below the bottom of the ship, supported by two shafts which led directly into the hull.

Nikolev turned to them, his face beaming with boyish pride. "Yes, Captain, we had to rebuild this whole section of the dock and keep it dry." He waved to the massive concrete blocks, capped with oak beams, which were taking the weight of the central section of the ship, enabling them to install the pod. "And putting those in made us scratch our heads. I reckon there's as much technology involved in fitting that nacelle as there is in making the thing in the first place." He laughed, even though none of the others joined him: they were subdued, awed by the enormity of the civil engineering works around them.

"You see, Captain, I know you've seen the drawings, read the specifications and know what it does, but I think it is very important that you understand exactly what it is you have beneath you when you are at sea." Captain Vasili Golitsyn surveyed the nacelle impassively, as though not a hundred percent sure what was being foisted upon him. Nikolev caught the expression. "You think it looks ugly. I tell you it is no more than an airborne radar pod. Radar, sonar, they're just the same, except that this one's retractable. I'll show you how it works. Please excuse me."

There was a telephone on the balcony. He picked up the receiver and gave orders.

Slowly, and very smoothly, the nacelle moved back, up and into the hull, fitting snugly into the slot provided for it. Captain Golitsyn timed it with his watch: it took exactly two minutes. Nikolev went on ebulliently, heedless to the silence of his guests. "Yes, Captain Golitsyn, it is a bit like the centreplate of a dinghy, it goes up and down. The shafts are hydraulically operated in tandem. Obviously one of our greatest problems was in sealing. . . ." He looked towards Evgeni Kirienko, the smartly uniformed KGB colonel from Moscow. "To prevent water from getting up the shaft and into the ship."

Nikolev turned back to the captain. "It means that as long as you have ultra sonar extended, you have a maximum speed of five knots. Any more and you are putting dangerous stresses on the shafts and the shaft seals. And after all we've been through, we wouldn't like you to leave it lying on the sea bed." He laughed again, totally blind to the humourless faces around him.

An impish glint came to Golitsyn's eye, "Is there any hope that the ultra sonar will make the *Kharkov* perhaps a little more stable in the water?" Even the admiral smirked at this one. Like her sister ships, the *Moskva* and the *Leningrad*, the *Kharkov* wallowed unpleasantly in any wind over force four. The helicopter pilots hated it. Nikolev pretended not to hear.

"Wait, I will lower it again. It is very important in a workplace to leave things exactly as you find them." He reached for the telephone, spoke a few words and replaced the receiver. Slowly the nacelle came down, back into its extended position.

Nikolev carried on talking. "You must forgive my pride, comrades; this refit represents the climax of my career. I don't believe there is another yard in the world that could have done this; not just the ultra sonar, but fitting it as well. I think we have good reason to be proud." The others smiled dutifully. "Come now, comrades, we are cold. You have seen the nacelle, you understand what it means to the *Kharkov*, let us go back to my office for some refreshment and further discussion. It will be warmer there and we can take our coats off."

Nikolev led the way back up the stairs. Though the only civilian, long experience in the naval shipyard had conditioned him to take uniforms for granted. It was the two KGB officers who made him slightly uncomfortable, they and the GRU director of Naval Intelligence, Konstantin Rodichev, and he knew why they were there. In addition to them and Captain Golitsyn, there was Vladimir Belinski, admiral of the Northern Banner Fleet; his flag officer, Commodore Orchenkov; and the senior commissar on the *Kharkov,* Fedor Tyutchev. Nor was he surprised by their impassiveness: he was sure that the admiral and his young captain were the only two who could really trust each other.

The only grand thing about Nikolev's office was the enormous window that flanked one complete wall. It gave a panoramic view of the whole dry dock, and the *Kharkov* which filled it. His own furniture was cheap and functional, the colours slightly garish. Black-and-white photographs of other vessels the yard had built or serviced lined the remaining walls. Whilst the visitors were taking their coats off and using the washroom, a secretary brought in coffee, brandy and vodka. Nikolev poured for each man as he sat down. The drinks brought warmth to their eyes as well as their bodies.

Surprisingly, it was not Admiral Belinski who brought the meeting to business, but Commodore Orchenkov, his flag officer. At first sight Orchenkov appeared a dissolute man: overweight, ruddy-faced and with thinning grey hair. He looked like a man who smoked, drank and ate too much, which he did, and who was more interested in women than naval matters, which was not entirely true. But his eyes were quick and alert, continually shifting from one person to another, assessing them, marking them, continually probing. He laughed like Khrushchev, but nobody was fooled. Nobody, however, not even the KGB or Rodichev from the GRU, was going to browbeat him. He coughed to draw the attention of the others before speaking, almost apologetically.

"Forgive me, comrades, I have some knowledge of sonar and I am aware that ultra sonar represents an impressive stride forwards, but," he pointed to the sheaf of papers as though it was a dead animal, "can somebody please explain to me in simple, straightforward Russian exactly what it is we have just seen under the *Kharkov*? Perhaps if you would not be too technical, so that our friends from the KGB can also understand what is involved?"

"Ah." Nikolev got to his feet. "I have a feeling that this is one of those moments when I ought not to be around. I suggest you take advantage of all the facilities." He waved towards the drinks tray. "If you want me back, use the telephone and have me paged; I shall be somewhere in the yard." He started to search for his coat on the overloaded coat-stand when another thought came to him. "Regarding Commodore Orchenkov's question, we've got Professor Uvarov working in the ultra sonar nacelle right now. Would you like me to send him up?"

"You are most kind, comrade." Belinski clearly approved. "Straightaway, if you would."

There was desultory chatter whilst the group waited for Uvarov. When he did come in they were taken aback by his youth, having half-expected a bespectacled sixty-year-old boffin. Instead they saw a young man, still in his thirties, and fashionably dressed. For his part, Uvarov was taken aback by the sight of so many officers' uniforms; suddenly his work had become real.

Belinski welcomed him in. "Commodore Orchenkov would like a more simple explanation of what the ultra sonar is all about. Come to think of it, so would I."

The others laughed. It was genuine laughter and it put Uvarov at ease. "I suppose it's the paper I prepared for you. I'm sorry. Some of your naval officers know as much about sonar as we do. When writing a report on this sort of thing it is very difficult to avoid being too technical for some of the readers and not technical enough for others. Let's see if I can help. I think all of us know that sonar is the use of sound waves under water to detect objects. Sound travels much more effectively through water than it does through air, and about four and a half times as fast. By timing the echoes, and noting how they change when they bounce back, we can identify what is around us: rocks, sea bed, fish, other vessels, and most importantly, submarines.

"But only for a short distance, eight kilometres at the most. That much I'm sure you understand."

The others nodded. Uvarov continued. "The problem has always been with long-range detection. Since the acoustic absorption co-efficient in water increases roughly with the square of the frequency, sonar fails in long-range detection at high frequency..."

"Please." Belinski was frowning. "I don't understand that. Please try to explain in a way which we can all understand." He finished with a smile.

"OK." Uvarov returned a distinctly frosty smile before continuing. "Well, for long-range detection we need a low sound frequency, but the lower the frequency, the more power we need to get that sound out in a beam. Ships just don't have the power needed. Hence the current limitation.

"But not only is Murmansk blessed with the naval base at

Polyarny, but also with our Research Institute of Marine Fisheries and Oceanography. We have spent a lot of time studying whales, who use sonar instead of sight to find their way around. If two whales over a hundred miles apart can find each other, then their use of sonar must be infinitely superior to our own, and using only a fraction of the power.

"There are other creatures that use sonar: bats. They are tiny and many of them quite blind. Some of them issue a sound pulse which lasts for less than two milliseconds, and in that time they will change the frequency from a hundred thousand cycles per second to forty thousand. In other words, they are using a minute time span to give them an enormous amount of information, using a sound which we humans cannot even hear.

"Our scientists at the Institute made their breakthrough just over twelve months ago. We still need the power, which is why an extra turbine has been fitted in the *Kharkov*, but if everything goes to plan, then with the nacelle dropped, the *Kharkov* should be able to detect a submarine ninety kilometres away."

Orchenkov sat bolt upright. "Ninety kilometres away?"

"Certainly. Ninety kilometres."

"Does that mean that with just a handful of *Kharkov* we can identify and establish the positions of all the NATO nuclear and Polaris submarines in the North Atlantic?"

"No. What it does mean, though, is that the *Kharkov* will be able to detect any enemy submarine at a much greater depth and range, and then she can despatch her helicopters to deal with it, and simply wait for their return, totally out of harm's reach."

Captain Golitsyn explained further. "You see, at present, by the time the *Kharkov* has detected a submarine on her sonar, she is already within range, at risk. This means she can stay well out of danger whilst each offending submarine is being neutralized."

"Mmmm." Orchenkov was silent. Suddenly his face changed. "Why wasn't I told about this before?" He held up a sheet of paper. "I had been told to expect thirty kilometres, not ninety."

Uvarov adjusted his tie. "I said 'we can,' not 'we will.' Ultra sonar needs testing. There is no advantage in raising expectations until they are based on fact. I believe the trials will be commencing in three weeks' time. You will know all about the practicalities of ultra sonar then.''

"Quite." Admiral Belinski stood up. "Thank you, Comrade Professor, you have been a great help."

Uvarov understood that he was being dismissed, said he hoped that he had been of use, and left.

Belinski turned to Orchenkov. "You will of course be on board, won't you, Commodore?"

"I wouldn't miss it for anything." Actually, Orchenkov would if he could. He hated the sickening, wallowing movement of the *Kharkov* as much as anybody else, but there was nothing he could do about it.

"Then let us drink to the successful outcome of these trials." Belinski was beaming. But looking around at the desultory way in which the others were toying with their cigarettes and pencils, he realized that something was wrong.

"Yes," said Rodichev, the director of Naval Intelligence from GRU. "There is one other factor which I am very sorry to report. It appears that knowledge of the ultra sonar may already be in the hands of NATO."

"Oh?"

Colonel Evgeni Kirienko, who had also travelled by train from Moscow, sighed. His sigh made the others focus their attention on him. He spoke slowly, with a heavy Ukrainian accent.

"Yes, Commodore, that is why I am here to assist Captain Kaledin. This shipyard employs over four thousand people. I suppose it is inevitable that one or two of them might be dissidents. They are lucky to be Russians, to have work to do, and even though they know that there are millions of Westerners who have no work, who live in abject poverty, they still bite the hand of their mother who feeds them.

"These are Karelians. Murmansk, as you know, is a new town and many of its inhabitants are from Karelia. Amazingly, some of these people would still prefer to live in Finland. It makes them susceptible to actions of this kind."

"How much did they learn?" Orchenkov snapped.

"We found one of them taking photographs, a very foolish thing to try. After we had shown him the error of his ways, he was only too pleased to tell us about his other two colleagues, one of whom, regrettably, also worked in the yard. For some peculiar reason, these two were unwilling to help us. We assisted them with Pentothol but they merely burbled all kinds of nonsense. We gave them psychiatric help, but it seems they were too far gone . . .'' Kirienko trailed off into silence.

"What did they learn?"

"They knew the nacelle's size, they knew how it is installed, they knew the *Kharkov* has been fitted with an extra turbine to power it, and they knew that its range is vastly superior to anything previous. Beyond that I believe they knew very little. Certainly they hadn't a hope of knowing how it worked."

"And they got this information out?"

Captain Kaledin answered for Kirienko. "During the last stages of their treatment, well, we couldn't wipe that stupid, self-satisfied, smug expression off their faces. I'm afraid it upset the nurses."

"You speak of them in the past tense. I take it they are no longer available for interrogation?"

Kaledin swallowed. "That is correct."

"Bit careless, wasn't it?"

"Director Rodichev made it known that he wanted to learn as soon as possible what the damage was. I was ordered to produce results. As we, quite clearly, did not produce the results expected, Colonel Kirienko has been seconded here to lend further instruction and to supervise secondary screening at the yard. I should imagine that it will be scarcely likely that such a thing could happen again."

Orchenkov sat back and lit another of his foul-smelling cigars. Nobody else spoke. Presently he turned to Rodichev.

"Comrade Director, does it really matter if ultra sonar is known to NATO? I mean, couldn't it strengthen our hand at the bargaining table? Isn't this the sort of information that is needed to prove to our Comecon brothers that we, as much as ever before, are the strength and bulwark to which they must turn?"

Rodichev was unhappy. "It is really up to our people at Strategic Studies in Moscow to decide. Such information could be dangerous, in the worst case encouraging NATO to order a pre-emptive strike. Certainly they will be handling all their submarines very differently. The element of surprise has been lost. And I'm sure our Comecon brothers would be far happier if we could keep our own secrets to ourselves, let alone theirs.''

"Mmmm." Orchenkov pulled a face but brightened almost as quickly. "Well, we've got these trials in three weeks' time. It is three weeks, isn't it, Captain?"

Captain Golitsyn was never really happy with Orchenkov on board; it meant two masters on the *Kharkov*. He was not quite able to keep it from his voice. "Yes, Commodore. Initial shake-down on the twelfth and thirteenth May and then, subject to all systems being operational, major exercises commencing on the fifteenth.''

"Do you know, I really am looking forward to it."

— CHAPTER 2 —

*The Atlantic Ocean,
fifty miles southwest of Rockall, 10th May*

The subdued red lighting in *Saturn*'s control room was neither cosy nor eerie, but somewhere in between. The men seated at their control panels neither joked nor chattered, but used their voices only to acknowledge and confirm orders, to report findings. They were professionals. Their detachment added to the atmosphere of surrealism, the whole unit being totally alien to the wild environment in which it operated and of which it had become part.

The captain, Commander James Henderson, was standing in position between the two periscope tubes, facing the attack systems computer. In his left hand he held a sheaf of papers and a clipboard. Tall, powerfully built and neatly dressed, he had dark hair that was perhaps a little too long, falling shaggily around the back of his neck. It was the same for all the crew: they had been at sea for five weeks.

On his right, but further forwards, the coxswain, Chief Petty Officer Tate, sat behind the steering console. Tate had turned on the automatic pilot, "George," and was sitting with both hands in his lap. The steering column, which doubled as helm and depth control, quivered slightly, responding to George's command.

Behind Tate, and just behind the captain's right, Lieutenant Commander Sykes, second in command and presently officer of the watch, was sitting at the systems console, in charge of power, vents, valves and electrics. On Henderson's left, the navigation officer, Lt. Peter Howarth, was sitting behind another console which governed the SINS, radar and communications. In front of the control room, out of sight but within easy earshot, was the sonar compartment, presently being managed by Lt. Crooke.

The low deckhand only just cleared Henderson's head. Given the confined space, the men did not have to raise their voices. Though the air was continually being cleaned by carbon dioxide scrubbers, the array of electronics gave off a faintly acrid smell, making the atmosphere slightly clinical.

Henderson gave a soft grunt and rearranged the papers on his clipboard. He turned to Sykes at the Systems Console. "Report reactor status, Number One."

Sykes flashed his eyes quickly over the panel: a last visual check to confirm that nothing had changed. It was automatic. "Reactor in full power state and turbine temperatures normal, sir. We are ready to carry out Section Six of the Engineering Trial."

Henderson sighed. "Thank you, Number One. I will address the ship's company now." He reached up, pressed a switch on the overhead communications panel, and pulled down the microphone. "Do you hear there. This is the captain speaking." It was not a question. He waited a few seconds so that men all over *Saturn* could stop whatever they were doing and hear the PA loudspeakers. "I know the last few weeks have proved difficult and exhausting. I am aware of the great deal of effort you have all put into proving *Saturn* during her trials period. However, we still have the final section of the Engineering Trial to perform. During this trial we shall work up to maximum speed and make various depth changes. Yes, gentlemen, 'angles and dangles.' I want you to remain on constant alert for the next thirty minutes. Upon completion we shall surface and head back to base for a well-earned rest. Thank you." Henderson's voice was a firm baritone; it carried well.

He gave his crew a few minutes to prepare themselves: the chefs to check that deep fat friers were securely hatched, as also the stores, crockery and cutlery; the engineers to check that nothing was lying around loose where they had been working; the men off watch to check that wardrooms, messes and bunk spaces were securely stowed, and that internal hull valves were operational.

Trials on a new submarine are always tense. During a period when complex machinery has to "bed down," captain and crew never know what might fail during a fresh manoeuvre. It is that difficult period when men and vessel are learning about each other, trying to gain confidence in each other, never quite sure when they are going to presume too much, always prepared for some unknown weakness to appear, always ready to react quickly when and where it does. Hence the tension. Commander Henderson and his crew had been living with it for five weeks. During this time *Saturn* had fully matched all expectations, proving that she was "Clyde built." The men were beginning to feel comfortable with her.

Tate was sitting back in his pilot's chair, quite relaxed, when he caught Henderson's eye. He reported. "Speed four knots, depth four hundred feet, planes and steering control in automatic, sir."

"Very good, Coxswain. Planes and steering in manual control."

"Aye, aye, sir." Tate cradled the steering column with one hand whilst with the other he reached forward to the control panel, flicking off three switches. His grip firmed on the steering column and he took it in both hands. "Planes and steering in manual control, sir, and responding correctly." His voice sounded casual but Henderson knew it wasn't: he was just good at his job.

"Roger. Increase revolutions to five zero."

Tate pressed two buttons on his console. "Five zero revolutions on, sir."

Henderson peered over his shoulder and watched the numbers on the digital speed gauge flicker until they passed twenty knots. "Take her down to one thousand feet, Coxswain, using five degrees bow down, and then level off."

Very gently, but firmly, Tate moved the steering column forwards. "One thousand feet, five degrees bow down and level off. Aye, aye, sir." Always the mechanical repeat and confirmation of orders given: total clarity. Equally gently, Tate brought the steering column back, his eyes on the depth and the speed gauges. "One thousand feet, sir, and steady. Speed twenty-eight knots."

"Thank you, Coxswain." Henderson turned to Sykes. "Are we trimmed, Number One?"

Sykes checked the "bubble" on the spirit level set into the systems console before replying. "The trim is 'on,' sir."

They could hear the panelling around them squeak as it bent a little, responding to the awesome pressure on the hull, pressure that tightened around it in a rigid grip. The noise was slightly disconcerting, even if it was expected. Henderson narrowed his eyes, some sixth sense warning him that *Saturn* was still new, that he couldn't be too careful.

"Number One, have the Engineering Department check for leaks."

For an instant Sykes raised his eyebrows, surprised because the instruction was not expected, but then immediately recognized what was in the captain's mind. "Aye, aye, sir." He spoke into his own microphone, and like the captain, used the same speculative tone of one playing a hunch. "Engineering Department. Check for leaks."

Lieutenant Commander Angus MacDonald, the marine engineering officer, was sitting at his own panel in the Reactor Control Department. His acknowledgement was brief: "Engineering Department. Roger." He swivelled round on his seat to face the men behind him. "OK, you all heard it. Winters, you go forward, Hunter, you check aft." The men helped themselves to torches; they knew where to look.

It was while this was going on that Henderson noticed the thin trickle of water making its way down the attack periscope shaft. For a second he wondered how long it had been there, but its irregular progress down the thinly oiled shaft told him it was new. He frowned, and spoke to Sykes without turning. "Number One, have the outside ERA report here right away."

"Aye, aye, sir." Sykes reached for his microphone.

Presently, CPO Stephen Fettler, the outside ERA, or Engineering Room Artificer, came in. He had a torch in his hand and appeared slightly harassed. Henderson spoke.

"Chief, take a look at this, will you?"

Fettler ran his finger round the joint at the top of the shaft, and licked it, to check that it was saltwater and not condensation. Like MacDonald, he had a strong Scots accent. "Aye, we've a wee trickle. It can happen with a periscope gland, probably because it's new. I should have thought that if we go any deeper the outside pressure should seal it for us. Probably what it needs to get it to work properly. If it doesn't, it'll have to be changed in Faslane."

"Very good, Chief. I was thinking much the same myself." Henderson was still frowning at it. "Just the same, I would like you to remain here in the control room whilst we do our next descent. Just to keep an eye on it."

"Aye, aye, sir. If I may, sir, I'd like to bring a spanner, just in case we need to use the emergency lock."

"Very good, Chief."

MacDonald had reported that the ship was clear of leaks by the time Fettler had returned from the workshop. He took up a position between the captain's cabin and the communications console, safely out of anybody's way in the control room. Knowing he was there, Henderson tucked the matter away in the back of his mind, looked down at his clipboard, and gave the next order. "Coxswain, take her down to twelve hundred feet and level off, using five degrees bow down."

"Twelve hundred feet, five degrees bow down and level off; aye, aye, sir."

Henderson squinted over Tate's shoulder to check the depth gauge, then glanced back to Sykes, who had his fingers poised over the systems console.

They all heard the splash and spray. A thin jet of freezing water shot out onto Henderson's shoulder, spinning him round and throwing him against the search periscope. His footing slipped on the wet deck and he fell down, banging his head on the shaft base. Coolly, Fettler stepped forward with the spanner and began attaching it to the nut.

Confused, Henderson tried to gather himself together. Dimly, he heard Tate call from behind him, "Primary system hydraulic failure."

And Sykes's reply: "Roger, switching to secondary system."

Henderson could feel a slight increase in the angle of the submarine; he knew that he had to act quickly. But his head was spinning, and he couldn't pick himself up. He heard Tate's voice again, this time with a distinct edge on it. "Passing twelve hundred feet, secondary hydraulic systems failure."

"Shit." Sykes was working the changeover switch but nothing was happening. His teeth were bared in frustration. Desperately he looked round for the captain and saw him still on the floor, dazedly trying to bring himself up from his hands and knees. He understood immediately that Henderson could not give an order, that he would have to do it himself. "Planes and steering in emergency. Coxs'n." The rush of words betrayed his urgency.

Tate reached over for the changeover lever and jerked it down. "Planes and steering in emergency. . . . Passing eighteen hundred feet." His voice was brittle, knowing that *Saturn* was already beyond her maximum depth.

Sykes knew they were close to losing control. "Stop main engine. Full rise on the planes, Coxs'n." The incoming rush of water had stopped. He turned and saw Fettler give the spanner a final turn, his face red with the effort. And he heard Tate's reply: "Full rise on the planes, sir. Passing two thousand two hundred, fifteen degrees bow down."

The depth alarm was sounding. Fettler bent down to help Henderson up, steadying him on the back of Tate's seat. Henderson clearly understood the danger they were in. He barked out his command. "Full astern, starboard thirty." He passed his hand on the side of his head where he had banged it on the periscope shaft and saw blood on his fingers.

Saturn was sinking faster than a stone. Not only had she got the impetus from twenty-eight knots driving her down at an angle which had increased to fifteen degrees, but the pressure of depth had compressed her, making her heavier in relation to the water. The momentum derived from the combination of these two forces meant it was impossible for her to drive herself out. By ordering the rudder to its maximum of thirty degrees, Henderson knew he could go some way towards stopping her. By ordering full astern, he hoped he would be able to pull her up backwards. He also knew it would take all the power he could find to reverse the force of five and a half thousand tons on its wild headlong descent.

Tate acknowledged the order, relieved to hear the captain's voice again. ''Telegraph full astern, thirty of starboard wheel on, sir.''

Henderson looked around, aware that the eyes of everyone in the control room were fixed on himself and Tate. He also became aware of the insistent, jarring tone of the depth alarm. ''Turn that bloody row off, Number One.''

Sykes snapped out of his trance and flicked the alarm off. The sudden silence was broken by the last of the water gurgling down the drainage vents and the bulkhead panelling popping away from the aluminium holding strips. Both noises held terrifying implications. Then the whole control room began to shudder, just as all of Saturn was shuddering: thrown into reverse, the pump jet had begun to cavitate, its rotor blades thrashing at nothing as they tried to bite into the rushing water.

There was fear in the room and Henderson felt it. Tate's face was ash grey as he held the steering column back, his eyes flickering between the depth gauge and the speed log. Henderson turned and saw Sykes, his face shining with perspiration, and noticed him pulling the fingers on each hand, making the knuckles crack, each one clicking until all eight were done. He recognized it for a reflex action, but found it slightly irritating. He glanced down at his own hand and saw the blood-smeared fingers biting into the upholstery on Tate's chair. From over Tate's shoulder, he stared at the speed gauge, willing it to slow down.

They could feel Saturn slewing uncomfortably in the water as the rudder took hold and forced her to one side. The vibration eased as the pump jet rotor blades found water. Gradually the numbers on the digital gauge slowed down, then paused. The headlong rush was broken; *Saturn* was slowing. Henderson was counting with the gauge as the speed was winding back towards zero. At two knots he gave the order. "Stop main engine, wheel amidships."

Tate's voice was distant. "Main engines stopped. Wheel amidships, sir."

Henderson sucked in his breath; he knew he had got it right as he saw the speed log come to rest at zero.

Sykes reported, his tone still brittle. "The bubble's amidships, sir."

Henderson nodded; the silence complete, the fear still with them. Then Tate, stunned with disbelief: "The depth gauge, sir. It's reading three thousand two hundred and fifty feet!"

Henderson had already seen it. The green numbers were dead already at three thousand two hundred and fifty. He managed to keep his voice firm. "Number One, situation report, quick."

Sykes called out the information from his console. "Depth, three thousand two hundred and fifty feet. Speed zero. Reactor in full power state, functioning normally. Hydraulic systems one and two inoperative. Steering and plane control in emergency. Main and auxiliary electrical systems functioning normally. The submarine is clear of leaks." He hesitated, looking back at the emergency bolt on the periscope shaft that Fettler had tightened. "Including the attack periscope gland."

"Thank you, Number One." Henderson returned to his place between the two periscope shafts. "Coxswain, can you bring her up in emergency control?"

"I think so, sir. She responds."

"Very well. Coxswain, slow ahead, two degrees bow up, level off at three thousand feet."

"Aye, aye, sir. Slow ahead, two degrees bow up, three thousand feet and level off."

"Number One, have the Engineering Department ready to check for leaks at three thousand feet. We'll be checking again at two thousand five hundred."

"Aye, aye, sir."

There was no knowing what damage the pressure of over half a mile of water might have done to the hull, pressure which had compressed it and made it several inches smaller than it was on the surface. During her ascent, *Saturn* would re-expand. All it needed was one section to re-expand faster than another and the hull would shatter. By checking at these depths, Henderson felt that they might be able to detect an incipient leak before it got out of hand. He was not sure how they would deal with it, but he would handle that problem only if and when it arose.

He watched Tate on the steering column for a few seconds before reaching for the microphone. "Engineering Room. What the hell happened to those hydraulic systems?" MacDonald's puzzled voice replied on the loudspeaker. "No idea, sir. We're checking the system computer right now." The information was useless, but there was something reassuring about his voice, as if confirming that there were other people still alive on *Saturn*.

Henderson hung the microphone up and glanced to his left. In the dim light he could see Peter Howarth at the navigation console, his face pale and his jaw working with an involuntary tic. The fingers on his left hand were tightly crossed, and Henderson wondered how many others of the ship's crew were doing the same. He brought the microphone down again, pressing the switch that would carry his voice throughout *Saturn*.

"Do you hear there. This is the captain speaking." He waited, as he knew he had to, for men to sort themselves out. It also gave him time to collect his own thoughts. "We have just descended to three thousand two hundred and fifty feet. As you know, our normal operating depth is one thousand two hundred and fifty. Due to a failure in both primary and secondary hydraulic systems, we have exceeded that limit. We are now in emergency plane and steering control and have already begun our ascent. Afterwards we shall surface and return to Faslane."

He replaced the microphone and watched Tate easing the steering column forward a fraction to level off. With the reassurance of commands being repeated and the standard routines being practised, normality returned to *Saturn*. Henderson felt the soggy packet in his breast pocket and remembered his crew again. "OK, gentlemen, one all round."

It was a signal that officers and crew may light a cigarette if they felt like it. They all did. There was a brief shuffling and snapping of cigarettes lighters while they waited for MacDonald to confirm that the submarine was clear of leaks. Howarth, who had been feeling useless at the navigation console, uncrossed his fingers and passed Henderson his dry packet. This small gesture gave him at last a feeling of purpose, of contributing to the activity in the control room, and his jaw finally relaxed. Henderson smiled his thanks. The tension was abating.

The laborious surfacing procedure was going to take at least thirty minutes. Each stage upwards represented another milestone at which men could breathe more easily. Defying the temptation to head straight for the surface, or to skimp on checking for leaks, put an additional strain on the crew.

At two thousand feet, Henderson unclipped the microphone again. "Sonar Compartment, two thousand feet. Clear stern arcs."

Crooke's voice was firm and positive. "Aye, aye, sir."

"Starboard ten, Coxswain."

"Starboard ten, aye, aye, sir."

They could feel *Saturn* change direction as she described a tight circle, corkscrewing her way upwards.

Sonar's report was brief: "Sonar clear, sir, no contacts."

A submarine is most vulnerable when she comes to the surface. Her sonar is mounted on the bows, so she can only "see" in a hundred-and-thirty-five-degree arc in front of her. The command to the coxswain was an order to take her off course so that sonar could check that there was nothing to impede her ascent. Again, just before surfacing, but still well below periscope depth, Henderson would give the same command to check that there was no surface vessel, perhaps a tanker or trawler, about to run her down. It is surprising how easily this can happen.

At two hundred and fifty feet, the final stage where Henderson ordered Sonar to clear stern arcs, he also ordered Tate to bring *Saturn* up to seventy-two feet. Measured from the base of the keel, seventy-two feet is periscope depth. At a hundred feet he gave the order "Up scope." By the time *Saturn*'s periscope was breaking through the water, Henderson was already behind the eyepiece, panning the horizon in a three-hundred-and-sixty-degree sweep, first in high power for short-range vision, and then in low power.

Satisfied that there were no vessels near him, he gave the next order, ''Stand by to surface.'' Sykes repeated the order on his PA. The control room became a hive of activity as each officer and crew member set about new tasks for a different routine. Sykes began receiving reports from all over *Saturn* that each department was ready to surface. The officer of the watch, together with an able rating, both dressed in Navy foul-weather gear, with binoculars hanging from their necks, moved into the control room and took up their positions below the hatch to the fin. Finally, Sykes sat back and reported to Henderson. ''The submarine is in all respects ready to surface, sir.''

Henderson nodded briefly at him. ''Surface.''

There was a rushing, roaring sound all around the control room as Sykes flicked the switches that sent high-pressure compressed air into the ballast tanks, forcing *Saturn* upwards to breach the surface of the sea.

IMMEDIATE SECRET

FM   :   SATURN
TO   :   F.O.S.M.
INFO   :   CINCNAV

ENGINEERING TRIAL SECTION 6.
INCIDENT REPORT.

1. PRIMARY AND SECONDARY HYDRAULIC SYSTEMS FAILURE 1200 FT. OPERATION NOW IN EMERGENCY CONTROL.

2. SUBMARINE INADVERTENTLY EXCEEDED PERMITTED OPERATING DEPTH AND REACHED 3250 FT. RPT 3250 FT.

3. NO EXTERIOR HULL DAMAGE APPARENT . . .

4. ATTACK P'SCOPE GLAND FRACTURE AT DEPTH IN PARA 1. BUT UNRELATED TO HYDRAULIC SYSTEMS FAILURE. URGENT DOCKYARD ATTENTION REQUIRED.

5. RETURNING FASLANE ETA 1800.

BT

''Jesus Christ!''

Admiral Harold Dawson, flag officer of submarines at

Faslane, had been woken up with a telephone call at six fifteen that morning. The rush into HMS *Neptune*, the operations base at Faslane, had left him without coffee, without breakfast, and badly shaved. His only remaining clean white shirt had a crease in the collar and to cap it all, he had a slight hangover from a very successful dinner party the evening before. He was irritable before he had even reached his office.

Now, reading the top priority message for the third time, his mouth had stopped working. He was beginning to sort out his emotions and reactions into some sensible order.

He was angry with Henderson for having put *Saturn* at risk. Why, he thought, it should be automatic that once both hydraulic systems fail you switch into emergency. So a periscope gland fails, that's no excuse! And there was *Saturn*, the most modern and expensive submarine in the fleet, probably limping home like a crumpled-up bit of scrap metal, written off before she had even seen active duty. Not only *Saturn*, but all fifty-five officers and men had been put at risk; fifty-five highly able men who together represented several hundred years of intensive training and experience.

Then there was relief. Relief that *Saturn* was coming home, relief that he did not have to go about organizing some dreadful salvage exercise in the middle of the Atlantic, relief that he would not have to sign all those difficult letters to wives and mothers.

Finally, there was pride, and a little admiration; *Saturn* had reached a depth so far attained only by sophisticated bathyscaphes, never submarines.

He sipped his coffee. It was cold, watery and floury. He put the cup down and grimaced. It was going to be a busy day.

First priority was to check with the Ministry of Defence (Navy), London. Really it ought to be the Commander-in-Chief Navy, Sir Richard Hardy; after Sir Richard could do what he liked with the information.

Then Kendall's: he would want a team from the yard alongside *Saturn* as soon as she came alongside. Christ, I'll wipe those buggers' noses in it, he thought. After all, it could only be sloppy workmanship. His knuckles went white as he scratched the item on his memo pad. There would have to be an inquiry; as soon as possible, while it's fresh in everyone's minds. No, tomorrow, give them all a rest. I expect they're a bit shaken.

I'd better get *Saturn* cordoned off, order a base radiation alert, get our own engineering staff down there. Christ, what a farrago! Dawson seldom swore but this was one of those occasions.

A difficult routine, involving, as it did, a lot of paperwork, had been broken up by an emergency which meant excitement for everyone else but twice as much work for him. And possibly difficult questions from London. Oh, hell.

Karen Henderson had been both surprised and delighted to hear that *Saturn* was returning earlier than she had expected. Either James had been able to get through the trials faster than planned, which was unlikely, or something was malfunctioning; either way it was good news.

Those five long weeks without him, fighting both boredom and loneliness, suddenly compressed themselves into a fortnight, then a week, and then were forgotten, over. Excited, she ran upstairs to tell Skip, their son, who was in bed with a slight temperature and a headache, instead of being at school. Skip had been christened Alan, but James had always called him Skip, or Skipper, ever since his first smile, and the name had stuck. Skip was all of eight years old.

He looked up when Karen came in, saw the excitement in her eyes, and smiled expectantly.

"Hey, Skip, guess what?"

"What?"

"Daddy. He's coming home. He'll be here tonight!"

"Oh, goody. Can I come down with you to meet him?"

Karen pulled a face. "That depends on your temperature, young man. If it's down this evening you can come with me. Otherwise I'll ask Mrs. Campbell if she'll look after you."

Skip screwed up his own nose in response. "Stupid Mrs. Campbell; she always reads me 'Peter Rabbit,' and I want her to read Biggles, or Doc Holloway." He thought for a moment, a flash of mischief crossing his eyes. "Can I watch television then? Until you come back?"

Karen had a feeling that he would anyway, despite Mrs. Campbell's blandishments. If "Top of the Pops" was on it would be almost impossible to stop him. Besides, if he still had his temperature, it might cheer him up. She drew herself up in mock severity. "Young man, Mrs. Campbell is not stupid, and we are very lucky to have her. Why, supposing we had somebody who was an absolute dragon?"

"She is a dragon."

"No, she isn't, and don't interrupt. Yes, you may have that blasted box on, provided it's switched off when we come back!"

"Thanks, Mum." Skip thought again for a moment. "Will Daddy have a present for me?"

Karen wagged an admonishing finger at him. "What's wrong with Daddy on his own, then? He shouldn't need to be bringing you presents. Besides, there are no shops on the bottom of the sea, silly, because nobody else would go there; it's too wet."

Skip giggled and then lay back, his headache obviously troubling him. The next time he spoke his voice was quieter. "What time is he coming, then?"

"Oh, we should be back around seven thirty, about your bed-time. Now, you try and get some sleep; it's the only way you're going to get better, and then you can come with me." She moved over and felt his forehead, frowning a little as she realized that the temperature was still there, and then smiled again to reassure him.

"Promise?"

"I promise."

Karen spent most of the rest of the day getting ready for James's arrival. She vacuumed the floors, polished the shelves, prepared an evening meal, tidied the kitchen, and finally checked that there was a bottle of whisky in the drinks cabinet, which there was. With each chore completed, she felt that James was that much nearer home, and she found it oddly exciting.

In the afternoon she helped Skip with a jigsaw puzzle and then, when she realized he was not going to be able to come down with her, she telephoned Mrs. Campbell. Mrs. Campbell told her not to fash herself; of course she would come round.

In her room Karen went through her wardrobe, randomly tugging at dresses, uncertain what to wear, but knowing only that she could not go in the jeans and ''T'' shirt she now had on. She peeled them off and studied herself in the mirror. She drew her shoulders back, smoothed her waist and stomach with her hands, and as she did so felt her body glow with a tremble of urgency and sensed the ripple of a deeper excitement welling up within her. Heavens, she thought, I hope he's felt the five weeks as long as I have: I *want* him.

After that the choice was easy. She pulled out a simple pale blue dress with long sleeves and a high collar, and a zip which ran down the front neck to navel. That, she decided, would give her enough austerity to survive the wardroom, but also the hint of enough promise to put her James in the right frame of mind, just in case he wasn't already. To make absolutely sure, she left her bra off, but tied a large dark blue silk scarf around her neck.

She was still smiling to herself when she opened the door to Mrs. Campbell, and grinned like a little girl when she saw the Beatrix Potter book in her hand.

Karen knew there was something wrong when she drove over the hill from Portincaple. Usually she would pull up beside the road to see if she could see a submarine alongside the pier. Now, in the late afternoon sun, she could see *Saturn*'s fin and hull cutting water about four hundred yards out, in the Gareloch. She narrowed her eyes at the Marine Guards on the end of the pier, wincing as she realized that there were far too many people milling about. But though her heart quickened, she was not unduly worried; after all, there was *Saturn* approaching the base, and they would have told her if anything was wrong.

Her unease deepened a little further when a Marine Guard suggested that she park in the compound: no private vehicles were being allowed on the pier that evening. Slightly cross, she let her tyres squeal as she accelerated away, and was only partly mollified when she found a gap among the parked cars by the exit. She slotted the little sports car neatly into the space.

As she strode briskly down towards the pier, anxious to know what was up, her thoughts were interrupted by a familiar voice from behind.

"Hello, Karen, you're always a sight for sore eyes. How are you keeping?"

Karen spun round and flicked a wisp of blonde hair from her face. "Hello, Admiral. I'm fine, thank you. How are you?"

The twinkle in Dawson's eyes was only there for a moment. "Oh, all right. Look, Karen, I have to go on board and speak to James for a while. Could I ask you if you wouldn't mind going to the wardroom and waiting there with the rest of the wives? I promise I won't keep James very long."

"Of course." She hesitated a moment before asking, "Is there anything wrong, Admiral?"

"No, Karen, everything's fine. Just a few minor things I have to sort out with James before he leaves."

"That's unusual, isn't it? Will you tell James I'm in the wardroom?"

"Yes, of course. I won't keep him more than a few minutes; that I promise."

Karen changed her direction and walked slowly off to the wardroom. She wondered if she ought to ring home; she had promised Mrs. Campbell she would only be away an hour at the most. Still, Dawson had said only a minute or two, promised it, and she was sure Mrs. Campbell wouldn't mind waiting.

Promises. She sighed. There seemed to have been rather a lot of promises today; she hoped they would all be kept.

Dawson was not standing on ceremony. He jumped the gangway as soon as it was lowered, automatically returning the salutes from the officers and ratings on the casing, but paying them scant attention. Sykes was there only just in time to meet him. He saluted crisply and welcomed the admiral aboard. Dawson returned his salute, but made no comment. Sykes caught the mood and led the way down, through the accommodation space hatch, equally grim-faced.

There were only two junior officers left in the control room: one on the communications console, the other opposite the systems panel. Both leapt to attention when Dawson came through. He didn't appear to notice them.

The officers in the wardroom sprang to their feet when they heard him coming in. Dawson halted at the entrance and surveyed them one after the other. "At ease, everybody." He glanced at the table and took a seat at the end furthest away from the entrance so that he could face anyone who came in. Seated, he looked as uncomfortable as the others. He smacked his lips. "Well, is nobody going to offer me a drink, then?"

Howarth was the most junior officer there. He jumped up. "Sorry, sir. Your pleasure, sir?"

"Whisky. Large and with very little water." He peered up at them all with tired eyes. "And by the looks of you lot, you'd better join me." Howarth bustled off to the drinks locker.

Sykes was still standing at the wardroom entrance. "The captain is in his cabin, sir. I'll inform him you're here." Dawson nodded his agreement.

Henderson and MacDonald were absorbed in a pile of the ship's drawings. Between them they were trying to identify common elements of *Saturn*'s primary and secondary hydraulic systems. Basically, these were to be found in the computer programme, the plane rudder operating valves, the actual hydraulic drive for these systems being on different circuits. Sykes's discreet knock on the door came as yet another irritant.

"Yes?"

"The Old Man's in the wardroom, sir. He's opened the bar."

"Oh."

"Yes, sir. And he's ordered a stiff one."

"Shit."

"Quite, sir."

Dawson had a reputation for using his drink. Unlike most people who will drink to relax or to revive spirits. Dawson would drink to make himself unpleasant. Henderson's foreknowledge was the only weapon he had. He sighed resignedly and stubbed out his cigarette.

"OK. Let's go show the Old Man that we still exist. Angus, you had better come with me."

Because there was no door to the wardroom, they had no opportunity to collect themselves before going in. Henderson did the best he could.

"Good to see you, sir. It's kind of you to come."

Dawson wasn't feeling the slightest bit kind. "It's good to see you safely back, James. It's my business to be here." He had spoken quietly and paused to let the last sentence sink in. "Well, aren't you going to offer me another drink?"

"But of course. I'm sorry, sir. Your glass should never have got that low. Peter!" Howarth was already refilling it.

Dawson ignored the possible double meaning. He swallowed half his drink, put down the glass, and narrowed his eyes at Henderson.

Curiously, there was a final check to be made in the torpedo room, the computer log needed attention, there were some papers left on the navigation console, and the sonar compartment was not completely closed down; most of the other officers quickly left. Only Henderson, Sykes and MacDonald remained to face the admiral. Dawson was sharp.

"Right, James. What the bloody hell have you been doing with *Saturn*?"

Henderson was disconcerted by the abruptness. "It was explained in the signal, sir. The computer log will be ready for analysis and inspection any moment now." He paused, not quite sure whether Dawson wanted excuses, explanations, reasons or an apology. He chose the last. "We nearly lost her, sir."

Dawson exploded. "We? We? Who are we? You and me or you and your crew? You, James. You nearly lost her. And I want to know why. I didn't give you command of the most expensive 'S' class submarine to hear you say 'we nearly lost her.'" He parodied the words.

Henderson bit back the words he wanted to say. Dawson glowered at Sykes. "Sykes, you bring that report and the log to me in my office or at my home as soon as possible. We shall need them both at the inquiry." He was getting up as he said it, but stopped on his way out. "Oh, and James, Karen's waiting for you in the wardroom inboard."

"Thank you sir." Henderson wasn't sure if Dawson had heard him. He was already on his way out.

The wardroom at HMS *Neptune* was humming with animated but brittle conversation. Submarines were coming and going all the time at Faslane, but this time every man there knew that something, somewhere had been amiss for *Saturn* to have returned early, especially with a radiation monitoring team for a welcoming committee.

Karen was sitting at a table with Penny Sykes. Thoughtfully sipping their Coca-Colas, neither had very much to say to the other. They knew something was wrong, but not knowing what it was made them slightly irritated, as well as nervous. They fidgeted with their cigarettes between anxious glances towards the wardroom doors and wished for the nth time that their husbands, or whatever it was that was keeping them, would hurry up.

The fragile talk in the wardroom slackened. Karen and Penny glanced up, looking again towards the doors, and at last they saw them: Sykes holding the door open to let MacDonald pass through, followed finally by Henderson. All three looked equally grim, and all three seemed at that moment quite unapproachable. The hush deepened, and became the silence for a leper.

Henderson felt the atmosphere. He surveyed the wardroom, read the silence for what it was, and something inside him snapped. The anger and frustration from having to deal with Dawson changed into something else: perhaps a hint of rebellion, and those nearest him could see it. His expression became, if anything, cocky, and knowing he had their attention, he spoke quietly, in a deep voice.

"The big three . . . and back!"

The effect was electric. To a man every officer stood up with total incredulity.

"What?"

Henderson held up his hands, smiling now. "Like I said, the big three . . . and we're still here. Alan and Angus will fill you in on the details. . . ." He corrected himself. "Well, some of them, anyway."

"The big three" meant three thousand feet; that had been done before, but coming back had not. Anxious to know more, men were leaving their tables, surging forward to find out what had happened on *Saturn*. Karen sat back in her chair, slightly jealous, knowing that James was going to have trouble in extricating himself, that other people were demanding his attention, and that, for the moment anyway, she was taking second place.

But it was only a twinge. Karen could see something else too, that James was liked as well as respected. The men were impressed, and she could see a degree of pride reflected in the faces of Sykes as well as MacDonald. She stood up, could see James looking for her, and their eyes met. She wanted to run up and hug him, feeling proud, relieved, and ever so glad to have him back, but she couldn't, feeling the restraints of wardroom etiquette restricting her.

Instead it was James who took the initiative. Disengaging himself from the other officers, he moved to meet her on her own. He kissed her on her forehead, holding her tightly for a second before leading her back to her table. Penny had gone.

Somebody had set out fresh drinks for them. James scanned the crowded bar to see who could be responsible, and caught a glimpse of his sonar officer, Lt. Crooke, his glass held high, giving him a knowing smile. James acknowledged him with a silent toast before concentrating on Karen.

"Good to see you, love, and thanks for coming." He held her hand tightly.

Karen responded with a squeeze of her own. "Lovey, I wouldn't have missed it for anything. So you did the big three. What happened? I saw Dawson and he told me to wait here. Are you in some kind of trouble. . . . ?"

James put a finger to his lips and changed the subject. "You look stunning, just what I've been dreaming about all those weeks at sea. How's Skip? Where is he, by the way?"

"Skip's at home. I kept him off school today because he wasn't too well. He's dying to see you. He wants you to take him crab-hunting along the beach."

James looked concerned. "What's the matter with him?"

"Oh, just a slight temperature and a headache."

"Mmmm. I should have brought him something." He studied his watch. "Tell you what, are the Corner Stores will open? They've got some toys there, haven't they?"

Karen wiggled her shoulders in mock self-congratulation. "Who's your clever girl, then? I got him one." She pulled a book out of her bag and passed it over. "Skip's into dinosaurs, but you'll have to help him with the long names. Anyway, it's better than comics."

James glanced at the cover. It showed a rampant Tyrannosaurus Rex, its foul teeth bared, its blood-streaked eyes glinting evilly at the death throes of some unfortunate but equally loathsome creature pinned down by its enormous foot. Suddenly his boyish grin showed again, and he began to shake with silent laughter.

"Well, come on, then," said Karen, "tell us the joke. What's so funny?"

James spluttered, "I must say, that creature looks uncannily like Dawson."

James drove. He drove fast, whipping through the gears and keeping the revs up. Karen could sense that he was using the car to vent some of the tension that was responsible for the anger in his face: that anger which she had only glimpsed for a second when he first entered the wardroom. She didn't know why it was there, but she did know it would be futile to ask: she would only get generalities.

But when they turned left out of Portincaple to follow the tortuous dirt road that led them along the western shore of Loch Long, James eased up; his face softened. A clear sunset was developing, flooding the moorland behind them with golden tones and dramatizing the peak of Creachan Mor on the other side. The sea was deep blue, rippled by a slight breeze. A small sailboat was tacking northwards, its sails iridescent in the dying sun. Their cottage was beside the loch, facing the junction between Loch Long and Loch Goil, with a view over three miles of water to Carrick Castle. It was a different world, magnificent, serene, yet only four miles from Faslane.

Mrs. Campbell scurried out to meet them, clasping the Beatrix Potter book and her knitting, which had been untidily bundled into a plastic bag. She beamed at James. "Well hello, Commander, and welcome home. I know somebody who'll be glad to have you back." She indicated Karen, but then, pointing back at the cottage, she became more serious. "His temperature's on the up, Karen. I took it just now and it read a hundred and one, and he's still complaining about his headache."

"But children do get these things, don't they, Mrs. C?"

"Aye, so they do, but I'd watch him just the same." She smiled at James and did a half curtsey. "Ye're dinner's in the oven, so if ye don't mind, I'll leave ye now and fix up Jack's."

"Bless you, Mrs. C. I don't know what we'd have done without you."

"Och, ye've nothing to thank me for, Karen, but I'll be on my way now."

They went inside, James climbed the stairs to Skip's room and found him waiting in bed, a big grin all over his face.

"Daddeee!" Skip squealed with delight and held his arms open.

"Hi there!" boomed James as he bent down to hug him. "So how's our invalid, then?"

"Oh, all right, I suppose. Mrs. Campbell says that if I sleep I'll be better in the morning." He paused, looking his father squarely in the eye. "If I am, will you take me to the beach? I want to race crabs again, but it's no fun on my own, and Mummy's frightened of them."

"When you're better, yes, I will. In the meantime"—he said it slowly, rolling his eyes around—"in the meantime, we've got a small coming-home present to keep you out of mischief." James pulled the book out of his jacket, and Skip reached up for it.

He laughed when he saw it. "How did you know? I bet Mummy told you."

"It's a present from Mummy and me."

Skip was flicking through the pages, seeing just the monsters he wanted to see. "Will you read it to me? Now?"

"Tomorrow. You will read it and I will read their names. Now, I think it's time for young Skips to go to sleep. . . . Otherwise they won't be better in the morning."

"I suppose so." Skip snuggled down. "Will you be back for long this time?"

James tucked him in. "Should be at least three weeks. We've got plenty of time."

Downstairs, James found Karen beside the drinks cabinet, cracking ice cubes into a bowl. She had drawn the curtains and lit the fire, which crackled with the liveliness of dry kindling, blazing brightly. James liked a good fire, and he realized it was one of the things he missed at sea. Karen passed him a whisky, neat.

" 'Fraid dinner's not ready yet. Mrs. C forgot to switch the oven on." She stopped, feeling slightly awkward. For, seeing each other, with time on their own and together at last, they found themselves acutely aware of each other. Karen put her glass on the mantelpiece and opened her arms. She was slightly hoarse. "Welcome home, lovey."

James could feel his heart thumping. For the first time he noticed her dress, and took in her special smile which was for him alone, her square shoulders and proud breasts. He took her in his arms and kissed her, feeling her mouth with his tongue, and sensing an urgent response. He put his hand to the top of her long zip, and her eyes were a mixture of pure adoration and pride as he pulled it down.

It was then that he noticed there was nothing underneath. "Why, you little minx! You did that to turn me on!"

Karen giggled and they fell on the floor in a tangle of arms, legs, zippers and buttons. Unable to help themselves, they flew together into ecstasy at a dizzy, headlong speed until finally they lay together, spent, embracing each other by the fire.

Karen broke the silence. "That happened rather quickly, didn't it? Was that the way you wanted it?"

"No," said James. He stroked her hair gently. "I'm sorry, I was a bit rough. It's just that, with someone so fetching as your beautiful self . . ."

Karen put her finger over his lips and passed him his whisky. "I think it's time we had something to eat, don't you?"

In bed that night, they made love again. And though each tried to be gentle with the other, somehow it turned out to be

a rather mechanical performance. Afterwards, Karen lay on
her back, her voice soft in the darkness.

"Darling, there's still something on your mind, isn't
there?"

James grunted, almost half asleep, so Karen carried on.
"It's just that you don't seem to be able to relax, to let go.
It's as though you are still on duty, determined, but deter-
mined to do what?"

"Determined? That's a funny word to say right now. . . ."
His voice trailed off. Karen could hear his rhythmic breathing, and knew he was already asleep.

Skipper was at the steering column. Water was rushing in
from the bulkheads and his face was contorted with terror.
He was screaming that he couldn't bring the bows up.

James woke up. Skipper was screaming. He felt quickly
beside him but Karen wasn't there. He sat up, tried to shake
the dream out of his head, and bumped his way through to
Skipper's bedroom. Karen had him on her lap, trying to
soothe him out of his own nightmare. She looked up at
James with worried eyes.

"He's hot, very hot."

James took the thermometer from the glass on the mantelpiece and began to shake it down. Skipper suddenly became
quiet. He woke up and peered around the room with wide
questioning eyes. James winked at him. Skipper could only
briefly smile. His stomach cramped and Karen was just able
to bring the bowl under his face in time. He retched and
vomited, gasping for breath while he did so.

Presently it was over. He sipped a glass of water and
lay back. His voice was faint. "Ooh, Mummy, my neck
hurts."

"I'm sure it does, dear. Now keep this under your tongue
like a brave submariner and I'll watch over you." Karen
popped the thermometer in. Skipper gazed at her with
trusting eyes; he tried to smile at his father.

Karen was uncertain of herself. "Do you think we should
call the doctor?"

James shrugged his shoulders. "It's hard to say. As you
said, children do get these high temperatures and they come
down just as quickly. I wouldn't want to call Dr. MacRae

out at this time of night only to find that Skip's got a dose of flu.''

Karen held the thermometer up to the light. ''It reads a hundred and three. What do you think?''

''We've got some junior aspirin. Give him one of those and try to keep the temperature down with a wet cloth. We'll call Dr. MacRae first thing in the morning.''

They were up most of the night. James tried to sleep; he knew he needed it, but nightmares about *Saturn* kept recurring.

He was woken up for the last time by the telephone at eight o'clock. It was Captain Peter Forbes, the officer in charge of submarine operations at Faslane, effectively Admiral Dawson's aide-de-camp.

''Good morning, James. Peter here.''

''Oh.''

''I'm sorry to disturb you, but it is important. The inquiry is at eleven hundred hours today, in the conference room.''

''So soon, Peter?''

''Yup. We've been up half the night with the Kendall lads and now the old man wants to clear this thing up as soon as possible. Good thing too, if I may say so.''

''Couldn't agree with you more. I'll be there, Peter. Thanks for calling. 'Bye.''

'' 'Bye, and good luck.''

He put down the receiver and saw Karen standing in the doorway. ''Inquiry at eleven o'clock, Honey. I'll call you when it's all over. Good luck with Skip.''

Oak panelling, brass wall lamps, dark green velvet curtains and studded leather chairs lent the conference room on HMS *Neptune* an atmosphere of Victorian solidity. It might even have been Victorian were it not for the gilt-framed pictures depicting modern ships in action off the Falklands, the easel which held cheap white paper and telephone at one end of the long oak table. In front of each place on the table was a blotter, notepaper and a tumbler. Crystal water jugs stood in a perfect straight line down the centre.

The doors opened and an ill-assorted gathering of men made their way in; some in crisp dark uniforms, others in civilian clothes, some holding themselves erect, other with sloping shoulders and backs. Their ages ranged from late twenties to mid sixties and each represented a complex discipline. They were serious, talking in subdued tones, uncertain of themselves and where they should be sitting, worried about the outcome of an inquiry which they all felt was premature. Captain Forbes was the exception; being anxious to get the best out of everybody, he saw his immediate task as relaxing tension. He took Henderson and steered him by the elbow to a tall, balding man with a face as tough as leather.

"James, I don't believe you've met Sir Ralph Waters, Managing Director of Kendall. Sir Ralph, Commander Henderson, *Saturn*'s commanding officer." They shook hands, though neither knew what to say.

Henderson tried. "*Saturn*'s a very impressive submarine, sir."

"Ah, about that you should talk to Dr. Forsyth, our chief design engineer. Have you met him? Dr. Forsyth?"

Dr. Forsyth was tweed-suited, wearing gold-rimmed spectacles and a mildly academic expression. He smiled hesitantly as he turned round in answer to his name.

"Yes, of course. Commander Henderson, we met at the commissioning ceremony before *Saturn*'s maiden voyage. How are you, Commander?" He shook hands warmly, conveying a confidence in his design and workmanship which seemed to indicate that any mishap could not possibly be his responsibility, though he would clearly do all he could to help put it right. Sir Ralph clearly approved of the impression he gave; Forsyth was the sort of man who belonged on a board of directors.

He waved expansively at the rest of the team. "As you can see, we've pulled out all the stops for you. Tom Collins, there, is our computer engineer. Archie Franks is in charge of hydraulics. Arthur Coates is works inspection supervisor and David Schneider is in charge of the Hull and Gland Sealing Department." He added by way of explanation, "The periscope gland."

"Ah, well," Henderson replied, "you've just got me, Lt. Cdr. Sykes, the chief executive officer, Lt. Cdr. MacDonald over there, he's our chief engineering officer, Cdr. Andrews, the base's chief engineer, and, oh yes, Captain Forbes, of course. You have us outnumbered."

"I don't think so. Admiral Dawson will see to that." All three smiled.

Admiral Dawson chose this moment to enter. "Good morning, gentlemen, and thank you for coming and being so punctual." He smiled at Sir Ralph. "Sir Ralph?" They shook hands and Dawson indicated the place on his right. On cue, the Kendall team moved over to the opposite side of the table and sat down, sorting themselves out in their natural order of seniority. Dawson turned to Henderson. "Commander?"

Henderson sat down on his left, joined by Sykes, MacDonald, Forbes and Andrews. It had become very formal. They began unsnapping briefcases, pulling papers out and arranging them on the table. Nobody smoked.

"Gentlemen." Dawson's voice was brisk, but grave. "This is an unofficial inquiry. Depending on the results, we may or may not have to have an official one later on. There are three things we need to ascertain. Firstly, why did the periscope gland fail? Secondly, why did the hydraulic systems fail, and thirdly, why did *Saturn* exceed her operating depth? These are our terms of reference. Commander Henderson will interpret the computer log. Are there any questions before we begin?"

Sir Ralph glanced at Dr. Forsyth and Forsyth answered. "No, Admiral. We have all had time to study the report and it seems quite clear. Thank you."

"Then I think we will start with Commander Henderson and ask him to present the situation to us as he saw it himself. Commander, if you would be so kind?"

Henderson pushed his chair back and got to his feet. He had used the time since leaving home to make sure he was as fully prepared as he was able. "As you know, gentlemen, Section Six of the Engineering Trials requires that the submarine be brought up to maximum speed and then rapid changes of depth and course be carried out to check the submarine for watertight integrity and control system response.

"At zero two hundred hours I ordered the reactor room to bring the reactor up to the full power state. This was confirmed at zero two fifteen with turbine temperatures normal and all reactor control systems functioning normally. Next, as required by Admiralty procedures, I ordered the exercise area cleared by sonar. Sonar reported the area clear for approximately seventy nautical miles."

Henderson paused to take a sip of water. The difficult part was coming. "Having satisfied myself that the submarine was in all respects ready, I ordered revolutions five zero to be rung on. At this moment we were at a depth of four hundred feet. When we had reached a speed of twenty-eight knots, I ordered the coxswain to take her down to a depth of one thousand feet and level off. I then had the Engineering Department check for leaks. During the check I noticed that the attack periscope appeared to have a thin trickle of water running down it from the hull gland. I then ordered the outside ERA to investigate it."

He glanced at MacDonald. "His opinion, and I agreed with him, was that this was not of any immediate danger. Periscope glands have been known to leak in this way before, and we both felt that the outside pressure on the hull would squeeze it in, sealing it tight as we descended further. I then ordered the submarine to be taken to a depth of one thousand two hundred and fifty feet, our normal operating depth. Just in case, I had the outside ERA remain with me should there be any emergency attention required on the gland's emergency tightening bolt. . . ."

Henderson stopped, his eyes looking into the distance as he tried to marshal the events in their right sequence. "It was while we were descending that the gland split, sending a powerful jet of water into my shoulder, and momentarily causing me to lose my balance. I slipped on wet tiles and fell down, knocking my head on the base of the periscope shaft." He touched the small piece of elastoplast on his temple, as if to illustrate the point. "I was half-stunned for a few seconds, and CPO Fettler, the outside ERA, immediately tightened up the emergency lock on the for'ard periscope gland.

"Whilst on the floor, I heard the coxswain report that the primary hydraulic system had failed. Immediately the executive officer switched over to the secondary system, but nothing happened and valuable seconds were lost. I was still on the floor and I could feel the inclination of the submarine increasing, forcing her bows further down. The executive officer then ordered planes and steering in emergency but by this time we had already passed eighteen hundred feet. Immediately afterwards, Lieutenant Commander Sykes ordered the main engine stopped, and full rise on the planes. The coxswain was quick to react but *Saturn* was already passing two thousand two hundred feet.'' He heard Captain Forbes and Dr. Forsyth sucking in their breath, clearly aware of the fear the crew must all have felt in those vital seconds.

''Meanwhile, the outside ERA had secured the emergency bolt on the periscope gland, and helped me up, steadying me on the back of the coxswain's seat. I knew what was happening and I knew what to do. I ordered full stern and thirty degrees of starboards rudder.''

Henderson was silent for a while, using the moment to take another sip of water.

''Go on.'' It was Dawson.

''It seemed an age before she pulled out, but she did, and when she did the depth gauge was reading three thousand two hundred and fifty feet. The wall panelling was prised from its aluminium holding struts. Apart from that, and of course the primary and secondary hydraulic systems being inoperative, the executive officer was able to report that *Saturn* was functioning normally. I ordered her to be taken up to three thousand feet, and then we would ascend in five-hundred-foot stages, a leak examination being made at every stage.''

Admiral Dawson broke the silence. His eyes fell on Sykes and MacDonald. ''Do you concur with this sequence of events?''

Sykes replied, ''So far as I can remember, sir, this is an accurate description.'' MacDonald nodded.

''Thank you, Sykes, and thank you, James.'' Henderson was relieved to hear Dawson use his Christian name, but not for long. Dawson was not through yet. ''Commander Henderson, why did you conduct this trial at zero two hundred hours when most of your crew should be asleep and the lighting dimmed?''

The team from Kendall leant forwards, studying Henderson, searching his face for any sign that might betray uncertainty. But Henderson knew his ground. ''*Saturn* is an instrument of war, sir. She should never have to do these manoeuvres in peacetime. Probably the most powerful instrument of war is the element of surprise. *Saturn* must be prepared to attack or defend herself at any time, night or day.''

Dawson was clearly enjoying himself. This was exactly how he liked his officers to behave. He turned his attention back to the team from Kendall. ''Does anybody have any questions regarding Commander Henderson's handling of *Saturn*?''

Sir Ralph Waters spoke. ''I would like to reserve judgement on that issue. We have the computer log to support the description of the failure of the hydraulic systems. However, the periscope gland failure cannot be recorded by the computer log. Clearly events are happening very quickly and it would be understandable if the commander, especially when stunned, were to be confused about the precise timing of events. Periscope gland assemblies are tested to seventeen hundred feet and it could equally have failed when beyond that depth. You see, on the tape we don't hear the commander's voice from the time he ordered *Saturn* to be taken down to twelve hundred feet until the coxswain had reported that they were past twenty-two hundred feet.'' He stopped to clear his throat. ''Which begs us to ask the question, why weren't the emergency systems immediately activated?'' He smiled but quite without warmth; it was more like a threat.

Bastard, thought Henderson. Dawson pursed his lips. ''Very well, we'll take the periscope gland.''

David Schneider stood up. His hand was shaking slightly, making his papers rustle. ''We have examined the gland packing assembly and tested the components for tolerance and materials integrity. It can happen that a gland will weep at certain depths, and the commander and his engineer were probably correct in surmising that the pressure from increased depth would squeeze it into a tight fit. That is why a periscope gland works freely on the surface but is locked tight below a certain depth. All our gland packings are X-ray tested prior to fitting, to check for any latent flaw. X-ray testing is the best method available for this sort of examination and it is ninety-nine per cent certain. Of course, we don't know for certain at what depth this happened: these were designed for normal operation at a maximum depth of seventeen hundred feet.''

Dawson was appalled. "Are you implying that the commander has misrepresented the facts?"

Sir Ralph was quick to take over. "No, sir, we wish to make no such imputation, just to reserve our position."

MacDonald had lifted his pencil, begging the admiral for leave to speak. Dawson let him.

"But the search periscope and the other five masts all remained tight. Besides, the failure of the periscope gland does not account for why *Saturn* exceeded her operating depth."

"Your point taken, Commander, but we are here to establish why it failed. You still haven't told us, Mr. Schneider."

Schneider had sat down again, and this time did not get up. "That's the point, sir. We are still mystified as to why it did fail. We have a team presently replacing the gland and we are confident that the new one will operate as effectively as the others. We will be taking the old one back to the lab for further tests. I can assure you, we want to know the reason for its failure as much as anybody else."

Dawson stared at him, his eyes reading the message clearly: if they could prove that it failed below seventeen hundred feet, then it would be outside their responsibility, irrespective of what caused the failure. It smelt. "Very well, let us for the moment turn to the hydraulic systems." He glanced at Dr. Forsyth. "Have we established yet why they failed?"

Dr. Forsyth was remarkably composed. "Not yet, Admiral. Our engineers and fitters are still on *Saturn* now. If I may say so, we would like to reserve our position on this one too. We feel the failure of both systems is by no means certain to lie in our hands."

Dawson clenched his fists. "The purpose of this unofficial inquiry is not to apportion blame, but to establish why these failures occurred, so that they don't happen again. Official inquiries apportion blame and they are not chaired by lone admirals."

The telephone rang. Dawson snorted and grabbed at the receiver. 'I said we were not to be disturbed."

"Lieutenant Briggs here, sir. First assistant engineer on

Saturn. Can I speak to Commander Henderson, sir? It's vitally important.''

"Hrumph." The admiral passed the receiver over to Henderson. "It's for you. Important."

Oh, Christ, not Skip! Henderson's heart was thumping as he took the receiver. "Commander Henderson here."

"Briggs, sir. We've found out why the hydraulics systems failed. The hydraulic fluid in the primary system was contaminated. We don't know how the stuff got in, but it was enough to jam the by-pass valve on the primary system in the 'open' position, so that the systems computer could not declare the primary system inoperative and switch over to the secondary system. Because to all intents and purposes, the primary system was still operative. We are draining the systems now, sir. It shouldn't take long. That's all, sir."

"Thank you, Simon. Do you mind repeating all that to Admiral Dawson?" Dawson nodded and took the receiver. He listened intently, closing his eyes as he tried to follow exactly what Briggs was saying. Then: "Thank you, Briggs. I'm going to ask you to say it once more so that we can all hear it." He pressed the switch that activated the telephone loudspeaker, and Briggs's earnest voice spread through the whole room.

Dr. Forsyth turned pale. He scribbled a note and passed it to Sir Ralph, who simply raised his eyebrows. Dawson hung up and gazed intently at each of them in turn. "Well?"

Sir Ralph answered. "You know we can't be responsible for contaminated hydraulic fluid. There's your answer."

"No, sir, it is not our answer." Dawson was fighting to maintain self-control. "There are any number of reasons why hydraulic fluid can become contaminated, and you are well aware of that fact." He looked hard at Dr. Forsyth. "You know and I know that we have a design fault here. If the crossover on a by-pass valve doesn't register failure on the systems computer, then it's not surprising that vital seconds were lost when trying to make that changeover. Seconds that could have turned *Saturn* into a sinking coffin!" There was cold fury in his eyes as he turned back to Sir Ralph. "It is not surprising that Sykes lost those vital seconds; the computer not only was unable to tell him what was happening, but was effectively giving him the wrong information!'' He glowered at Schneider. ''This makes it irrelevant whether the gland failed at twelve hundred feet or at two thousand, doesn't it?

''Gentlemen, you have thirty-six hours to get *Saturn* fully operational. That is all.''

''But . . .'' Dawson's glance froze Sir Ralph into silence. He stood up and nodded at the admiral. ''Thirty-six hours and you shall have *Saturn*. Good day, sir.''

Dawson grunted. White-faced, the other engineers from Kendall stuffed their briefcases and hurried out. They left a different kind of silence behind them. Henderson, Sykes, MacDonald, Andrews and Forbes sat quite still, thrown by the latent forces that had so nearly surfaced in Dawson's voice, aware that he had been fighting for self-control.

Then, like a ray of sunshine from a heavy sky, Dawson threw them a wink. His voice softened. ''You know that nothing else is wrong with *Saturn*, that she descended to over three thousand feet and surfaced without a single blemish on her structural integrity or her other systems.''

''Yes, sir. We felt that would be the case,'' Henderson said.

''They're not a bad yard, really. It's just that man Waters who puts them up to it. He reads the bottom line too much for my liking.''

''The bottom line, sir?''

''Profits, damn you, what makes the country tick.''

''Mmmm.''

''James, I'm glad you managed to handle yourself well during the incident and were able to conduct yourself correctly this morning. It spares me from having to rustle up another commanding officer for *Saturn*, but I'm afraid there will be no leave for you or your crew yet. Tomorrow morning we are off to Northwood for a briefing with CINCNAV and COMSUBATLANT. It seems the Admiralty have got something up their sleeves for you.''

''Oh?''

''No, James, I can't tell you any more than that. We'll find out tomorrow. Be here at eleven hundred hours, will you?'' Dawson was getting up as he said it. Forbes followed him out of the room.

When they were quite sure Dawson and Forbes were well

out of earshot. Sykes let out a wild cry. "Yeeeah-hoo! We did it! Well done, sir!"

Henderson hardly heard them. Events were crowding in on him; first the inquiry, now the briefing, and then there was Skip. My God, Skip. He got up briskly to find a telephone.

— CHAPTER 3 —

London, 13th May

It was raining. The two policemen on duty outside the door of Number Ten Downing Street stood as close as possible to the wall in an attempt to avoid the worst of it. One of them spoke into his walky-talky as soon as he saw the staff car drawing in to the kerbside in front of them. Almost immediately the door was opened by Martin Taylor, the prime minister's youngish personal secretary. Admiral Sir Richard Hardy, commander-in-chief of the Royal Navy, clambered briskly out. A gust of wind tore at the dark raincoat which he had hung loosely over his shoulders, revealing for an instant the gold braid that bedecked his dress uniform. He was followed by Sir James Hythe, director of Naval Intelligence, equally impressive in clothes that could only have been cut in Savile Row, sombre but elegant in their cleanness of line.

Both police officers saluted them as they darted through the rain to the sanctuary of the open door awaiting them. Inside they shook hands with Martin Taylor, who took their coats and waved them to the comfortable leather chairs in the anteroom to the prime minister's office. They paused before sitting down. Arthur Wainscott had only recently been elected, and already he had changed the furnishings to suit his own taste; previously there had been pastel-shaded fabrics, now it was leather, but chiming slightly off-key with the paintings of Yorkshire woollen mills, reflecting a man who was trying to ride two horses at the same time. Both men caught the same impression and their eyes met, each confirming the other's thoughts, before they sat down. Sir Richard Hardy, the admiral, reached for the *Times*, folded it and began the crossword. Sir James Hythe took the day's *Financial Times* from his briefcase and opened it at the last page but one. Neither of the two knights spoke to each other, though clearly they were comfortable in each other's presence.

Four minutes later, Martin Taylor re-emerged and told them that the prime minister was waiting. Both stood up and left the newspapers on their seats, almost as if reserving them, and moved through the open door.

Arthur Wainscott stood up to greet them. He had all-white hair, angular lines to his face, and blue eyes which glistened, making him look younger than he really was. His politics were basically middle-of-the-road except that he was strongly pacifist, though not necessarily out-and-out for complete unilateral disarmament. His election as leader of the Opposition and then prime minister had come as the result of compromise between the major factions in his party. In the event neither faction got what they wanted, but then neither had they got what they did not want. The only clear winner was Arthur Wainscott, with a strong electoral mandate for nuclear arms reduction and detente. All of which suited him fine.

He was certainly affable enough to Hardy and Hythe when they came in, introducing them genially to David Hogarth, the defence secretary, and Julian Randall, the junior defence minister, whom they both already knew. Hogarth had been appointed for his ability to deal with the chiefs of staff, to keep them in line with ever-diminishing budgets, and yet perversely to see that they were still effective in defending the realm. His appointment was made to appease the multilateralists. Julian Randall was better known to them as the minister directly responsible for the Navy, but he worked very much under Hogarth's shadow. Neither of them expected to hear much from him that morning.

The conference table in the prime minister's office was of a curious oval shape, with stub ends, so that the prime minister, on the one side, could see everybody on the other with an identical profile. Blue-backed mission files were lying spread open on the table, evidence that they had been talking about the mission whilst Hardy and Hythe were waiting outside. And it was correct, Hardy thought, that political decisions should be made separately from military ones. He saw Hythe frown briefly and smiled to himself, knowing that Hythe felt otherwise: that a valuable intelligence mission could too easily be thwarted by political aims.

They took the two empty chairs next to Randall and brought out their own files. The prime minister came straight to the point.

"Why does this have to be done with a sub? What can possibly be gleaned from a submarine, a vessel that spends most of its time under water, that we cannot glean from Satellite, or Nimrod, or our normal intelligence sources? MI5 and MI6 are collecting defectors all the time; surely it's only a matter of time before we get the right Russian naval officer?"

This was Sir James Hythe's preserve. "Not Russian naval officers, Prime Minister. They're never allowed ashore except under strict surveillance. It is very difficult for them to defect even if they want to. The point is that with a submarine's recording facilities we can get a very clear idea of how effective the *Kharkov*'s ultra sonar is, what power she is using for her sonar transmissions, indeed, what sonar transmissions they are. We can find out an immense amount of information about this ultra sonar and when we get all this, we'll know if we have to alter the operating procedures of our own submarines. It may even be that we'll find that many of them have become obsolete. Only a submarine intelligence-gathering mission can give us this, not satellite or air reconnaissance."

The prime minister was still unhappy. "But if you suspect the *Kharkov*'s own sonar to be so good, how do we know that our sub won't be spotted before it picks up the *Kharkov*?"

"Submarine, Prime Minister, not sub. Two reasons: only the day before yesterday, the *Saturn*, our newest 'S' class hunter-killer submarine, reached a depth of three thousand two hundred and fifty feet. She is also remarkably silent.

Both her depth and her silence should prove an adequate defence; with these combined, she should be completely undetectable. It is the *Saturn* we want for this mission, precisely because of her capabilities.''

"I am still very unhappy." Wainscott snatched up his half-moon spectacles and put them on. He flicked over a page. "It says here that this is a live firing area. That's missiles, depth charges. You can't send one of our subs . . . submarines in there. It's an area which the Soviet Union has specifically warned the Western Alliance is hazardous to foreign navies.''

Sir Richard Hardy chose to field that one. "It's where the *Kharkov* is doing her trials. That is where the information is and we need it." He paused, adding as an afterthought, "She'll only be operating with the two diesel submarines. It's nothing we haven't done before.''

"But not with this Government.''

"No, sir. But they won't even be looking for her. And even if they did find her, they wouldn't believe it. Of that much we're certain.''

"So what do you think are the chances of success for this mission?''

Sir Richard continued to defend the mission. He had not bargained on authorization being quite so sticky. "Obviously we can't be one hundred per cent certain. I'd give it a ninety-nine per cent success factor. It's a straightforward slip in, lie low, listen to the *Kharkov*, record her transmissions, and when we've got 'em, slip out again.''

"And if it goes wrong?''

Sir James Hythe felt his help was needed. "But it won't.''

"But Sir Richard, here, has just said that there's a one per cent chance that it will." The old politician: keep them divided.

Hythe sucked in his breath. "OK, so there's a one per cent chance that things will go wrong. Surely the importance of this mission outweighs those odds. Suppose we find that all our submarines are obsolete ten years ahead of time. By 'obsolete,' I mean unable to defend themselves, therefore useless. Suppose we find that our planning for the new generation of Trident submarines will need to be rethought. It's a damned sight better to be doing this now than after they've been built."

"I wish we weren't going to have Trident."

Sir James's voice became tight. "That, Prime Minister, is a separate issue. The point is that all our defence strategy hangs on the effectiveness of our submarines. We have got to be certain that they *are* effective. Look, even if you want to scrap the lot, and heaven forbid, I'm sure you don't want to be doing the scrapping under duress, with your arm twisted behind your back. This is the sort of mission whose success leaves you firmly in command of this country's destiny, and able to conduct a firm and positive foreign policy. It's information you must have and this is the only way to get it."

Silence. Arthur Wainscott took off his glasses and laid them slowly on the desk in front of him. He turned to his defence secretary. "David, what do you think of it?"

"It is my job to see that this country is properly defended from enemies without. I don't like this mission any more than you do, but having heard these two gentlemen, I see no alternative but to give it my sanction."

"Mmmm." The prime minister looked out of the window, feeling the drabness of the weather as yet another incubus on his shoulders. An idea came to him. "If that one per cent chance occurs, can we deny the existence of this sub . . . marine?"

Hythe and Hardy glanced at each other, a glance that said: At long last he's coming round our way, but how do we handle this one?

Hythe pursed his lips and smiled archly at Wainscott. He spoke softly. "You can, Prime Minister. And if the Russians do find out, you had better put my head firmly and publicly on the block. Does that satisfy you? After all, I believe that the information sought by this mission must be far more important than my career, which isn't far off coming to an end anyway."

Wainscott smiled thinly. He was already on to another tack. "Who is in command of *Saturn*?"

Admiral Hardy replied. "Commander Henderson, sir, an extremely able man, if I may say so."

"Reliable?"

"Oh, absolutely; very cool and highly competent."

"Of course, all your officers are. Nevertheless, all officers, just as all individuals, will react differently in a crisis. Is this man a risk-taker?"

Hardy bridled. "No, Prime Minister. I think it worth stressing that the first priorities of any Navy captain are to his ship and her crew. That is inbuilt in them from Day One of officer training. Commander Henderson, though, is exceptional; he is the only submarine commander so far to have beaten the attack computer at HMS *Dolphin*. Perhaps he can be criticized for being slightly unorthodox, but this is what gave him the edge over his fellow students. More than anybody else, I believe he is the right man for *Saturn*, and *Saturn* is the right submarine for this mission."

"I seem to remember *Saturn* as being the most expensive of our 'S' class submarines. Kendall built her, didn't they, at something like twice the cost of the others?"

"That is correct. But it now seems as though that extra investment could pay off handsomely."

"Mmmm." The prime minister replaced his glasses and continued flicking through the mission papers. He stopped at the last page, his forehead crinkling into a frown. "This last paragraph. I see you have amended it to read, and here I quote, 'The captain shall at all times ensure the safety of Her Majesty's submarine, and its crew, and its safe return to harbour, using all means at his disposal.' Surely this is ambiguous? It means he has *carte blanche* to go and start his own mini-war if he wishes to do so."

Hythe replied, very coolly, "This is really just a formality, Prime Minister, because of the area Henderson will be operating in. He should never have to interpret that paragraph to the full: as you will have seen on the previous page, his orders read . . ." Hythe turned to the last page of his Mission File, " 'to abort the mission if he is detected.' "

The prime minister sighed. He looked at Hythe and Hardy thoughtfully for a few seconds before turning to his defence secretary. Hogarth nodded his head, almost imperceptibly, giving the impression that he didn't like it either, having no alternative.

The prime minister reached for his pen, signed the last page with a bold flourish, and passed the Mission Order back to Hythe. "I sincerely hope he *would* abort it, gentlemen, I sincerely hope so."

Neither Sir Richard Hardy nor Sir James Hythe spoke to one another on the drive back to the Admiralty. But back in Hythe's office, relief overcame both of them. Hardy was the first to speak.

"Whew. During my whole time as C-in-C I don't think I have ever had such a tough time getting one of those signed."

"Sign of a new broom." Hythe was opening the drinks cabinet. "I think we could both use a little refreshment. A clear dry sherry?"

"Would do nicely." Hardy perched himself on the edge of Hythe's desk. "Did Fredenberger know what we were in for?"

"Now it's signed he will." Admiral Joe Fredenberger, NATO Commander Submarines Atlantic, was, as his title suggests, commander of all the submarines in the Atlantic that were part of the NATO force. It was only because *Saturn* was still in her trials programme that she had not yet been seconded to NATO.

Hythe rubbed his forehead and eyes with his hand. "You know, knowing that the Russians don't know how deep *Saturn* can operate . . ." He broke off and started again. "If you were given a new weapon, and found that it didn't work, what would you do?"

"Throw it away, use one which I know does work." Hardy stopped abruptly, realizing the implications of what he had just said. "Are you thinking what I think you are thinking?"

"The temptation is strong, isn't it? Sort of gives the mission a dual purpose, a treble one really; we get the information on the ultra sonar, we prove it's ineffective, and we will know a lot more about *Saturn*'s capabilities. Still, it's a silly thought, isn't it?"

"Is it?" Hardy was silent, deep in thought. "I did convoy duty on a frigate in the Barents Sea during the War. It's an interesting stretch of water. I should have thought the Baltic, or the Black Sea, would have been a better place to test the *Kharkov*."

"Ultra sonar was developed at Murmansk. They've got the scientists and the facilities there. The Barents Sea is the only place they can test it."

"You know, the Russians know we've got *Saturn*. They know she's hunter-killer class, they probably know who most of the crew are. All they don't know is her operating depth and her quietness, and those two features are vital." Hardy was speaking slowly. "If we were to relax our security just a little, just so that the Russians would know *Saturn* had departed northeast with full provisions and a war load, then we don't need to do anything else."

"Isn't that a mite rough on Henderson?"

"Nothing he can't handle. He will know he mustn't be detected and he's very good at that sort of thing. If the *Kharkov* knows he's there and can't find him . . ." His voice trailed off.

Hythe carried on for him. "And the *Kharkov* would be trying all sorts of sonar transmissions. It does sound very attractive."

"Supposing we put it to Fredenberger. He was as anxious as we were to get this Mission Order signed, possibly because the Americans don't want to involve one of their own submarines, I don't know." Hardy smirked roguishly. "It adds a whole new dimension to the mission, doesn't it? I should think he will be tickled to death."

Hythe nodded, smiling with him. "I see no harm in that at all."

Henderson hated flying. For one thing, the helicopter's speed and gravity pull on take-off always reminded him just how slow submarines were by comparison. For another, he felt exposed and vulnerable in the open air, quite the opposite to his ability to tuck himself invisibly away somewhere in deep water. And then there was the purpose of the flight: secret briefings always made him feel nervous. . . .

Admiral Dawson had been just as morose, but for different reasons. Even though they were his superiors in London, he did not like other people ordering his vessels around. He was an admiral, and he commanded a submarine fleet; his business was in deploying his fleet to execute objectives set out by the Ministry. It did not lie in having his vessels poached to carry out missions which were not of his making.

They looked out of the windows as the helicopter made its noisy descent to Northwood, noting the modern three-storey building with its impressive array of NATO flags around the courtyard by the entrance; the wooded grounds adjacent, studded with white accommodation blocks; and the grassy hill behind with its satellite scanner dishes among the trees. Beneath these, Dawson knew, was the massive amphitheatre, the much-spoken-of but rarely seen Operations Room, whose complex electronic and satellite machinery enabled wars in any part of the globe to be conducted from there. Involuntarily he shuddered as the helicopter landed, and unfastened his safety belt. Henderson had done the same.

The helicopter landing pad was beside the car park. They both stepped out, thankful to be away from the noise, to be feeling firm ground beneath their feet, and made their way round to the main entrance. They walked slowly up to the huge glass doors, tinted to give one-way vision from inside, and showed their passes to a Marine guard. He saluted them, allowing them both to pass through. Once inside they approached the security desks where more Marine guards were waiting. They all wore dark blue dress uniform, with red stripes down their trousers, gleaming black boots and white webbing, and white caps with red bands on their heads. As the guards checked their identities and passes, Henderson noted wryly that they were all fully armed, the sergeants with pistols, and the privates with light machine guns, and he knew that the guns were loaded. Dawson clearly knew the form, and Henderson took care to do as he did, until the sergeant gave him the clearance to go through.

They turned left at the back of the reception hall and walked down a long carpeted corridor to an unmarked door, with another immaculately dressed Marine guard standing to attention outside. Without speaking to the guard, Dawson knocked and entered. Henderson followed.

Inside they found Hardy, Hythe and Fredenberger seated around a medium-sized conference table in a room that was, though sparsely furnished, opulent. The table was of rose-wood, the carpet was thick, and the brown hessian-lined walls bore the photographs of previous NATO commanders-in-chief. Crystal decanters and cut-glass tumblers had been laid neatly on the table, their symmetry marred only by the blue files haphazardly spread on it. There were no windows, but they could hear the gentle rush of air conditioning. At one end of the room was a projection screen, and this was patched in to the War Room, enabling them to see Satellite and Nimrod coverage of any hot spot in the world, be it the Middle East, Central America or Southern Asia. Beside the table was a complex communications console, also linked in to the War Room.

The three men rose to their feet immediately. Admiral Sir Richard Hardy was clearly presiding in an expansive mood.

"Hello, Peter, and you must be Commander Henderson?" He shook hands with them both. "You've made good time; you must have had a good flight down?"

Dawson replied. "Er, yes, thank you, I suppose we did, all things considered." He looked questioningly at the other two, a half-smile on his lips.

"Yes, of course. Allow me to present Admiral Fredenberger. I'm sure his title explains everything: NATO Commander for Submarines Atlantic, and Sir James Hythe, director of Naval Intelligence."

Fredenberger went straight to Henderson. "Call me Joe," he said. His handshake was firm, dry and positive.

Henderson smiled back at him. "James," making sure his own hand was equally firm. Their eyes met and in that fraction of a second established a mutual feeling of trust.

"So you're the sub killer I've just been hearing so much about. I'm very pleased to be meeting you, James."

"I've often wondered what you looked like. Now I know." He turned to Hythe. "Sir James, how do you do?"

"How do you do, Commander?" Curiously, they did not shake hands. Neither felt the need or the wish to do so.

"Well, why don't we all sit down?" Hardy knew that activity was another way of breaking tension. He passed Dawson and Henderson their files, then poured himself a glass of water. "I think now is as good a time as any to begin. . . . That is, if I can get all these knobs and buttons to work." He had taken the seat beside the communications console. He reached for the microphone, pressing a button on its side. "Blue Peter One Zero. This is Northwood Control. Please project our friend. Over." His eyes focused on the others. "We have a Nimrod reconnaissance plane in the area right now."

There was static, broken by a voice coming over the console speaker. "This is Blue Peter One Zero. Roger, stand by."

Hardy turned to Henderson. "What you are about to see, Commander, is the Soviets' antisubmarine carrier, the *Kharkov*. She is currently exercising with two diesel submarines in the Barents Sea." He gave Hythe a quick glance. "We have good reason to believe that during her last refit in Murmansk she was equipped with a new type of sonar system. They call it 'Ultra Sonar' and it is possibly superior to anything we have. When I say 'we,' I am including the Americans. If we are to be able to assess this 'Ultra Sonar,' it is absolutely vital that we have intelligence recordings . . ."

He was interrupted by a voice over the speaker. "Northwood Control, this is Blue Peter One Zero. Patching you in now. Over."

Hardy squeezed the microphone button. "This is Northwood Control. Roger. We copy."

At that moment the large screen opposite flickered into life. The other four swung round on their seats to face it, and Hardy chose the moment for a little drama. "There you are, Commander, your quarry!"

The pilot on the Nimrod was giving a running commentary. ". . . Eight Hormone helicopters on the flight deck. There, alongside the superstructure, you can see emplacements for SAM Twos and SAN Threes. Just forward of the superstructure you can clearly identify the bridge. There on the foc'sle in front of the bridge you can see the flat hatches for the twelve-barrelled ASROCS. Current speed estimated at twenty-eight knots, steering two six five degrees west." The screen was showing her box now, and the pilot was silent for a while. He came back again on the loudspeaker. "Northwood Control, this is Blue Peter One Zero. Do you require further coverage of our friend? Over."

"Blue Peter One Zero, this is Northwood Control. No, that's fine, just what we wanted. Thank you. Breaking contact, out."

In an instant the screen went blank. Hardy let the silence continue for half a minute before going on. "The *Kharkov* is sister ship to the *Moskva* and the *Leningrad*. Six hundred and twenty-four feet long, one hundred eleven-foot beam. Deadweight sixteen thousand tons, can weigh anything up to twenty thousand tons with a full wartime load. She can carry eighteen 'Hormone' anti-submarine warfare helicopters or twelve VSTOL 'Forger' YAK—thirty-sixes, or a combination of both. She carries SAM Two and SAN Three surface-to-air missiles as well as four emplacements of fifty-seven millimetre anti-aircraft guns. Also, one twin-barrelled SUW-N—anti-submarine missile launcher. There are two sets of the twelve-barrelled RSU. Six thousand series ASROCS, both carried on the foc'sle. In other words, she's a very prickly piece of equipment. What else? Oh yes, her size and configuration give her very poor handling capabilities in choppy weather. That's why there are only three of them."

The others were still silent. Henderson spoke first. "What's her maximum speed, sir?"

"I'm sorry, I've overlooked that part. Cruising speed thirty knots, can probably make thirty-five flat out. Peacetime range nine thousand miles at eighteen knots, wartime two thousand eight hundred miles at thirty knots. Powered by two screws driven from geared turbines, each rated at one hundred thousand SHP. Another gas turbine has been fitted to power her Ultra Sonar. Keel laid in 1973, launched in 1975 and commissioned one year later into the Northern Banner Fleet. She carries a full complement of eight hundred and forty men, but we don't know how many are officers." He paused. "Don't worry, it's all in the file. You've really got Sir James to thank for that information, and I think now is a good time for him to take over."

Hythe stood up and looked Henderson squarely in the eyes. But the look told Henderson nothing: what little bonhomie Hythe had displayed during their introductions had now evaporated, leaving a man who was deadly serious, intimately bound up with his own grey and murky world, trusting only those who he knew from a long past experience. His voice took on a metallic echo when he spoke.

"Commander, those pictures you have just seen came by

courtesy of the Royal Air Force. There was nothing particularly special about the information: the Russians don't even bother to hide it.

"But what you are now about to see required a very different kind of skill, one that took years to develop and, as a result of what you are now going to view, has been smashed." He switched on the projector and attempted precise focusing, then gave up. It hurt the eyes. "This is an overall view of the *Kharkov* in dry dock. If you look here," he pointed to the screen with a baton towards the bow section, "you will see that there is considerable activity. In fact all the equipment, and the position of the gentry crane, is here at the forward end."

He flicked to the next slide. "This is an enlargement of the bow section. You will see that whatever it is they have been fitting in required some considerable civils; they've just about rebuilt this section of the dry dock, and they have made it very much deeper."

The third slide showed a long streamlined canoe-shaped object. The men working on it gave the scale away. Hythe continued, "And this is what it's all about. Our informants told us that they call it 'Ultra Sonar,' but beyond that there was nothing they could tell us, except that it is extensible. I'm sorry these pictures aren't too good, but we're very lucky to have them: beggars can't be choosers. Sadly, there will be no more pictures coming from the same source." He switched the lights on again, speaking directly to Commander Henderson and Admiral Dawson.

"Now then, gentlemen. We don't really know anything more about this Ultra Sonar, but we do have these pointers. Firstly, it is large. Using these men for scale, we estimate it to be at least fifty feet long. Secondly, we know the *Kharkov* has been fitted with an extra turbine to power it. Thirdly, as you have just seen, they have gone to an immense amount of trouble to fit it in. Fourthly, they are not testing it in any old merchantman which is easily expendable if things don't pan out right, they are testing it in one of their most modern and powerful anti-submarine warfare carriers.

"All of which adds up to them being pretty positive

they've got something that works and is worth their effort. We want to find out what it is."

Henderson's expression was uncomfortable; he already had a good idea what the objective of this briefing was going to be. "If this is being mounted in an ASW vessel, then it looks very much like long-range detection . . ."

"Especially for hunter-killer submarines." Hythe said it softly. Hardy was examining his fingernails. Fredenberger was studying Henderson, biting the end off a cigar as he did so.

"OK, we'll carry on." Hythe switched off the lights again. This time the screen showed a picture of two officers mounting the gangway. Their faces were circled and the next slide was an enlargement of the leading and older face. "This is Commodore Orchenkov. He flies his flag on the *Kharkov* as flag officer of the Soviet Northern Banner Fleet. Fifty-eight years old, he saw North Atlantic service as an officer cadet during the War. One of the products of Stalin's new Naval Academies, now close to retirement. Highly patriotic, but competent."

The second enlargement appeared on the screen. "This is Captain Golitsyn. Age thirty-five. Very much a technocrat, works by the book as opposed to Orchenkov's 'seat-of-the-pants' philosophy. But he's bright just the same."

The picture of the two of them climbing the gangway returned to the screen. Hythe let it remain for a few seconds before switching on the lights. "It's all in your files, gentlemen, so please take care of them." He went back to his place and gathered up his blue file. "This is the moment when I take my leave of you. Admiral Fredenberger will fill you in on the other details. Good afternoon, and"—he looked pointedly at Henderson—"good luck." He raised his hand in salute before disappearing through the door.

There was a pause for a few seconds as the remaining four collected themselves.

Hardy cleared his throat. "Admiral Fredenberger."

"Surely." Fredenberger took Hythe's place behind the projector. The screen lit up with a map of Northern Europe, extending from Glasgow on the bottom left to the Franz Josef Land islands, just off the Arctic Circle, on the top right. The upper right quadrant showed the Barents Sea.

Fredenberger walked towards the front of the screen, collecting a long baton stick on the way.

"You sail tomorrow morning, James, at zero six hundred hours. Here, just south of Arran, you will dive and cruise at maximum speed, to arrive here, a hundred miles south of Bear Island, in the Barents Depression, no later than seventy-two hours after diving. That means an average speed of twenty-eight knots.

"As you know, the Barents Sea is quite shallow. If the *Kharkov* is testing her Ultra Sonar, she will want depth, and this is where she will find it, between Bear Island and Murmansk.

"There you will lie low and maintain complete silence for one hundred hours, monitoring all sonar transmissions. You will return by the same route. The mission clock starts at oh-six-hundred tomorrow morning. Is that all clear, James?"

"So far, quite clear, sir."

"Good. You will find all the co-ordinates and charts in the blue file."

Dawson had a nasty feeling that this was all the briefing there was going to be. "Er," he began awkwardly, "will *Saturn* be in communications contact throughout the mission?"

Hardy replied, his face quite impassive. "No. Once *Saturn* dives, she will stay in communications blackout until she surfaces after the mission. Clearly, if Ultra Sonar is as good as they think it is, then any kind of contact will increase our risk factor."*

"I see." Dawson was worried; it meant temporarily losing control over one of his submarines, his best one at that.

Henderson took that point matter-of-factly. His mind was already on other things. "What sort of activity are we likely to find in that area?"

"I was just coming to that." Fredenberger faced him again, something of a smile coming to his face. "By

---

*Communications have nothing to do with sonar. But if *Saturn* was to get a message, she would have to rise to three hundred feet or less below the surface to receive signals, which would increase the risk of detection by ultra sonar.

courtesy of the United States Navy Satellite Network, we've got something all set up. Hold on a second." He picked up a telephone receiver from the console and jabbed at the digits. "Western Control? . . . This is Admiral Fredenberger. I want priority control on Navstat Two for the next ten minutes. . . . Thank you." He laid the receiver on the table without hanging up. "We have a Navy satellite permanently monitoring the Barents Sea and its coastal approaches. With infra-red detection we can pin-point the precise location of every surface and subsurface vessel in the area." He picked up the receiver again. "Give us the northeast quadrant, will you?"

The screen started flickering again and steadied with a new map, this time showing Spitzbergen on the top left, Bear Island south of it in the middle, and North Cape, the most northern part of Norway, below. Murmansk was clearly shown to the left of the bottom. On the right was the upside-down New Zealand configuration of Novaya Zemlaya. The Franz Josef Land islands were shown on the top. Fredenberger spoke a few more words into the receiver and the screen altered again. This time red crosses were superimposed on the map, each with a serial number alongside.

"Can the Russians do that?" Henderson asked.

"We don't think so. At least, not the way we can. With infra-red we can detect a subsurface vessel up to three hundred feet below the surface, and up to five hundred feet if we use magnetic anomaly detection. So if *Saturn*'s deep enough, they won't detect you. Now then, let's see what we've got. Unit X26 is a 'Q' Class nuke on its way into the Atlantic. She won't pick you up; by the time you're past the North Cape she'll be a long way away. Units X29, 27, 28 and 30 are the Civtor Class nukes the Soviets have, and they are exercising in the vicinity of Franz Josef Land. That's over six hundred miles from where you're going to be. That's too far north, and clearly they won't be involved in the trials.

"That leaves us with these two diesel class submarines and the *Kharkov* herself, there. Those red crosses on the base denote coastal traffic; they don't concern us. So you see, with the depth that *Saturn* can reach, they won't even know you're there.

"Any questions, James?"

Henderson scratched his head. He was about to speak when Fredenberger continued. "There are a few other points I might mention while we're here.

"Firstly, this area is classified as a live firing area. That means live torpedoes, surface and subsurface missiles. Mostly they use icebergs for practice. It is therefore imperative that you remain deep throughout the whole mission."

Henderson, sitting with his hand over his mouth, glanced at Dawson, who simply raised an eyebrow, acknowledging that this was going to add an extra dimension to the mission. Hardy remained impassive, using his composure to stress that there was nothing unusual in this factor.

"Secondly, you will be taking onboard, tonight, a full war complement of torpedoes and missiles, together with provisions for a hundred and twenty days."

Henderson thinned his lips. Fredenberger appeared to pay no attention, though he knew it was the tense part of the briefing. He went on by way of explanation: "It's a very sensitive area; we have to cover every possible kind of eventuality. If Sir Richard thinks there's a one per cent chance of trouble on this mission, then it's up to us to cover for that one-in-a-hundred risk. Clearly we will be most unhappy if you use any hardware."

Hardy got to his feet and came round the table. "I shall cover Joe's last point. This is the original of the Mission Order with the prime minister's countersignature. Obviously it's not a good thing to have on board. Yours is identical in every respect except that it doesn't carry the countersignature. Now you'll see that we have amended the last paragraph to ensure that you use all means at your disposal to bring *Saturn* back.

"Very careful now. This is not a declaration of war, Commander. It's just that, as Joe so succinctly puts it, we don't want another *Pueblo* on our hands." Fredenberger was nodding his head.

Henderson was frowning, his tongue in his cheek. He spoke quietly. "I get the drift, sir."

Fredenberger grinned at him. "I think that wraps it up. Any questions, James?"

Henderson's voice was tight. "No, sir, it's all quite clear."

"Good luck, son." Instinctively Fredenberger thrust out his hand. Henderson took it, but though he shook it as firmly as before, his shake lacked the warmth it had then.

Sir Richard Hardy accompanied them back through the building, then out and over to the helicopter pad, talking to Dawson most of the way. The helicopter was waiting, its floppy rotors idling slackly and its motors humming in neutral. Hardy had smelt their disquiet but was not sure how to alleviate it. In the event he decided not to try. They shook hands with him coolly before climbing the steps and disappearing within. The engine noise increased and the rotors accelerated, their wind forcing Hardy to run back, holding onto his hat. In seconds the helicopter was up and on its way, leaving a comparative silence behind, and Hardy with a slightly puzzled expression on his face.

Admiral Joseph Conrad Fredenberger helped himself to a weak black coffee from the Cona pot before returning to his office. He was slightly puzzled too, and he wanted a few minutes to collect his own thoughts before transmitting his confidential report on the briefing to the Pentagon.

Fredenberger had been very carefully chosen for this appointment: Pentagon staff officials had been worried for a long time about morale and cohesion within NATO. Not that there was anything wrong with the armed forces in the European member countries, but certain political movements did concern them. Holland had prohibited nuclear missiles on her territory. In Germany, the surge of leftist peace movements had made German politicians evasive during discussions with their American counterparts. In Washington, U.S. officials who were under increasing pressures to withdraw their troops from Germany were more reluctant to do so than ever before, knowing that West Germany was the lynchpin for the whole NATO defence strategy.

Opinion polls in Britain had long told them that they could expect a change in Government. They had discreetly changed their NATO staffing accordingly, replacing the brash, all-American staff officers with a new breed: men who understood the subtleties of European politics, who realized that diplomacy and a low profile were what was necessary, that strategy in politics as well as defence was the order of the day. And Fredenberger, despite his sometimes colourful language, was just such a man.

And now the British had elected their own pacifist prime minister. It had happened before, in 1936, with almost disastrous results, and the circumstances today were not too dissimilar.

It was not only the pacifism that worried Fredenberger: he was equally worried by a Ministry of Defence which he was damned sure did not allow the full and free exchange of information they so frequently promised. The unions at GCHQ in Cheltenham were still there, grumbling on, and he wondered how much attention they paid to their precious Official Secrets Act. Furthermore, it seemed that a fresh mole was being dug up almost every year. Hell, even Members of Parliament had been known to pass secrets on to the East.

So when Hardy and Hythe had suggested the mission, Fredenberger jumped at the opportunity to endorse it, and willingly offered his services for the briefing. A mission like *Saturn*'s meant a commitment by the British, and as far as Wainscott's new administration was concerned, a precedent. Hythe's idea of letting the Soviets know, if only obliquely, that *Saturn* was up to something, was a brainstorm. For it might just encourage a certain amount of frostiness from the Soviets, and that frostiness might just discourage Wainscott from pushing through his disarmament policies too precipitately. . . .

Fredenberger smiled for an instant, clasped his hands behind his head, and leant back in his enormous chair. But the smile lasted only for an instant. Something still niggled, and he narrowed his eyes at the photograph of President Mallory on the wall opposite.

With a pacifist government and a mole-ridden Defence Intelligence Service, *Saturn* was too good for a weak ally. With her quietness and her depth-reaching capacity, she could outclass any other submarine in the world, including any American submarine. It would be all right if Britain was wholeheartedly committed to NATO, but he didn't think Britain was.

Henderson bothered him too. At first he thought he had liked him, but now he was not so sure. Fredenberger had been told Henderson was good, and he had studied him very carefully during the briefing. There was no hint of nervousness, as well there might have been in a man surrounded by two admirals and an Intelligence chief, but rather a self-assurance that had made Fredenberger feel as though he were briefing somebody bigger than he was. Yes, that was what made him feel uncomfortable, and he felt more uncomfortable acknowledging it.

Now, he thought, addressing himself to the pad in front of him, how in hell do I go about putting that on paper?

Inside the helicopter Dawson rummaged in his briefcase, producing a flask and two silver-plated beakers. He suggested that a whisky might help them relax, and surprisingly, Henderson agreed.

Dawson filled both beakers and passed one over to Henderson before taking a swallow from his own. He smacked his lips. "Feeling better now, James?"

"Thanks, thanks a lot. It's not just that we've had five weeks at sea, we've had a hell of an experience when *Saturn* was at risk. I know my crew are frustrated, I've just had to go through an inquiry, and inquiries are always unpleasant, and now I've just had a briefing which, if I may say so, stinks. We don't know if *Saturn* is vulnerable and it's a live firing zone. I don't know how you would feel, Admiral, but I feel, yes, pretty damned angry. You give those little gods a new toy and like five-year-olds, they want to play with it straightaway."

Dawson looked down at the countryside passing below them, but his thoughts were in Faslane. "It's only ten days at the most. You get three weeks' leave when you come back. Besides, isn't this what being a commander is all about?"

Henderson recognized the danger signal. He gave a wry grin. "Just how long does a commander have to keep proving himself?"

"As long as he's a commander, old boy, as long as he's a commander."

— CHAPTER 4 —

Scotland, 13th May, evening

The helicopter landed at HMS *Dolphin* at twenty-five minutes past six. Henderson and Dawson made their way over to the main building before splitting up, Dawson to his office and Henderson towards the pierhead. *Saturn* was moored at trot* number one, at the end of the pier.

Henderson found Alan Sykes, Commander Andrews and a Kendall engineer standing on the quayside. The engineer was explaining something to the other two with a mechanical drawing spread out on a packing case. Sykes saw him approaching and broke off, stepping briskly forward to salute him.

"I'm glad you're back, sir. We don't know what's going on but leave has been cancelled and there's a whole pile of signals which needs your attention. Most of them are urgent."

"I'm sure they are, Number One. Look, I want all hands back on board. Summon all officers to the wardroom now, immediately."

Sykes nodded. "Aye, aye, sir," as if the order confirmed what he had been expecting. He half-ran down the gangway, over the trot, and into *Saturn*. In the control room he would use the ship's telephone, which was hooked in every time *Saturn* entered harbour. All he had to do was phone the base Security Commander and simply ask him to recall all

---

*Trot: a pontoon between the pier and the submarine. The trot moves up and down with the tide, giving the submarine a safe berth, without continual attention needed on her moorings.

Saturn's hands. A simple request, but one that involved sending a patrol wagon throughout the married-quarter estates, searching the bars at HMS *Neptune*, and sending a patrol to search the pubs in town.

Henderson turned to Andrews. "How are we shaping up?"

"Hello, James. So far as I can see we're all tidied up. You'll find MacDonald on board. He's been giving these lads one hell of a time, but I think you'll find he's happy now." The engineer gave a sick grimace to confirm Andrews's words, and began folding up the drawing. Henderson smiled to himself; it was typical of MacDonald, and so far as he was concerned, a good thing too.

"Thanks, David. Sorry I can't talk now, but I've got my hands full. I'll see you anon, and thanks again for your help."

"Sure thing, James. Only try and bring her back in one piece this time." He was laughing but Henderson had hardly heard him: he was already climbing down the gangway and onto the pontoon.

In his cabin, Henderson shuffled through the messages which were waiting for him. Most of them concerned the release and loading of stores, munitions and fuel, but there were others regarding personnel, meteorology and, of course, the repairs. And because they were due to sail in twelve hours, they were all urgent. He felt for a pencil and began to answer the most pressing. He found that the answers were automatic, and that he could deal with them all inside half an hour.

By this time he could hear the rest of the officers talking in the wardroom, speculating on why their leave had been cancelled, and what they were about to hear. He rinsed his face in the small basin on the cabin wall and smile grimly at himself in the mirror. Apart from the smudges under his eyes looking a little darker, he had not worn too badly, considering what he had been through in the last three days. It was a pity he had not had the time to get himself a haircut.

The officers stopped talking as soon as he stepped into the wardroom. Some of them had glasses in their hands, but none were smiling. Henderson asked them all to sit down, and helped himself to a whisky whilst they took their places. He drank half a finger and washed it round his mouth, singeing his gums, before swallowing. Feeling better, he spoke to them all.

"Right, gentlemen. Unfortunately we shall be returning to sea at zero six hundred hours tomorrow morning. In their great wisdom, the Lords of the Admiralty have decided that we have one further exercise to carry out before we can have our rest." He scanned the tight, resigned faces that were focused on him, before turning to Sykes and the weapons officer, Bayliss. "So there we are, Number One, at twenty-one hundred hours tonight, a munitions barge will be brought alongside, and you will embark a full warload of torpedoes and missiles. We are also taking on provisions for a hundred and twenty days." He swung round to MacDonald and asked him, "Have the repairs been done yet on the periscope and hydraulic systems? To your satisfaction, I mean?"

MacDonald was known to be a stickler for getting work properly done. "Yes, sir. And the systems computer programme has been updated to ensure that the same thing cannot happen again. It's been demonstrated to me, and I'm happy."

"Good." He sipped a little more from his drink and frowned. "I know you have a lot of questions to ask, and so will the men, but right now I can't answer you. We will follow the usual form and I will address the ship's company tomorrow, after we dive. That is all."

He finished the drink, put down his glass, and left them. Nobody dared speak a word, instinctively knowing that he was as bitter about the loss of leave as they were.

Lt. "Shorty" Soanes, the second assistant engineer to MacDonald, broke the silence. "D'you know, I didn't even have a chance to . . ."

"Shaddup."

It was dusk when the taxi dropped Henderson by his home at Portincaple. He watched it drive away and stood still, savouring the heavily-scented twilight air, hearing the birds calling in the moorland behind him. *Saturn* slipped away into the back of his mind, along with Dawson, the briefing and his sullen crew. He became James Henderson, a free man, a family man, with at least a few hours in which to relax.

There were no lights on. Usually Karen or Skip would have come running out to meet him, but the cottage looked dead, empty. He frowned, shuffled through his pockets for the key and hurried up to the back door.

There was a note on the kitchen table. He turned on the light, lit a cigarette, and glanced through it.

Darling,
    Skip's got meningitis. I've gone with him in the ambulance to the Glasgow Royal Infirmary. The key's underneath the driving seat in the car. I'll see you there.

Love you, K.

Oh. What was meningitis? All they had was a dictionary and he looked it up: "inflammation of the membranes of the brain." Oh, hell, he'd better get over there.

It was a thirty-five-mile drive to Glasgow, and James drove like never before, cursing the slow drivers, swearing at the traffic lights. But he completed the trip in forty-five minutes. He asked at the main reception for the Pediatrics Department, and a young doctor pointed the way. He found himself in and out of lifts and wandering through corridors, awed by the size and complexity of the building, his pace ever quickening, but his mind telling him not to run. He found that the Pediatrics Department had its own reception and they were waiting for him. A nurse took him through.

Karen was reading a two-year-old *Country Life* in the waiting room outside the intensive care ward. Her face lit up when she saw James, and she crumpled in his arms. The nurse interrupted them briefly. "I'll tell Dr. Holroyd you're here, Commander. He'll tell you what it's all about."

James thanked her, and drew himself away from Karen. "Now, tell me what happened."

Karen had been crying. Her eyes were red-rimmed and the crow's feet below them told him she was all in. "Dr. McRae came round after breakfast. The antibiotics he gave

Skip yesterday had made no difference at all, so he called
for an ambulance there and then. It took over three hours to
arrive and I was getting frantic. I left a message for you at
the base . . . .''

"I went straight home. How is Skip?"

"They've put him under sedation. He's sleeping."

The door opened. A man with a clean, tidy face, trimmed
moustache and longish grey hair looked in.

"Commander Henderson?"

"Yes, are you . . . ?"

"Dr. Holroyd, yes. I'm glad you could make it. Skip's
asleep, but I'll take you along to see him, and then you can
go home. Do you know what meningitis is?"

"Not really. I looked it up and all I could find was that it
is some sort of inflammation of the membranes around the
brain."

Dr. Holroyd held the door open for them. "That's right,
but it's a very serious condition, especially among children.
All headaches should be treated with the gravest suspicion,
and this is one of the reasons why." He led them down the
corridor. "Fortunately, I think we've got Skip here in the
nick of time. Dr. McRae told us the antibiotics he pre-
scribed yesterday, so we've put him on something else.
Don't be alarmed by the oxygen tent; it's there as a
precaution."

"What causes it?"

"Meningitis? It's a virus. Anyone can catch it, but it's
not contagious or infectious, just one of those things which
crop up from time to time." He knocked on a door and
showed them in. A nurse was reading beside the tent, and
she put the book down as soon as she saw them coming
through. She stood up and straightened her skirt. Dr. Holroyd
evidently knew her. "Evening, Sally. How's he coming
along?"

"Much better now, Doctor. His temperature's coming
down and his pulse is back to normal." She showed him the
card.

"Ah, that's the antibiotic doing its stuff. Well, we'll see
in the morning. Meantime, don't hesitate to call me if
anything happens, will you?" The nurse nodded and smiled.
James and Karen peered through the tent, saw that Skip was

comfortable, breathing evenly, though there were still a few beads of sweat on his forehead.

"Does he still have a temperature?" James asked.

Dr. Holroyd replied. "A hundred and two, but that is a long way down from this afternoon." He took them both by their shoulders. "It'll be a while before we know how successful this antibiotic is. Sometimes a virus will fight back, and then we have to find another. So it may be four or five days before we can let you have him back, and then it's a long, slow recovery; lots of rest and sleep."

He was holding the door open for them. James and Karen thanked the nurse, wishing her a good night. Outside, James turned back to the doctor. "And if it doesn't work, like the first?"

"Then we keep him here longer, and find one that does."

"Just how worried should we be, Doctor?"

Dr. Holroyd scratched his head. "Ach, I never like to see parents worried. Skip's got a very serious condition here, but there's a good ninety per cent chance he'll pull through. The point is, there's nothing you can do, so there's no point in worrying." He looked at them kindly. "I know, I'd worry myself, but if you're good Christians, you'll pray. It's the best thing you can do. Ach, I said ninety per cent; it's not very often, though, that we lose a child to meningitis."

"We'll do as you say, Doctor. What else can we say, but thank you?"

"That's the stuff. I'll be seeing you tomorrow then?"

"Yes, we . . ." James stopped himself, realizing that he wouldn't be there, but Karen would. "I may be tied up, Doctor, but Karen will be here."

"Good. Skip needs all the support he can get. Good night."

"Good night, Doctor."

They were standing by the lift and shook hands briefly, before the bell chimed and the doors slid open.

Karen and James spoke very little on the journey home. They were sure that Skip was in safe hands, but that ten per cent chance of disaster niggled. Both knew that to pretend to be confident would be callous, and both knew that to worry openly only made matters worse. So their conversation was humdrum, skirting around the problem that weighed on them so heavily.

It was past eleven o'clock when they finally reached home, and James heated up coffee for them both before turning in. They were sipping it quietly when Karen remembered that James had been in London.

"I never asked you. . . . How was your trip to London?"

"Oh, all right. The Old Man came with me, which made it hard work. I'm afraid we sail tomorrow."

"What?" Karen put her mug down, shaken.

"We have to sail tomorrow."

"When?"

"Six o'clock in the morning."

Karen stared up at him, bridling. "You can't just push off at six o'clock! What about Skip?"

"I know. Darling, I have to sail."

"What do you mean, 'have to'? Doesn't your son count for anything? Don't I?"

"Of course you do, love, so does Skip, you know that. But you heard Dr. Holroyd say there's nothing I can do. Skip's in safe hands, and it's a very important exercise. They wouldn't have briefed me in London if it wasn't."

"I don't see how any exercise can be that important."

James knew she was right. But this wasn't an exercise, it was a mission. Now that he had been briefed, by CINCNAV and COMSUBATLANT in person, and that his crew were preparing *Saturn* for sea, he knew there was no way he could opt out without postponing the mission for at least another twenty-four hours. Besides, it might look like funking. And as the whole thing was so secret, he knew he couldn't tell his wife. He sighed. "Well, this one is. If I'm not there in the morning, I might as well forget about the Navy."

"Then I'll ring up Admiral Dawson, tell him what's happened, and he'll give you special leave."

"If you do, then I am out of the Navy."

"Then just what is this exercise?"

"Oh, come on, honey, you know I can't tell you."

"I don't see how any exercise can be more important than your wife and family. For heaven's sake, James, don't we mean anything to you? Your business is here!" Karen was close to tears again. She took the two empty mugs and turned the hot tap on full, angrily swilling them out. James took a drying-up cloth, and had to raise his voice to make himself heard.

"Darling, Skip should be better in a day or so, a week at the most. If I funk this one, I'm out for good. It's not on."

There were tears in her eyes as she rounded on him. "Damn you, James; we put up with your being away for weeks at sea, we put up with not knowing what you are up to, but when it comes to really needing you, you push off. It's either us or your precious submarine!"

James froze. Suddenly the inquiry, the briefing, the flight, the trouble with his crew and now this, all welled up inside him, breaking the restraints of reason. "That's blackmail!" he shouted, and flung the mug he was drying onto the tiled floor, scattering a thousand pieces across the room. Karen blanched, in that instant realizing she had gone too far.

James looked aghast at what he had done, as though somehow the mug symbolized the breaking up of their marriage. He sat down and held his head in his hands, trying to press back the pain inside. "I'm sorry, darling. I really didn't mean . . . . I'll ring up Dawson now."

"No!" Karen rushed to the telephone and put her wet hand on the receiver. James's expression told her she had nearly broken her man. In that second she saw that she had trodden on some forbidden piece of ground, that it was vital her husband sailed. "You're quite right. I've been stupid. Stupid . . . stupid and selfish. You sail. I'll get your things ready. You'll want to be there by five in the morning."

James shook his head. He felt tired, grey and old.

"No, darling, I do belong here. I should never have put you through all this. Let me call."

"Certainly not. You're still young, and you'll be a captain soon. I don't want a broken old man around my neck for the rest of my life. You go." She smiled at him, the tears staining her cheeks, but real affection showing through. James took her hand and squeezed it, smiling back. He stood up and embraced her.

"Well, where are the *Saturn* lads?"

"You're better off without them tonight."

"Why? What's up?"

"Leave cancelled. We damn near blew a gut getting their stuff alongside. You've no idea how much fifty-five men can eat in four months. And drink too," he added as an afterthought.

"Four months? That's a heck of a long time without a break."

"Oh, it doesn't necessarily mean they are going to be at sea for four months, but they've already been away for five weeks and they're none too happy about it."

"I should think not." The landlord paused, taking a sip from the shandy he kept below the counter. "Wasn't it *Saturn* where I heard about the radiation alert? What's going on with her?"

"Tch, tch. Those were just routine precautions. They're very funny about nukes, slightest technical hitch and they're all over them."

As it was a Friday night, the bar was busy. Most of the customers were servicemen, some with their girlfriends, and the landlord naturally kept an eye on the arrivals and departures from Faslane, because they affected his trade. Besides, he liked submariners, who seemed much more easy-going than their surface counterparts. He had expected at least a dozen in from *Saturn*, and spending about a fiver each, that would have meant sixty pounds.

On his left, Jimmy Handol couldn't help overhearing the conversation. He continued washing glasses, but his ears were pricked up, listening to the talk between the landlord and this man from Faslane, obviously somebody from the Supply Department. He had been working behind the bar for three months, and it was two months since he had met Alistair MacKintosh during one lunchtime. They each quickly found that the other had a passionate interest in Scotland's independence. They had both agreed that what they wanted was a proud independent Scotland, able to defend herself, and not to have to rely on the English and Americans. Their presence with their nuclear submarines could only put Scotland at risk, and would inevitably make Scotland do the suffering for another people's wars. It wasn't right.

During another lunchtime, when the bar was empty and they were alone together, MacKintosh explained that he worked for the Scottish Nationalist Party Information Service, with a special brief on oil and defence, that the job was becoming too much for him, and that he could no longer keep travelling from Sullom Voe in the Shetlands to all the ports on the Clyde. The Party had suggested that he build up a network of information gatherers, and that he use his own office as a collation point for information as and when it came in. Jimmy seemed ideally placed, and obviously had the right political views. Could he keep MacKintosh informed of anything he got wind of that related to Scotland being put at risk, more specifically, on happenings in Faslane? Because above all, the Party needed to know what was going on there, on their soil, in their water, and the Royal Navy was not going to tell them.

It made sense; Jimmy could see nothing wrong with that, particularly because the information was so easy to come by; which vessels were coming in, which were leaving, any odd little anecdotes. This wasn't spying, no cloak and dagger stuff, no Official Secrets Act, just to keep his ears open and his feet on the ground. And if he kept it up, well, barmen like Jimmy Handol were hard to come by, and it was worth forty pounds a week. Just for little snippets, like this one, and all he had to do was keep feeding it back.

Apart from getting paid for it, the thought that he was actually doing something to free Scotland from foreign rule gave Jimmy a new purpose in life. This was something he had never felt before, and MacKintosh found he had to take pains to explain that Jimmy was never to try asking for any information, just to keep passing on what he had heard.

"I said two pints of heavy and a rum and Coke, please, barman!"

Jimmy snapped back to life. "I'm sorry, sir, you've caught me dreaming. Two pints of heavy coming up, and a rum and Coke. Morgan's or Bacardi?"

Jimmy had never asked himself how or why the Scots Nats would pay him so much. It never entered his head that if this was what they wanted, they should be able to find plenty of helpers for free. That is, if they really felt the information would be of use to Scottish Nationalists.

At ten-thirty he slipped out to the telephone booth and called MacKintosh's Glasgow number. MacKintosh was in, and Jimmy gave him the news: *Saturn*, no leave, departing soon, radiation alert and four months' provisions. MacKintosh thanked him and told him he was absolutely right to have called; this was exactly the sort of stuff they wanted, well done.

MacKintosh was nothing to do with the Scottish Nationalists. He believed fervently in a doctrine that was clear and precise: a doctrine that preached total equality of all individuals, which meant common rights to all property. Human misery was the result of inequality, and it would stay that way so long as those with property continued to exploit those who had none. The limpid clarity of this view was overwhelming; he could see the evidence all around him.

He had sought and received help from the Communist Party. It was not long before a minor Russian diplomat arranged a meeting to see if they could help each other. Both men agreed that the achievement of such a State could be messy, as it had been in Russia and China, but certainly worth it. The Russian explained what MacKintosh could do, and a week later he was admitted for a short training course in a lonely farmhouse, not far from Crieff.

He sighed when he put the phone down, not sure whether Handol's information was really worth following through. Then on an impulse, he put on his raincoat and reached for his car keys.

Forty minutes later he was driving through Faslane, though there was nothing he could see. He took the ageing maroon Maxi into Garelochhead and turned left, where the road led him down the other side of Gare Loch. He stopped beyond Rockville, in Garelochhead Forest, and parked his car in a small lay-by. The night was quiet, its stillness only interrupted by the Friday night music floating across the water from Garelochhead.

He found his path and clambered up, using only a pencil torch to guide him. It was a path he had used before for surveillance on Faslane, and it led to a small clearing below short, squat oak trees. From there he could sit, totally invisible, and watch what was happening on the other side of the loch through high-power infra-red binoculars. He was less than a mile from *Saturn* and could see her clearly.

There were no floodlights, which was unusual, but he

could see men working around her, and they were using small hand torches. His interest soared when he saw the torpedoes being loaded at the forward end.

He grunted and wriggled to make himself more comfortable; it could be a long wait before *Saturn* sailed.

The heavily rust-stained Russian trawler, more brown than white, stationed between Malin Head off Northern Ireland and the Island of Islay, is well known to the Royal Navy. She bristles with antennae and eavesdropping devices, but despite this plethora of electronic hardware, is singularly unlucky in catching fish. She is known to the Navy as an AGI, an Auxiliary Gatherer of Intelligence, or else as an "ELINT" vessel, "ELINT" being the acronym for electronic intelligence.

The main feature of the Russian trawler lies below the water line: her passive sonar involves the most powerful hydrophones available, with which she attempts to monitor the passage of naval vessels passing between Scotland and Northern Ireland to the North Atlantic. What she really wants to hear is the "signature tune," the special sound by which any vessel can be identified, so that her masters could eventually plot the passage of British and American warships and submarines wherever they went, or recognize them wherever they were found.

She has a difficult time. Not only is it extremely unpleasant wallowing on the Atlantic swell, but British warships, frigates or destroyers, will accompany each nuclear submarine emerging from the Clyde, making such a noise with their screws that it is impossible for her hydrophones to decipher which is which. But the Russians get full marks for tenacity; they are still there now, and occasionally their efforts are rewarded.

Commander Henderson was at his usual place in the control room, making a sweep with the search periscope, checking that *Saturn* was well clear of all surface shipping. The North Channel from the Irish Sea is a busy traffic route and submariners cannot be too careful; in the event of a collision, however minor, the submarine is bound to be worse off.

He was interrupted by a voice on the loudspeaker. "Captain, sir, WT I am in communication with *Sirius* and *Phoebe*. *Sirius* says she has us on radar, we bear zero two zero and they will be with us in three zero minutes."

"Roger." Henderson swung the periscope round to three four zero degrees and could clearly see the two frigates closing in on him at high speed. He came away from the eyepiece, stood up and took down his microphone. "Officer of the watch, Captain. I am opening up for diving."

"Roger, sir." Lt. Hansen, the officer of the watch, was on the bridge on top of the fin, from where he was conning *Saturn*. It was a wet and uncomfortable position. Both he and Philips, the able rating who was with him, were looking forward to the comfort of being inside *Saturn* again.

Henderson motioned to the CPO on the Systems Console. "Order Diving Stations."

"Aye, aye, sir." The CPO flicked the PA switch and intoned. "Diving Stations, Diving Stations, open up for diving."

The executive officer and the outside ERA, that is, Sykes and Fettler, immediately began checking the valves and vents for smooth operation, an exercise which, though routine, is done thoroughly and taken seriously. It was twenty-five minutes before Sykes returned to the control room and reported to Henderson, "The submarine is opened up for diving."

Henderson was already reaching out for the microphone as he said it. "Roger." He flicked another switch. "Officer of the watch, I have the con. Come down and shut the hatch."

He heard Hansen acknowledge and took the search periscope again. He scanned to port and starboard and found *Sirius* and *Phoebe*, one either side, waiting for him to dive. He was ready.

"WT captain. Make to *Sirius:* I am diving now."

"Roger, sir."

Henderson barely noticed the two figures appearing from the hatch, the water dripping from their wet foul-weather gear, but nodded when he heard Hansen report, "Upper and lower hatches shut and clipped, sir."

Henderson stood back and spoke to the coxswain. "Half ahead, Coxswain."

"Half ahead. Aye, aye, sir."

"Dive the submarine, Number One."

Sykes replied, "Aye, aye, sir," and flicked open a series of switches on the Systems Console. They could hear water rushing into the tanks on either side. "One, two, three and four main vents open, sir."

"Roger."

He flicked open two more switches. "Five and six main vents open, sir."

"Roger."

Gracefully, *Saturn* slid below the surface of the water. She had dived. It was the moment all the crew, officers and men had been waiting for, the moment when the captain would address the ship's company. But Henderson would keep them waiting for a few minutes longer. He spoke to Tate. "One hundred and fifty feet and back to periscope depth, Coxswain."

"One hundred and fifty feet, back to periscope depth, aye, aye, sir."

He stood waiting, with a half-smile on his lips, until the coxswain informed him that they were at periscope depth. He took another sweep with the search periscope and saw *Sirius* and *Phoebe* as he had left them, one on either side. Satisfied that they were safe for a few minutes, he flicked down the PA switch.

"Do you hear there, this is the captain speaking." He looked around the control room, knowing that even if their eyes were not on him, everyone's attention was. "I am sorry we were not able to take our proper leave period when we were in harbour, but I can assure you that when we return from this mission we shall all have a long rest." He had used the word "mission" and not "exercise." "Now, the mission, gentlemen. The Navy have decided that because of *Saturn*'s performance on trials, as well as our own performance, that we are the most suitable crew and submarine for a particular intelligence-gathering mission. This will take place in a certain section of the Barents Sea. Our quarry, gentlemen, is the Soviets' latest anti-submarine carrier, the *Kharkov*." He knew that many of the crew would be familiar with the *Kharkov* and would therefore realize that this mission was for real. "I expect to remain in her exercise area for no more than one hundred hours, and this should give us the time to make all the sonar recordings we need. I would like to stress that the area we shall be operating in is a very sensitive one. Should we be discovered, then we shall leave immediately and return to base with all possible speed. Thank you."

He hung up and looked again at the faces around him. They were inscrutable. Or were they? Was that a glint in Sykes's eyes? And Peter Howarth, was that the ghost of a smile on his lips? Dammit, it was. The crew are excited. Yes, this is going to be a good mission.

He hoped the search periscope would mask his grin as he did another sweep, confirming *Sirius* and *Phoebe* on either beam.

"Captain, sir. Sonar."

"Captain."

"Stationary contact bearing three two five, approximate range four zero miles. Classified as the Soviet AGI as confirmed earlier by NIMROD sighting."

"Roger, Sonar. WT, Captain."

"WT. Sir?"

"Make to *Sirius:* 'My course will be two eight zero, speed fifteen knots. I am starting my run-out now, and thank you for your assistance.' "

"WT. Roger."

Sykes was watching him and thought he caught a glimpse of that grin. Funny, he thought, when you see a grin like that you know the man really is human, despite the iron, professional exterior.

On a submarine, the captain is not just king, but something more. He may not be liked, but he is revered and respected. Like a king, his decisions are absolute and he need give no reasons for making them. Like a king he exists in isolation, alone responsible for the well-being and success of his kingdom. But he is more than that: he knows more about the workings of his submarine than any other crew member. He has been tested to breaking point in endurance and stamina, both physically and mentally, tests that break down nine out of ten would-be Commanding

Officers, sometimes irreparably. The tests alone will prove the man, but the knowledge of those tests also gains him the confidence and complete trust of his crew. His officers envy him, but are afraid of those trials and the cost of their own possible failure. It is a distant envy, tempered by respect, reverence and complete trust. On board his submarine, the captain is father, leader and lawgiver: he is God.

Sykes knew that one day he would be a Commanding Officer, knew that one day men would feel about him in the same way he felt about his captain, knew he must think like his captain, though not behave like him, knew he must learn from him and use his example, knew he still had a long way to go, but couldn't be in a better place. Knew also that there was nothing wrong in feeling slightly excited about the mission, if his captain felt that way too.

His momentary musing was interrupted by the speaker over Henderson's head. "Captain, sir. Sonar. *Phoebe* and *Sirius* are doing us proud."

"Roger, Sonar." Henderson took the periscope and saw that *Phoebe* had dropped astern and was starting to weave behind him. Both ships would have their propellers on the roughest pitch setting possible, making bedlam in the water, cavitating most horribly, so that the sonar readings on the AGI would be totally indecipherable.

He caught sight of an Aldis lamp on *Phoebe*, signalling to the brown, rusty trawler. He grinned again as he tried to imagine what it would be saying, probably something like, "Nice to see you. Hope we didn't frighten the fish."

The trawler did not respond, but continued her aimless plod. Henderson could imagine the frustrated looks on her sonar operators' faces as they wondered for the nth time what good they could possibly be doing.

On the trawler, Captain Suslov frowned, as he always did, but his frown slowly changed into a grim smile. He called his radio operator and bade him inform Moscow:

"Unidentified submarine, possibly *Saturn*, exited North Channel accompanied by two RN frigates, direction NE. Unable to obtain sonar trace due to routine interference from accompany frigates."

* * *

Colonel Rodichev, director of Naval Intelligence (Submarines) was sitting erect behind a large mahogany desk, staring at the faded photograph of Lenin on the opposite wall. He was staring but not seeing, his mind wandering back to that meeting in Murmansk, there weeks before, when they were speculating about what the NATO forces would do with their flimsy knowledge of the *Kharkov* and her ultra sonar.

His hair was thin and grey, his face angular and his eyes heavily lidded. It was a face whose owner had grown up using it to mask his thoughts, a face well-trained in a discipline which held that to survive it was essential that nobody knew what was being thought. As a result, it was cold, never betraying warmth, hiding an animal within that was frightening because it was unknown, never understood.

In front of him was the signal from London. He read it for the fourth time:

TOP SECRET—PRIORITY 1
LONDON DATE 064514 MAY
FM 2ND SECRETARY
TO GRU NAVAL INTELLIGENCE SECTION (SUBMARINES)
SOURCE: AGENT SO3 SCOTLAND
ROYAL NAVY SUBMARINE ''SATURN'' LAST NIGHT UNDER COVER
OF DARKNESS IN FASLANE BASE RECEIVED WARLOAD RPT
WARLOAD OF TORPEDOES AND 4 MONTHS PROVISIONS

OBSERVATIONS:

1. CONFIRMED AGENT SO3 SCOTLAND

2. PROPOSED MISSION UNKNOWN

3. CIRCUMSTANCES HIGHLY UNUSUAL—SUBMARINE ONLY
   JUST COMPLETED TRIALS WITH BRITISH AND UNITED
   STATES NAVAL FORCES. ALL LEAVE CANCELLED.

4. SUBMARINE ''SATURN'' SAILED 0600 GMT SATURDAY

5. DESTINATION UNKNOWN RPT UNKNOWN

MESSAGE ENDS.

There was a discreet knock on the door. ''Come in!''

The door opened and an aide stepped in with a flimsy in

his hand. "Colonel, this has just come in from the *Volodya*, off Malin Head by Scotland."

"I know the one." Rodichev held out his hand and took the message, read it and put it down beside the first. "Bring me the file on *Saturn*, please, comrade, also her personnel file, as soon as you can."

"Yes, Colonel, immediately."

The aide saluted and left.

Rodichev closed his eyes and asked himself for the hundredth time what NATO would do with their knowledge of the *Kharkov*, now at sea, about a hundred and sixty kilometres north of Murmansk. Could this *Saturn* be linked? Was this the response they'd been waiting for? Was she coming up to try to listen in to the *Kharkov*'s ultra sonar transmissions? They know this area is sensitive: they would be crazy to try that . . . .

Unless they believed this *Saturn* was something special, that she might be able to listen in when others couldn't. Ridiculous! There are no submarines in NATO that we can't handle,' Rodichev told himself. There's another thing: a full warload of missiles is highly provocative. Except that we aren't supposed to know that she's carrying a full warload. In that case the full warload implies that they don't mind it getting messy. But one submarine against the entire Northern Banner Fleet? . . . Stupid.

No. Don't panic. This submarine has only just left Scotland. We don't know where it's going. It may well be to another Cold War brewing in the North Sea . . . except that they use destroyers to handle those. Well, then, perhaps target practice on icebergs. . . .

With four months' provisions? Where could a British submarine travel, that she would be unable to take on more provisions within two weeks? The only place he could think of was the Soviet Union's own northern coastline. Or else they were off on a very special exercise. . . . Very special, because this was the first he'd heard about it.

His thoughts were interrupted by another knock on the door. . . . He pulled himself together and sat upright again.

Lt. Granovski gave a brisk salute. "Your files, Colonel. *Saturn*."

"What do they say?"

The aide opened the first one. "HMS *Saturn*, Colonel, construction started May 1985, completed October '88. Gross tonnage five thousand five hundred. Length three hundred and thirty-five feet, crew of fifty-five officers and ratings. Finally handed over to the Navy in January this year, from a newly formed shipyard on the Clyde, Kendall's.

"She is the last in the line of the 'S' Series, ordered by the Royal Navy. Curiously, she was doing exercises in the Atlantic concurrent with her trials and these lasted for five weeks. We have reason to suspect that these exercises were centred on her and not on the other forces."

"Ah ha. Isn't that unusual? What makes you say that, Granovski?"

"NATO war games are usually reasonably well balanced, or with some specific purpose. In this one it was *Saturn* against a fleet of seven other vessels."

"I see what you're getting at. If I understand the British Navy correctly, no captain would ever be allowed the opportunity to boast his prowess against that sort of odds. It could have been some feature on *Saturn* they were testing. What else have you got?"

"That is it, Colonel."

"What? Is that all?"

"I'm afraid there's even less on the crew. Her captain is a Commander Henderson, believed to have done very well in officer training at their place in Gosport."

"Oh. Is that the best we can do?"

"Yes, Colonel. . . . I mean no. But that is all we have now. I am sure that we will be able to glean more information as time goes by, but *Saturn* is a new vessel."

Rodichev put on a baffled expression. "But didn't we have somebody in the yard who could have kept us informed? I mean, they've got people in ours."

"It is a new yard, Colonel." It suddenly hit Granovski that he was making excuses. "You're quite correct, Colonel, this information is hopelessly inadequate, quite insufficient to help you make judgements. I shall inform the United Kingdom Department immediately." He saluted and made for the door.

Rodichev watched him with the same expression that

other people might reserve for a cockroach on a dinner table. "Yes, I think you ought to." He sat back again, and closed his eyes.

Three minutes later he picked up the telephone and asked for Satellite Surveillance, North Atlantic.

"Rodichev here. There's a British submarine, believed to be the *Saturn*, which passed our monitor off Malin Head at thirteen-oh-six hours, direction northeast."

"We know the one, Colonel. We have infra-red recordings for that area at that time."

"Good. I want her tracked, and her position reported to me every four hours."

"Yes, Colonel. Pleased to be of help."

Rodichev replaced the receiver thoughtfully. Provided *Saturn*, if that's who she was, didn't dive below four hundred feet, he should soon know where she was going. If she did dive deeper, well, there was nothing else he could do, was there?

The Soviet Union is arguably the most powerful nation in the world, supporting one of the largest and most modern navies. Yet there are many Russians who are not at all sure why they have a navy of this size in the first place. Three quarters of all Soviet citizens live west of the Urals, in Europe.

Without proper sea access.

True, the USSR shares the Black Sea with Turkey, but to move out of the Black Sea into the Mediterranean, her ships must first pass the Bosphorus, into the sea of Marmara, and then through the Dardanelles. To reach the Atlantic they must pass Gibraltar. Many do during peacetime, but Russian admirals know only too well how easily defended these straits are in times of war; any attempt at naval deployment must involve treaties of access, or divisions of men to secure these passages.

Leningrad is Russia's largest port. But for between three and four months of the year, Leningrad is icebound. The Baltic can be likened to an enormous freshwater lake, its salinity so low in certain parts that the water tastes no more than slightly brackish. To reach the North Sea, her ships must pass the Baelt at Elsinore, another channel that is no wider than the Bosphorus. And to enter the Atlantic, they must either use the English Channel, or sail an extra thousand miles or so around the top of Britain. Militarily, the problems of the Baltic are as bad as those of the Black Sea; in times of war they are both non-starters.

Which leaves Russia with one main port she can use all year round, which doesn't freeze over, and where she can enjoy privacy from her neighbours, Murmansk. Here the warm waters of the Atlantic keep the ice at bay. The Norwegian coastline is virtually uninhabited, and she can give it a wide berth if she needs to. But Murmansk has a serious disadvantage: it is very remote, six hundred miles to the north of Leningrad, nine hundred miles north of Moscow, and well within the Arctic Circle.

But this is Russia's port, and because of its direct access to the open seas, it is very precious. From here her ships can carry out naval exercises and escape into the Atlantic. It was therefore no accident that this was where the *Kharkov* was stationed, and why Rodichev was so anxious about *Saturn*'s departure.

For once past the North Cape, the only landfall *Saturn* could make was Russian. Therefore her motives could only be clandestine.

— CHAPTER 5 —

17th May

"Joe seems very happy with the mission. I must say, I had expected him to be asking a lot more questions. Instead we're getting all the co-operation we could ask for, far more than usual." Sir James Hythe was half-standing, half-leaning, his backside resting on the edge of the table, in the conference room at Northwood. Admiral Sir Richard Hardy was absentmindedly drumming his fingers on the communications console.

"That tallies. I think he far prefers to see a British submarine doing the dirty work and not an American one. Besides, I don't think they have a submarine which can match *Saturn*." He pulled a face and sighed. "No, I suppose that's a bit cruel. I suspect they would also like us to feel that we are pulling our weight every bit as much as they are."

They were quiet for a while, each one absorbed in his own thoughts whilst waiting for Fredenberger to arrive. It was Hythe who broke the silence. "No, I think there's more to it than that. This ultra sonar on the *Kharkov* is common knowledge around NATO. I should imagine that there are some hotheads in the Pentagon who have been calculating some far more drastic action. What we are doing is pre-empting them with a passive operation. If that's the case, then I'm not surprised Joe's giving us all the help he can." He shifted his position. "What's happened to him? He should be here by now. It's nine-fifteen already and *Saturn* will be up there. I expect she's already gone deep."

Hardy checked his own watch. "Probably. If not, then she's just about to. Submarines have to slow down every four hours to clear stern arcs; that will have held her back a bit."

The door opened and Admiral Joe Fredenberger confidently smiled his way in. "Good morning, Admiral. Good morning, Sir James. What's the form now? Has *Saturn* gone deep yet?"

"We were waiting for you." Hardy was never sure whether to call him "Admiral" or "Joe." "We reckon she should be going deep about now."

"Well, let's see, then." He put his briefcase on the table and moved straight over to the communications console, picked up the receiver, and dialled. "Western Control? . . . This is Admiral Fredenberger. Patch me in to Navstat Two, please. . . . Thank you, Western." He put down the receiver and pointed to the screen. "Coming up any moment now."

They all turned to face the screen and watched it flicker into life. There were various red crosses dotted around it, but the one thirty miles to the north of North Cape indicated *Saturn*. "There she is," Fredenberger said, indicating the correct cross with a wave of his hand, "and she hasn't gone deep yet."

Hythe was speculative. "So the Soviets should know there's something there?"

"Oh, yes, and they'll detect a submarine. They won't know whose, though, only that it's not one of theirs."

"Which should set the alarm bells ringing. By the way, Admiral, has there been any change in Soviet naval activity up there since the briefing?"

"Nope. You can see it all here. There's the *Kharkov*, bang in the middle of the Barents Depression, and there are the two diesel submarines in escort. Apart from whatever the Soviets have in port at Murmansk and Archangel, the only hardware here are those four nukes around Franz Josef Land."

"Good." Hythe left a sudden twitch run through his body. He realized for the first time that he was slightly nervous about the mission, not sure that he had, after all, done the right thing in proposing it. Fredenberger saw it and smiled at him, asking the unspoken question.

"No," Hythe replied, not certain what was being asked. "They can't latch on to her with sonar, can they?"

Hardy answered. "Not *Saturn*. Henderson will take her in there quiet as a mouse. They'll look for her, which is fine, but I don't think they'll find her. She should give us everything we want, both of them really."

Hythe was mentally trying to assess what all the crosses meant on the screen. "Hello, *Saturn*'s red cross has gone!"

"Then she's dived." Fredenberger was pleased. "Gentlemen, the mission has begun." He took out a cigar, held it next to his ear, rolled it between his fingers, and finally tucked it into his mouth. He watched them both through narrow eyes while he lit it, making a cloud of bluish smoke. Satisfied that it was drawing nicely, he took it out and waved it towards the screen. "From now on we won't see *Saturn* on that, not unless she comes back up to four hundred feet. But we will be able to plot the *Kharkov* with this and your Air Force Nimrod, so we should have some idea of what is happening. I wish us all luck, gentlemen."

Fredenberger was jaunty, almost truculent; it gave Hardy

the uncomfortable feeling that somehow he was being used. Hythe noticed it too. He felt cold.

It was already twelve-fifteen in Moscow. Behind his desk, Rodichev felt the first tickle in his stomach, telling him he ought to be thinking about lunch. He looked at his watch, saw that it was in fact still too early for lunch, and then realized he was burning up more energy than usual, that he was more wound up than he had thought. During the past three days, *Saturn* had been monitored sailing north by northeast, and though he couldn't say why, he knew for certain that her destination was the Barents Sea.

Officially, Bear Island and Spitzbergen, which border the Barents Sea to the west, belong to Norway, despite the very definite presence of Russia on Spitzbergen. Norway is a member of NATO, so there was no reason why a NATO submarine should not be around these islands. It was perhaps a little cheeky, but not a *casus belli*.

Rodichev tensed again when Satellite Surveillance reported that *Saturn* was about to pass the North Cape, sailing in a more easterly direction, leaving, or appearing to leave, these islands well to port. Now he could inform Admiral Belinski without the danger of appearing panicky.

The telephone rang just as he was about to pick it up. He snatched at it, slightly irritated by the interruption, and frowned when he heard the voice at the other end.

"Director Rodichev, Satellite Surveillance here. We have lost *Saturn*. She's just disappeared."

"What do you mean, 'just disappeared'?"

"Just that, Director. One minute she was there and then she faded out. She must have dived below our detection depth."

"What was her last course?"

"Her heading was zero seven zero."

"Thank you, comrade. Continue to monitor the area, and inform me the moment you detect her again."

"Yes, Director, of course."

Rodichev tapped the receiver buttons on his telephone, impatiently waiting for the operator's voice. Finally it came.

"Switchboard."

"Get me Admiral Belinski at once, please. . . . No, he's

here in Moscow. . . . Yes, Naval Command Headquarters. . . . I don't care what he's doing, just get him for me straightaway.''

''Yes, Director.''

He pushed his chair back, stood up, and walked to the window, surveying the Moscow skyline: an impossible hotchpotch of skyscrapers, delicate spires, and the silhouettes of those ugly gothic ''wedding cake'' buildings, Stalin's most lasting achievement. He knew what had been nagging him: *Saturn*'s progress had been too obvious. Either her northeasterly heading was a feint, in order to distract attention from some other vessel which was moving into the Barents Sea, or London was trying to tell him something.

But what?

The telephone rang, and he stepped back to his desk to pick it up. ''Rodichev.''

''Belinski here. You do realize that you have interrupted a very important meeting?''

''Possibly. You know the *Kharkov* is presently doing trials with her ultra sonar in the Barents Sea?''

''Yes. Apparently they're going very well, so far.''

''Quite. I have reason to believe she is just about to be shadowed by a British submarine.''

''A what? You must be joking. It's a highly sensitive area, we've got SLBMs* up there!''

''No, I do not make jokes. Moreover, we don't know where she is, only that she's there.''

''What are we supposed to do about it?''

''I can see three options: chase her out, force her to the surface, or withdraw the *Kharkov* until she's gone. By the way, this submarine carries a full warload.''

''Oh.'' Rodichev could almost hear Belinski thinking at the other end of the telephone line. Then, ''I think we must inform the president. All these options involve wide international repercussions, but they all boil down to one thing: either we control the Barents Sea, which means our North Western exit, or we don't.''

''Good. Will you ask the president for a meeting, or shall I? There isn't much time to lose.''

*SLBM: Submarine launched ballistic missile.

"I'll ask him. I think we both ought to be there. I'll call you back." Belinski was never happy with GRU men coming between him and President Kirov. GRU men, though, were a fact of life, and it never helped to antagonize them.

Saturn had been making fast passage through the Norwegian Sea, travelling at speeds between twenty-eight and thirty-two knots, pausing only every four hours to slow down and clear her stern arcs.

The forenoon watch was closed up, the control room clock reading nine-twenty. Henderson had been constantly checking *Saturn*'s position with his navigation officer, knowing that he was leaving the North Cape to starboard and that very soon he would have to travel deeper and more quietly as he approached the exercise area.

"Captain, sir. Sonar. Stern arcs cleared, no contacts."

"Roger, Sonar."

He turned to David Hansen, the officer of the watch. "David, order the first watch action stations closed up."

"Aye, aye, sir." Hansen pressed the alarm signal on the navigation console and sent the alarms throughout *Saturn* sounding. He spoke into his own microphone. "Action stations, action stations. First watch action stations, close up."

It happened very quickly. Within fifteen seconds the PO on the helm had been replaced by CPO TAte, and the CPO on the Systems Console had been replaced by another. Sykes replaced Hansen as officer of the watch, and two more ratings took their places on the navigational and communications console. Within these fifteen seconds the control room was "closed up" and Sykes was in his position beside the Systems Console, acknowledging reports from the Manoeuvring Room, the Fore Ends and the Auxiliary Machine Space that all departments were "closed up," with the first watch at action stations.

Sykes took the last message and reported. "The submarine is closed up, sir. First watch at action stations."

"Roger." Henderson waited a full minute, giving the men time to check that they were comfortable, to familiarize themselves with the status of their consoles. He then spoke to Tate. "Coxswain, take her down to eighteen hundred feet, using ten degrees bow down, and level off."

"Aye, aye, sir. Eighteen hundred feet, ten degrees bow down and level off." They felt the angle of the submarine shift and heard Tate's voice calling out the depth, "six hundred feet . . . eight hundred feet . . . a thousand feet." The bulkhead panelling started to creak, but this time it was a friendly noise, somehow confirming that there was safety in depth. "Eighteen hundred feet and leveling off, sir."

"Thank you, Coxswain. Is the submarine trimmed, Number One?"

Sykes replied, "The trim is 'on,' sir."

Saturn had gone deep. Now she had to find her prey.

President Kirov was sixty-seven years old. Despite his luxuriant white hair and his white, slightly puffy complexion, his face also bore the hint of Asian features: high cheek-bones and slightly slanted eyes. The eyes themselves were blue, and twinkled, but they had the disconcerting habit of suddenly turning cold.

He remained seated behind his desk when Belinski and Rodichev were shown in. Though he did not get up, his eyes smiled in a faintly patrician manner, confirming that the presence of these two highly senior officers was yet another proof of his own indispensability. "Good afternoon, comrades. You have a problem, otherwise you would not be here and at such short notice." He motioned to the two seats in front of the desk, and Belinski and Rodichev settled themselves in.

Belinski came straight to the point. "We have a submarine, we believe the British submarine *Saturn*, which has entered the Barents Sea where our anti-submarine carrier, the *Kharkov*, is exercising. The *Kharkov* is currently testing the new ultra sonar device which was recently fitted in Murmansk. We hold this area as our own, excluded to foreign vessels, and we conduct live firing exercises there. We believe the *Saturn* is there on a mission of espionage."

"So." Kirov had taken it in quickly. He vaguely remembered the ultra sonar from a war briefing two days before the May Day Parade.

Rodichev knew that more information was necessary.

"There was something odd about her approach, Comrade President. She sailed directly from Scotland to the North Cape with no attempt at dissimulation. We were able to track her through Satellite Surveillance using infra-red. That is, until she dived out of range. I would have thought that if a submarine was going to go on this sort of spying exercise, she would have approached through Spitzbergen, anything to try and confuse us. Indeed a submarine would use every trick in the book to try and get in there without being detected. Certainly one of ours would."

"So?"

"So either *Saturn* is a feint to divert our attention from another submarine or London is trying to tell us something."

"Like what?"

"We can't say. I don't see what possible advantage she can gain by telling us."

Belinski interrupted. "*Saturn* is loaded. A war load, I mean."

"Ah." Kirov relaxed, having absorbed the information. He lit a black cigarette, drew on it deeply, and released a cloud of pungent smoke. He drank water from a glass on his desk, sat back and gazed at the ceiling. Finally he spoke again. "Tell me, comrades. In 1982 and 1983 we were doing similar exercises off Scandinavia. I believe we beached a submarine outside Stockholm, and for a while we had another one trapped in the Hardangersfjord. Is that correct?"

Belinski winced. "Lamentably, yes, President. Both submarines had a very difficult time."

"And the one in Norway, President Andropov had to claim was not one of ours."

Belinski was not at all happy about being reminded.

"And they fired depth charges and ASROCs* at it, didn't they, in an attempt to force it to the surface?"

"They very nearly got her. Fortunately, the captain kept his head."

"Precisely." Kirov bent forward. "Now this area is a free-fire exercise area, is it not? Good. And all the NATO forces know this, do they not? Now it does not matter if this

---

*ASROCs: Anti-submarine rockets.

Saturn is a feint for another submarine or otherwise. In either case there is a foreign submarine in our water, spying on one of our vessels. So the NATO forces have already shown us how to behave in precisely these circumstances.''

His eyes stopped their dancing and went cold. ''Admiral, you bring her up. We will show to the whole world what those Western powers are up to, and we shall make an example of her. And if you can bring her up in one piece, then so much the better.''

Belinski grinned. ''Yes, Comrade President. Then I take it I have your full permission to . . . to . . . to . . .''

''Yes?''

''To use all the forces at my disposal?''

Kirov stood up and walked round the desk, giving the sign that he was bringing the meeting to a close. ''Hadn't I made that clear? Please keep me informed, Admiral, I like to know what's going on.''

Both men came to their feet and shook hands with Kirov. They left together.

Rodichev brought Belinski back to his own office, ordered two black coffees, and handed over the two files on *Saturn*.

''Is this all you've got?''

Rodichev tried to look impassive, but saw that it made no difference to Belinski's more blustery attitude. Water off a duck's back, he thought, and that's how he made it to becoming an admiral. ''I'm afraid it is. *Saturn* is a new submarine from a new yard. It is difficult to obtain information in these circumstances.''

''But they've got people in ours.''

''I'm afraid that's how it is, Admiral.'' Rodichev found himself snapping and silently cursed his own department for letting him down. He decided to change the subject. ''How do you force a submarine to the surface?''

''Straightforward. You find her, dump ASROCs all around her, prove to her that she's pinpointed, and up she comes. Trouble is, it's a lot more easily said than done. Submarines can be slippery fish, and dangerous. They 'bite.' ''

''Can the *Kharkov* do it on her own?'' Rodichev was curious.

"She should be able to. In wartime she would have to. By all accounts she has the equipment to do it."

"With those two diesel submarines to help?"

"I don't think they'd be a match for *Saturn*, just a nuisance. I'll have them back in Polyarny."

"Can you guarantee, then, that the *Kharkov* can do it on her own? We wouldn't want a mistake. And supposing *Saturn* is a feint? Supposing that there are two foreign submarines up there?"

Belinski sighed. "I know what you're saying. Yes, we have four nuclear 'Victor' class submarines up by Franz Josef Land. We can bring them in and make the outcome certain. Trouble is, if we do that, then we aren't really proving anything with the *Kharkov*."

Rodichev leaned forwards, his hands tight together. "If it is the *Saturn*, then it's a nuclear hunter-killer submarine. I think it would be wise to minimize any possible chance of failure. How quickly could you bring those four nuclear submarines down?"

It was very simple mental arithmetic. Belinski reached for the telephone on Rodichev's desk and spoke at the same time, "About twenty hours."

Seasickness must be one of the most unpleasant conditions known to man. It induces nausea, sweating, violent retching, and total debilitation. Unlike other forms of travel sickness, there is no immediate possibility of relief: it can take days to reach a port. Those lucky ones who do not suffer cannot understand how strong men can be reduced to utter despair, genuinely wishing themselves dead. Many of the empty yachts found ghosting at sea are the result of just this: the movement in a storm can be so unpleasant that crew and captain will jump over the side—preferring any alternative, however temporary, to that dreadful sickening movement, that lurching which can send a stomach to the mouth, inducing waves of fever that beg for relief.

And yet this terrible condition can be cured within sixty seconds on dry land. It can also be cured with sudden activity on board ship: the need to secure a flapping sail, the need to throw a line to a man overboard, the need to secure a cargo which has shifted. The activity must be urgent, perhaps slightly dangerous, and must involve all of a man's physical and mental abilities. Then the cure comes instantly, even though the malady may return.

Commodore Orchenkov stood on the bridge of the *Kharkov*, trying desperately to focus on some part of the horizon. His face was very white and he was sweating underneath the eyebrows. The bridge was high up and located in the very centre of the ship, giving a long view forward over gun turrets to the two banks of anti-submarine rocket launchers. Behind, two more bridge windows on either side gave partial views of the flight deck. The bridge needed to be high up, but its height also accentuated the pitch and roll of the ship, swinging its inmates anything up to twenty feet from side to side. Orchenkov stood with his feet well apart, moving his weight from one foot to the other to compensate for the roll. He concentrated hard on doing it, in the hope that his concentrating would take his thoughts off his stomach, which had developed a rebellious mind of its own.

He had eaten bread and kolbassa, dried fatty pork sausage, for breakfast, and washed it down with sweet black coffee. He had had no lunch because he knew his breakfast was still there. He had a nasty feeling he was going to see it again, looking and smelling very different from the first time he saw it. He searched around for a paper bag or a bucket, and was relieved to spot a blue pail in a cubbyhole beside the chart table. He wondered angrily if the ship's architect had designed that cubbyhole for the bucket, knowing full well the potential for misery he had sketched into the ship's lines and calculated with her ballast to freeboard ratio. He tried to imagine that ship's architect, no doubt an arrogant, weak-chinned, bespectacled know-all from some highly theoretical academy, who had never been nearer to the sea than a pedal boat on the Khimki Reservoir. He began to conjure up all the most horrible tortures he could inflict on this man, starting on his most private parts and finally making him eat them; or filling him up with raw rice, and then, when his tummy had expanded, jumping up and down on him; or perhaps holding him over an enormous vat of boiling oil, enjoying the fear and terror in his eyes.

He began to feel better. Slowly a smile began to form on his face, not the smile of one grateful for the commiseration, pretending everything was all right when it wasn't, but a real smile of enjoyment. His eyes glistened and he licked his lips. No, he thought, I've got it all wrong. When I get back I'm going to find that stupid bungling idiot of an apparatchik and send him for seventy days' duty on the bridge of the *Kharkov*, and his official duty will be emptying the vomit bucket. No, better still, his only food will be from the vomit bucket. Maybe he will design better ships after that.

Orchenkov laughed out loud, and Captain Golitsyn gave him a sharp glance, wondering what it was he found so funny and hoping it was nothing to do with himself. Orchenkov caught the glance and stuck his tongue in his cheek, trying to keep his mouth straight. Then he saw him reach for his clipboard. Oh blast, he thought, that wretched man's about to do another stupid exercise with his ultra sonar.

Which meant slowing right down to four knots, and this meant in turn the *Kharkov* would increase her merciless wallowing. There was something he didn't like about Golitsyn, but he hadn't yet quite worked out what it was. He was damned correct, meticulous to a fault. He never shouted at anybody, but if one of his officers ever made a mistake he would go over that mistake time and again, making the poor fellow feel only a centimetre high. Much better to bawl him out and have done with it. And again, Golitsyn seemed to get upset over the most trivial of errors, like a coffee stain on the log. That had happened yesterday. Actually it was Orchenkov's coffee, but a young lieutenant had taken the blame. Orchenkov did not feel it was a particularly good moment to explain whose coffee it was. He would have to make it up with the lieutenant later, perhaps get him promoted onto another ship.

Then again, Golitsyn seemed so familiar with all the electronics; not just the hardware, but their programming too. Which was all very well, but enemy ships were controlled by human beings, and you had to understand that and try to work out how they were feeling, whether they were frightened, whether they were predictable. Clearly, if you'd got Golitsyn on board, you didn't need an enemy.

But worst of all, Golitsyn was not seasick.

"Message, sir." The coding officer had touched Orchenkov on the elbow and he came out of his reverie with a jolt. He took the slip of coarse white paper and unfolded it, reading it as quickly as possible. Reading made him even more seasick. His eyes widened as he came to the end, and then he read it a second time, slowly, and all vestiges of seasickness disappeared.

"Good God, we've got one!" He saw Golitsyn look across at him. "Captain, that thing we've got slung under our bows is like rubby-dubby shark bait. We've got a visitor! A real live hostile visitor, and we're going to fish him out!" He passed the message over and Golitsyn took it impatiently, annoyed at this slight delay in the next exercise. His expression changed to concern as he read it:

URGENT   TOP PRIORITY
TO   KHARKOV, FLAG OFFICER AND CAPTAIN
FROM   CINC NORTHERN BANNER FLEET

1. BRITISH NUCLEAR SUBMARINE SATURN REPORTED
    ENTERING YOUR EXERCISE AREA, BEARING FULL WAR
    LOAD.

2. MISSION OBJECTIVE BELIEVED TO MONITOR ULTRA SONAR.

3. YOU ARE ORDERED TO FORCE HER TO THE SURFACE. TAKE
    POSITIVE IDENTIFICATION AND ESCORT HER FROM THE
    AREA.

4. FOR YOUR SUPPORT WE HAVE ORDERED 4 RPT 4 VICTOR
    SUBMARINES TO JOIN YOU, ETA 0930 18 MAY.

5. YOUR TWO WHISKY SUBMARINES TO RETURN TO BASE
    IMMEDIATELY.

END.

Golitsyn also read the message twice. He passed it over to Commander Tyutchev, who was having less success in allaying his own seasickness. Orchenkov was delighted, his face cracking into a wide jovial smile.

"There, Captain. The British Navy have decided to come and have a look at us. So we shall have to put on our Sunday best, as the British would say." He breathed in, savouring the moment and the anticipation. "When all four submarines are in place and the two diesels have gone, yes, then, then we shall conduct live firing exercises with real anti-submarine rockets. Then maybe our British friends will have a little headache. We can send them all home without eardrums!''

Neither of them paid any attention to Tyutchev, who in that moment made a desperate lurch for the bucket. He held it tightly, retching violently and shrilly, struggling to bring something up that might allay the waves of nausea and the spasms of cramp that tore at his stomach. And while his face went red with the effort, he crumpled the message up against the side of the bucket.

Commander Tyutchev had not reached his rank through proven seamanship or naval academies. His academy had been the Communist Party Centre for Political Training at Leningrad. His responsibility was to monitor the actions and words of the officers and men aboard the *Kharkov*, and he had twenty subordinates to help him. They were to report on each man, indicating his fitness to serve in the Soviet fleet, not with regard to seamanship, but regarding his commitment, firstly to the Communist Party, and secondly to the Soviet Union. Even Tyutchev's rank could not reflect the importance of his position. He was second in command to the captain, but actually more powerful than Golitsyn or even Orchenkov.

But he was too busy with his bucket to note the disgust and confusion which showed on Golitsyn's face. The expression ''to force her to the surface'' meant war with kid gloves on. Very clearly he saw that, for propaganda purposes, there was all the difference between sinking her and escorting her away from the area.

Orchenkov misread his expression. ''What are you worrying about? We have the ultra sonar; we pinpoint her and make her life so uncomfortable she has to come up.'' His smile vanished for a moment. ''Or stay down for good.''

''But surely, Commodore, they don't mean us to harm this submarine?''

''Captain!'' There was condescension and a reprimand in Orchenkov's voice. ''When Belinski orders us to make an example of her, he doesn't mean for us to let her go. He wants us to make it very clear to other countries what happens when they send submarines snooping around in our exercise area. This is *our* exercise area, ours, and it's being violated by some foreigner. Don't you see, if they can come and go at will, it's no longer ours and the whole world will laugh at us. They must be very upset at Severomorsk*, not to mention Moscow.'' He strutted to the other end of the bridge, towards the companionway. ''Do you know, I think I'll go down and have some lunch.''

Golitsyn bit his lip. He said nothing.

Henderson was beginning to feel depressed. Time and again they had brought *Saturn* up from eighteen hundred feet to six hundred to take sonar readings, but they had located nothing that resembled the *Kharkov*. In fact the sea seemed devoid of any marine traffic and this worried them slightly more. The adrenaline they had generated when they first went deep had worn off, and they now found themselves wandering aimlessly around the Barents Depression, beginning to wonder if the *Kharkov* had gone home, and whether they shouldn't be doing the same too.

Wearily, Henderson reached for his microphone, ''Sonar, Captain.''

''Sonar, sir.''

''We are coming up to six hundred feet and going back down to eighteen hundred feet. I want you to report all contacts.''

''Sonar, roger.''

''Coxswain, ten degrees bow up to six hundred feet and back down to eighteen hundred feet.''

''Six hundred feet, sir. Ten degrees bow up and back to eighteen hundred feet, roger.''

The calm, slightly melancholy atmosphere in the control room was punctuated by Tate's mechanical readings: ''sixteen hundred feet . . . fourteen hundred feet . . . twelve hundred feet . . .'' Henderson stood quite still, letting his eyes wander around, half-resigned to another non-event. Finally, Tate finished. ''Eighteen hundred feet, sir.''

''Roger.''

''Captain, sir, Sonar.'' Crooke's definitive voice told

Henderson he had got something. "We have one contact, long range, bearing green one five . . . twin screws . . . no rev count as yet, sir, approximate range sixty miles."

Have we, now! "Roger, Sonar." Those two words spoke volumes: relief, decision, business at last. "Designate that contact 'Zero One.'"

"Aye, aye, sir. Zero One. Sonar signature indicates that this is probably the *Kharkov*."

"Roger, Sonar." A satisfied smile spread over Henderson's face as he caught Sykes's eye. "It looks as though we've found her. Number One."

"Yes, sir. Actually, I'm surprised we didn't pick her up before."

Henderson stepped sideways to the Navigation Plot and began to study it, plotting the *Kharkov*'s direction and where best to put *Saturn*. It immediately crossed his mind that something was missing. "Sonar, Captain."

"Sonar, sir."

"Have you any indication of the two 'Whisky' class submarines in escort with the *Kharkov*?"

"Stand by, sir." Lt. Crooke came back almost straightaway. "No, sir. The only contact we have is Zero One."

"Roger, Sonar." Henderson replaced the microphone thoughtfully. He turned back to Sykes. "That's strange, Number One. I wonder where they are, then."

Sykes seemed equally puzzled. "They could be masked behind the *Kharkov*, sir, or perhaps they're not there at all."

"No." Henderson had returned to the Navigation Plot, but was still talking to Sykes. "No, they must be there. If the *Kharkov* is testing her ultra sonar, she must have a subject to test on." He stood up, arched his back, and returned to his position between the two periscope shafts. The control room clock read fourteen twenty-four and he suddenly felt tired, realizing he had been on his feet for over eight hours. It reminded him that the mission had now officially begun, the moment they had located the *Kharkov*. He turned to Sykes again and gave the command, "Start the Mission Clock, Number One."

"Start the Mission Clock. Aye, aye, sir. Mission Clock started."

Above the attack computer, set into the bulkhead, the

Mission Clock began counting, in hours, minutes, seconds and hundredths of a second. It worked with the ship's computer log, enabling every event to be recorded, in the minutest detail, and timed accordingly. It would serve far better than any memory, should things begin to start happening at once.

LONDON, 18th May

Sir James Hythe had only been sleeping for two hours when the telephone woke him up. He came to groggily, fumbled for the receiver, and noted that the luminous hands on his alarm clock were showing half past one. He did not like being woken up at any time; this must be the worst of all.

"Hythe."

"Richard here. I'm at Northwood, in the Operations Room, and Joe's with me. Something's come up and we think you ought to be here."

"What do you mean?"

"Not on the phone, James."

"Oh . . ." He bit back the curse. "I'll be right with you, 'bout half an hour."

He hung up, swung out of bed, and shook his head to throw off the sleep. In the bathroom, he rinsed his face with cold water, brushed his teeth and asked himself what he ought to be wearing. He decided on an older suit, just in case he had to sleep in it.

Before going downstairs, he stopped by his bedroom door, peeped in and saw his wife fast asleep, dead to the world. Oh hell, he thought, I'd better leave her a note; she won't believe it anyway.

The drive to Northwood was fast. The streets were mostly deserted, peopled only by a drunk here and there, policemen in pairs, and the occasional fast driver. Litter fluttered across the pavements, and around the untidily stacked dustbins he caught glimpses of cats, dogs and rats, pulling at plastic bags and lids in quick jerky movements. Once he thought he saw a fox, but just as quickly dismissed it from his mind. The desolation, the rubbish and the scavengers gave London an atmosphere of wanton decadence and decay, though

Hythe was old and experienced enough to tell himself otherwise: the morning would bring back with it the bustle and activity, the vibrancy that made London London.

He left his car in the parking compound beside the main building, and walked across the compound, past the main entrance with its rows of flagpoles and down along the side. Instinctively, he checked for the second time that he had his security pass in his top pocket before making his way slowly and deliberately towards the massive "one-way" glass-fronted porch set back into the grassy knoll. He knew hidden television cameras were watching him, so he held his head up high to ensure that they had a good picture of him before he entered.

Once through the doors he paused, noting with satisfaction the mean faces of the Marine guards scrutinizing him from behind their desks, in front of him and fully forty-five feet away. These guards were not clad in the smart dress uniform used for the main entrance; they were in combat uniform. They carried hand grenades on their belts, their gun holsters were open and he knew that the safety catches were off. He knew, too, that on the long shelf behind their armour-plated desks were General Purpose machine guns, also loaded and cocked. For these guards were trained to trust nobody, not even the prime minister, and should anybody stray from normal practice, their instructions were to shoot first and ask questions later.

The sergeant knew him, but that did not mean he could relax. Hythe allowed himself to be searched and then produced his pass. The sergeant led him to a hand identification panel and checked his palm print. Satisfied, he nodded and disappeared into the office behind. Hythe waited, surveying the faces of the Marines around him, hoping for some glimpse of friendliness, but seeing none. In his own time the sergeant re-emerged, saluted, and handed him a second pass, granting permission to enter the Operations Room amphitheatre only, and Hythe knew that his progress there would be monitored on closed-circuit television too.

Now he was allowed access. Hythe walked down the slightly sloping floor to what seemed like a huge bank-vault door, only half open, which he knew would be sealed shut on the slightest alert. He stepped through and found himself in front of two lifts in a small foyer. He could use either one, but it could only be activated by his pass, and would only stop outside the entrance to the main amphitheatre, nowhere else.

Even Hythe did not know how deep the lift was taking him. Perhaps six hundred feet, he wasn't sure, but it was a long way down. He needed his pass again, when he left the lift, to take him through the double doors into the main amphitheatre, the Operations Room, where he knew he was expected.

The room was immense, its dim lighting enhancing the impression of size. Directly opposite him were three massive screens, each one able to project satellite, Nimrod or television coverage. Leading down forwards there was a thin catwalk, flanked on both sides by banks of desks and consoles, though it seemed that none of them was presently being manned.

He stopped for a moment, allowing his eyes to adjust to the dimness, first surveying the three screens and then looking round to see who else was there.

"Hi! Come on down here." He recognized Fredenberger's voice, squinted, and saw them sitting around one of the consoles at the front. There was an operator with them, a Navy lieutenant, who got up to leave as Hythe made his way towards them.

They stood up to meet him, Hardy, wearing a dinner jacket, and Fredenberger, who was still in uniform. Both had been waiting for him and his eyes, now accustomed to the dim light, could see the concern on their faces. He spoke softly; somehow the room did not encourage loud voices.

"Hello and good morning. What's up, then?"

Hardy spoke first. "It's about *Saturn*. Those four nukes up at Franz Josef Land, they've decided to join the *Kharkov*."

"But weren't they supposed to be six hundred miles away?"

"They were, but not now." He looked at Fredenberger, silently asking him to elaborate.

Fredenberger was equally grim. "It seems they started to move at eleven-thirty yesterday morning, our time. They were seen moving when Western Control did a routine sweep on NAVSTAT at sixteen hundred hours, but nobody thought much of it, assuming they were on another routine exercise. Then, a couple of hours ago, Western Control did another sweep and they found this." He pointed to the screen which showed it dramatically: the red cross, denoting the *Kharkov*, and four long arrows, emerging from the far north, already two-thirds of the way there.

Hythe was very quiet. "Where's *Saturn*?"

"We don't know. Not exactly anyway. All we know is that she's . . . somewhere in there." Fredenberger indicated a circle around the *Kharkov*, covering an area roughly a hundred miles in diameter.

Hythe was thinking, shaking his head in disbelief. "Why have they brought them down? Why aren't they using the *Kharkov* on her own, giving her a valid empirical test? It doesn't make sense, at least I can't see . . ."

He was interrupted by Hardy. "It could be that their ultra sonar isn't all it's cracked up to be."

"That is a possibility. In which case *Saturn*'s depth and quietness should keep her out of trouble. How well do you know your man?"

"Who?"

"Henderson, the commander of *Saturn*."

"I've met him a couple of times. Dawson's the one who really knows him, swears by him. Why?"

Hythe was resigned, knowing that the mission was going to be a failure before it had even started. "Because I hope that when he sees these units moving in on him he'll have the sense to abort the mission, to come back to base immediately."

Hardy grimaced at the implied lack of trust. "He should do. He's the right sort of man and it's written into the Mission Order. What I'm worried about is that he doesn't know those nukes are coming down and he may not know until it's too late. What if the Russians don't let him come back?"

Fredenberger regarded them both apprehensively, realizing that this was the one eventuality that had not been covered in the briefing, wondering how they were going to take it, and wishing that he had never got involved in the first place. He had long suspected that some of the strate-

gists in the Pentagon did not like seeing their allies with
superior weaponry, and that this was why those strategists
were so shamelessly prepared to use them. But this one
could get messy and he did not like being in the middle of
messes. He wandered back to the other end of the table,
towards the communications console.

"Gentlemen, I'm going to inform Western Control. We
are going to need full satellite coverage for the next twenty-
four hours." He gave Hardy a meaningful glance. "If you
can get your Royal Air Force to provide Nimrod surveillance, that might come in handy too."

Hardy nodded. "I'll do that now."

Hythe was still thinking about Hardy's previous remark.
"What did you mean when you said 'what if the Russians
don't let him'?"

"Just that. Henderson will give them one hell of a fight."

Hythe shuddered.

— CHAPTER 6 —

Barents Sea, 18th May

Deep in the bowels of the *Kharkov*, at the for'ends and well
below the waterline, was the Sonar Operating Department.
Here, eleven sonar operators monitored a bank of oscillo-
graphs and pen recording machines, from which papers
covered with rows of thin lines flowed in folds down to the
floor. Each hydrophone operated eight pens, and each pen
responded only to noises around its own frequency. The
operators were tense, having been told to expect something
but not knowing what, nor where or how it would appear.

One of these lines flickered into activity when *Saturn* rose
through eight hundred and fifty feet. She was there for only
a few seconds, doing her own sonar scan, trying to locate
the *Kharkov*'s escort, before descending again to the safety
of eighteen hundred feet. The flickering needle had subsided

before the operator had made up his mind to call the lieutenant on the watch. He shouted for him, at the same time desperately trying to turn up the sensitivity control knob. The lieutenant was quickly there to examine the recording, but he was as surprised as the young man who had called him. Taken on its own, the tightly oscillating line on the print-out indicated a submarine, but its sudden emergence and disappearance were unlike anything he had seen before. He picked up the intercom receiver and dialled the bridge.

"Captain."

"Captain. Sonar. I think we've picked up the submarine, bearing zero one five, range approximately eight zero kilometres."

"What do you mean 'think'? Either you have or you haven't."

"We only recorded her for a few seconds. We had a trace and then it was gone."

"That sounds more like a whale."

"No, Captain, this was definitely a submarine. There was no mistaking."

"Thank you, Sonar. From now on I want you to maintain the utmost vigilance around that bearing. Report to me the moment you detect anything the slightest bit abnormal."

"Yes, Captain. We already have all hydrophones turned on to maximum sensitivity."

Golitsyn hung up and regarded Orchenkov with a tight smile. "We've found her. Only for a second or two, but we know she's there."

"What?" Orchenkov jumped out of another reverie. "Where?"

"Bearing zero one five, range approximately eight zero kilometres." Golitsyn was pointing eastwards through the bridge window, towards an empty expanse of grey water.

"*Otshudo!*" Orchenkov was ecstatic. He slammed one fist onto the other. "The chart! Show me on the chart!"

The navigation officer stepped smartly back, allowing them both easy access to the chart table. He pointed from behind them. "We are here, Commodore, and the submarine must be round about here, in this direction, speed unknown."

"Good, good." Orchenkov was excited. He stuck his chin out and bit his lower lip as he feverishly began to calculate what was to be done. "Captain, have the *Vladimir* and the *Voronetz* here and here on our port side. The *Vitebsk* and the *Vologda* here and here to starboard. Have them keep their sonars on maximum alert and advise us of any detection. When they are in position, we will sail in a reciprocal direction and fire a pattern of four missiles, six kilometres ahead. We will do this every kilometre for twenty-four kilometres. She should be in there somewhere."

Golitsyn was aghast. "Do you realise you're putting us and the *Kharkov* at risk? What if we run over her? Suppose she fires back? We will have fired the first shots."

Orchenkov smelt criticism and he didn't like it. "No, Captain, that submarine is here on a mission of espionage. She will try to escape, not turn our attention on her. Then she will find that there is no escape. Ultimately she will have to surface." He turned to Tyutchev, subconsciously assuming his support. "How else can you get that submarine to surface? Eh, Commissar?"

Golitsyn would have preferred to have the submarine accurately pinpointed, to surround her very closely with all four of his nuclear submarines, and then instruct her, using underwater telephone, to surface. There would be no missiles. Orchenkov's plan was wildly barbaric, but one look at his face told him that this was how it was going to be done, and that Orchenkov was going to make damned sure he got the kudos for it, whether the submarine was intact or not. There would be no arguing, nor even reasoning with this man.

Helplessly Golitsyn turned to his first officer. "Sverdlov, did you get that? I want you to contact each submarine. Give them the suspected position of *Saturn* and give each one its new position. Tell them to use full speed to get there and full alert from now on, and to inform us if any one of them picks up anything that might be the *Saturn*, or otherwise alien, and explain what we are going to do. Got that?"

"Yes, Captain." Sverdlov had understood only too well.

"And tell them to hurry. We don't want to lose this one."

"Yes, Captain."

Golitsyn turned to Orchenkov. "And what if we should hit that submarine?"

Orchenkov grinned. "Tough titties."

The Mission Clock in the control room of HMS *Saturn* read zero five ten. The submarine was still at action stations, and Sykes had been relieved by the navigation officer, Peter Howarth. This time Howarth was beside the Systems Console and Coxswain Tate had been replaced by CPO Palmer. The five hours of uncertainty had drained them of the adrenaline they had initially generated when they first located the *Kharkov*.

For five hours and ten minutes Henderson had been periodically rising to eight hundred feet, and then descending, monitoring the *Kharkov*'s position, keeping her in range, and exploring the sea bed. Most of all he had been hoping to hear from sonar about her two escorts: it was extremely doubtful now that they were being masked by the *Kharkov*, and somehow that didn't make sense. Frowning, he reached for the microphone that was set in the bulkhead above him. "Sonar, Captain."

"Sonar."

"I am coming up to eight hundred feet. I am going to put us in that thermal layer you reported. I want you to make an all round sweep and report all contacts."

"Sonar, roger."

He replaced the microphone and turned to Peter Howarth. "Peter, rig for ultra quiet routine."

"Rig for ultra quiet routine. Roger, sir." Howarth stretched to reach his own microphone on the Systems Console and piped throughout *Saturn:* "Rig for ultra quiet routine. No movement throughout the boat."

Though there was no change in activity in the control room, they all sensed *Saturn* becoming much quieter, somehow expectant. Henderson picked it up too, and spoke softly to Palmer. "Five degrees bow up, eight hundred feet."

"Five degrees bow up, eight hundred feet. Aye, aye, sir."

Slowly *Saturn* drifted upwards, with Palmer calling out the depth every two hundred feet. Henderson took the microphone.

"Sonar."

"Captain speaking. Put all contacts onto the attack computer."

"Aye, aye, sir."

The attack computer was monitored by the screen immediately in front of the captain's position between the two periscopes. Henderson leant over it as it lit up, and then jolted his head back in disbelief. For there, very clearly, it showed not one, but five contacts. He grabbed for his microphone, but Sonar was calling him before he had got it down.

"Captain, sir. Sonar." The words were rushed.

"Sonar?"

"Contact zero two bears red four seven. Contact zero three bears red one three five. Contact zero four bears green six zero. Contact zero five bears green zero one zero. And contact zero one is steady on green zero four eight."

" 'Strewth! Sonar, confirm those contacts."

The voice from sonar came back over the loudspeaker. "Contacts checked and double checked, sir. We can only imagine that they were masked by a thermal layer."

"Give me a signature print-out as soon as you can, will you?"

"Sonar, sir. Roger, stand by."

Sonar were back in a matter of seconds, though it had seemed like an eternity. "Captain, sir, Sonar. The sound traces from contacts zero two, zero three, zero four and zero five indicate four Victor Class Soviet submarines."

"Captain, roger." He hissed at Palmer, white-faced behind the control column, "Eighteen hundred feet, ten degrees bow down."

Palmer repeated the command as steadily as he could, his hand already pushing forwards on the control column. Henderson's brain was reeling: my God, Victors, hunter-killers, nuclear. Where had they come from? What in hell are we supposed to do? He steadied himself, telling himself to keep calm, to try and work it out, remembering that the crew were counting on him for leadership. He saw Howarth at the Systems Console, looking at him expectantly, and noticed his jaw quiver as a slight tic passed through. "Peter, go into my cabin and get me the intelligence briefing pack, immediately."

"Aye, aye, sir." Howarth jumped up.

Meanwhile, *Saturn* was plunging down to eighteen hundred feet and Henderson could barely hear Palmer calling out the depth every two hundred feet. He called for Alan Sykes, and when Howarth was back, the three of them began shuffling through the briefing pack on the navigation console, trying to establish where these four submarines had come from. They were interrupted by the loudspeaker.

"Captain, sir, Sonar."

"Captain."

"Contact zero one, the *Kharkov*, has altered course. She is now bearing green one two, speed increasing."

"Roger, Sonar. What's the range?"

"Three zero miles, sir, and closing."

"Roger, Sonar." Henderson glanced at Sykes and their eyes met. "Sonar, Captain. Give me a range on those four Victor Class submarines."

"Sonar, roger. Stand by, sir. . . . Captain, sir, Sonar. Contact zero two, range approximately twenty-five miles. Contact zero three, range thirty miles. Contact zero four, range twenty miles. Contact zero five, range twenty-two miles."

"Captain, roger." Henderson tapped Howarth on the shoulder. "Peter, you take the con. Number One, get all officers to the wardroom, immediately. This stinks."

By the time Henderson had folded away the briefing pack and entered the wardroom, somebody had already served up eight steaming cups of coffee. The officers waiting for him were grim-faced, nervous and not sure what it all meant.

Henderson nodded approvingly at the coffee. "Those four submarines have come from Franz Josef Land. That's over six hundred miles away and my bet is that they've just arrived. They must have been going like the clappers."

"Does that mean they know we're here?" MacDonald seemed quite prepared to face unpleasant facts.

"Not necessarily, though it looks like it. We could have found ourselves in the middle of some extensive exercise. They've no reason to know we are here; we are very deep, and may not have been detected. Even if we have, we are in the middle of them. *Saturn* is very much quieter than they are, and there is every likelihood that they can have mistaken us for one of their own.''

Sykes was chewing the top of his pencil. He took it out and asked, ''How does this affect the mission, sir?'' He put the pencil back in his mouth.

''The Mission Order says we are to abort the moment we are detected. We don't know if we've been detected, but as soon as we try and do something I am very sure we will be. They are all around us. We must prepare to abort.''

''What do you mean, sir?'' Sykes was puzzled. ''If they move away with their exercise and we remain undetected, then we might as well stay where we are and record whatever transmissions occur.''

Henderson shook his head. ''No. I mean that they are all around us. Effectively we are boxed in. If one of those Russian nukes moves in any closer to us, then we are getting the hell out of here.'' He scanned the sombre faces around him. ''Does everybody concur?''

Sykes replied, ''I'm in total agree . . . ''

Ka-crump! The submarine shook with the force of the explosion. Stunned, the men looked at one another, unable to believe what was happening around them. Peter Howarth's brittle voice rattled through the PA system. ''Captain to the control room, captain to the control room.''

Hardy, Hythe and Fredenberger were sitting alone in the Operations Room at Northwood. It was eight-thirty in the morning, their coffee cups were empty and their ashtrays already full. Balefully, they watched the four crosses marked X27, 28, 29 and 30 on the screen in front of them, saw them move into a neat square formation, and noticed the *Kharkov* begin to change direction, as if preparing to run through. They had no idea where *Saturn* was, but there was something distinctly ominous about the way this exercise was progressing.

Hythe was feeling sick. The kind of sickness that comes when things go horribly wrong, when the stomach stops working and cheek muscles force the lips down. He was about to say something when Fredenberger forestalled him, speaking to Hardy. ''You reckon that Nimrod's there yet?''

The Nimrod is a curious-looking aircraft. Although built

on the lines of the Comet 4C, practically the only aspect of it left that still looks like a Comet is the four jet engines, built into the wings in pairs on either side. Both the nose and the tail are deformed by enormous swellings to house sophisticated radar and detection equipment. The wings are cut off at the tips to make places for extra fuel tanks. She is packed tight with electronics and communications equipment, and manned accordingly; in addition to the normal flying crew, she carries a tactical navigator, a radar operator, two sonics systems operators, an ESM/MAD operator and two observers. Airspace over the sea is considered international; provided the Nimrod keeps well away from land, there is little anybody can do about her without creating an international diplomatic fracas.

Hardy stood up and then slipped into the seat by the communications console. He lifted the telephone receiver, gave instructions, waited, and then took the microphone. He spoke carefully, the dynamism having left his voice. "Blue Peter One Four, this is Northwood Control. Are you in position to project our friend? Over."

There was static which cleared when the voice with a distinctly Midlands accent came over the speaker. "This is Blue Peter One Four. We are in position. Stand by for patching in. Over."

Hardy squeezed the microphone button again. "This is Northwood Control. Roger, we copy."

The screen was already flickering and then, suddenly, there was the *Kharkov*. But this time she was a hive of activity. Short, stubby Kamov helicopters were coming in and landing, others taking off, like bees around a hive.

The Kamov 25, codenamed "Hormone" by NATO, is a weird but very businesslike animal. Instead of one main rotor, she has two, one above the other, moving in opposite directions. This means she needs no tail rotor, and instead she carries three large square fins on a stubby tail. The four main jet inlets are mounted at ninety degrees, crosswise, above the fuselage, increasing the squat appearance, making her look like a fat bee. The design is effective. Hormones are capable of carrying and launching anti-submarine torpedoes, or "Fire and Forget" air-to-surface guided missiles. They also carry search radar, Magnetic anomaly detectors and sonobuoys. Sonobuoys are sonar transmitters coupled with hydrophones, which use the helicopter's power. They are lowered into the water from a hovering helicopter to transmit and record. As they can be moved around to compensate for their comparatively short range, a mathematically designed search pattern should be able to locate a submarine quickly. The Kamovs are very efficient at finding and destroying submarines; and like bees, they can sting, lethally.

The cameraman on the Nimrod panned forwards of the *Kharkov* and they could see three or four of these helicopters strung out in front of the ship, hovering over the sea with the long lines beneath them, disappearing below the water.

Hardy grunted. "Sonobuoys. They're listening for her."

Abruptly the screen blurred, fizzing back to the *Kharkov*, where for a fraction of a second they saw four white flashes from the forward end. Fredenberger croaked. "Goddamn. Is that what I think it was?"

Hardy groaned. "Yes, it is." His head shook with the shudder that rippled through him.

The captain of the Nimrod came through on the PA. "This is Blue Peter One Four. Have just received international warning from our friend that this area is unsafe and we are to stand off for fifty miles. I must comply with international laws. Over."

Hardy's knuckles tightened on the microphone, his voice staccato. "Blue Peter One Four, this is Northwood Control. Message understood. Return to base. And thank you. Over and out." He clipped back the microphone. All three of them were silent, stunned by the short but vivid camera shots of action thousands of miles to the north, knowing that it was against one of their submarines.

Hardy stood up and pointed his pen at Hythe. "James, I think we ought to be telling the prime minister."

"I was afraid you were going to say that. I'm not sure it is really necessary, not yet, anyway. After all, what can he do that we can't do?"

"He can't 'do' anything, but he can prepare himself for a difficult telephone call from the Soviet ambassador, if there is going to be one. I don't like it. I don't like it at all. This isn't how we planned it and it's gone very wrong.''

"But . . .''

Fredenberger interrupted them. "I don't know what you're going to do, gentlemen, but I sure as hell am going to tell our defence secretary. I'll bet the radio waves are fairly humming with traffic between that ship, Severomorsk and Moscow, and he's gonna wanna know why.''

Hythe was grey. "Oh.''

"Peter! What happened?'' Henderson had rushed into the control room as soon as the first explosion was over. He found the atmosphere very tense; Howarth was white-faced.

"ASROC, sir, at least I think so, from the *Kharkov*.''

"Order all compartments to shut off for depth charge attack.''

"Aye, aye, sir.''

Sykes and MacDonald had followed him into the control room. Henderson swung about to face them both, his face tight. "Well, that definitely confirms it. We are aborting this mission. Something has gone very wrong; they know we are here.''

They both nodded. Automatically, Sykes moved over to take Howarth's position on the Systems Console and MacDonald disappeared aft through the tunnel to the manoeuvring room. Thankfully, Howarth returned to his place on the Navigation Console. The only sounds came from the intercom on the Systems Console; departments reporting that they were shut off for depth charge attack. Sykes confirmed their status. "The submarine is shut off for depth charge attack, sir.''

Henderson nodded, his mind occupied with the attack computer. When he stood back, licking his teeth, Sykes spoke again. "Er, could be sticky, sir.''

"Yes, it could.''

"Perhaps if we tried that thermal layer again . . .'' But Henderson wasn't listening. His mind had switched to the crew, their need to know, to be reassured. He reached for his microphone. "Do you hear there. This is the captain speaking. It would appear that the Soviets know we are here, in their area. . . . By that ASROC attack it is obvious that they are going to try to force us to the surface . . . and that's not on. So as per our orders, I am going to abort this mission. We will endeavour to slip away and return home. That is all."

As he hung up, he noticed that Tate had replaced Palmer on the helm. Tate caught his look of surprise and explained, "I thought you might like a steady hand on the helm, sir."

"Yes. Yes. Thank you, Coxswain. Half ahead, revolutions three five, port twenty, steer two one zero."

Tate repeated the order as he moved the control column. "Steady on two one zero, sir."

"Sonar. Captain."

"Sonar."

"We are going to try and slip out in that thermal layer. Only report contacts if they come within range of detecting us."

"Sonar. Roger."

"Coxswain, five degrees bow up. Take her to eight hundred feet."

"Eight hundred feet. Aye, aye, sir."

The Barents Sea is a lonely and eerie stretch of water. Lonely because there is little traffic, there being few people who live north of the North Cape, and ships hug the coast. Eerie because here the warm Atlantic finally meets the freezing polar waters, generating "sea smoke," a weird phenomenon when the sea looks as though it is on fire, before forming a fog. From the torrid heat of Florida, the Gulf Stream becomes the North Atlantic Current, passing Ireland, and in turn becomes the Norway Current, the North Cape Current and finally the Murman Current. During this long journey the sea has been evaporating, making it more salty. This and its relative warmth keeps Murmansk ice free throughout the winter, when many ports over a thousand miles south are frozen up.

The polar ice cap is made from packed snow and glaciers. It is fresh, containing no salt. This melts into the Barents Sea, making the whole area one of confusing currents carrying different types of water. Though colder, because it is fresh the polar water floats above the salty Atlantic. In a sense the sea there can be thought of as a composite sandwich, the bottom layer being freezing still saltwater, the middle layer salt and warm, and the top layer fresh and cold. Sometimes the layers are dramatically distinctive, at other times they are hardly noticeable.

These different types of water affect sonar recordings, distorting them so that it can become impossible to "see" through one layer into another; a submarine captain can use them in much the same way as a fighter pilot can use cloud. Henderson was hoping that he could use the thermal layer, instead of his depth, in just this manner.

The day had gone badly for the *Kharkov*. Orchenkov's mood had progressed from elation to disappointment, followed by moroseness, frustration, and finally, outright bad temper. With all their helicopters, submarines and the ultra sonar, they had not been able to detect one further hint of *Saturn*, and Fleet H.Q. was getting worried.

Orchenkov was clutching yet another message in his hand, shaking it wildly at Golitsyn. "This is the third message we've had today, and this one's signed by Belinski. Why haven't we found this fucking submarine?"

Golitsyn said nothing. He was harassed, nervous of Orchenkov's posturing, angry with his bullying attitude and frustrated because he himself would have handled the matter differently. Secretly, he had been asking himself if there really was a submarine, but he knew it was there: nothing else could have made that recording.

The Kamov helicopters had been using their sonobuoys for active transmission, but all they got were traces of their own submarines. One of their sonobuoys had been damaged by the noise from an ASROC missile explosion, and Golitsyn was livid with the helicopter sonar operator for not switching it off when the missile was fired.

At three o'clock Orchenkov had ordered the ultra sonar to transmit, something else which worried Golitsyn, in case the *Kharkov* was within torpedo range. They had transmitted and transmitted, working their turbines at full power, but every time the response was negative. Perhaps they had sunk the submarine with a missile, but if that was the case, one of the two rear Kamovs should have noticed the explosion, seen the debris. Or perhaps they had disabled it, sending it to the bottom intact, but unable to get away. And all the time this wretched, stupid man had been strutting around like a banana-republic dictator, fuming, finding fault, and insulting his men.

Orchenkov was doggedly persistent. "Well, what are we going to do about it?" he demanded. Golitsyn didn't feel like answering: whatever he said he was going to have his head bitten off. He ignored the question, preferring to interpret it as rhetorical.

"Well, what?"

Oh, why wouldn't that idiot shut up and let him get on with the job? Golitsyn snapped back at him. "Tell them we are still trying; we've got all our helicopters up and we've fired over a hundred missiles. Tell them we've been transmitting on ultra sonar, using maximum power. Tell them . . . oh, tell them that as far as we're concerned the sea around is clear for a radius of over a hundred kilometres."

"But it isn't!" Orchenkov roared at him, waving his bit of paper. "We've already told them we've detected it for a few seconds. How can we tell them it isn't there now?"

Golitsyn busied himself over the chart table, wishing that Orchenkov would go away. At length he looked up, his eyes tired. "Well, figuring that out is your job, Commodore. Is there something else you would like me to do? Box G, for example?"

"Box G, yes, do Box G." This was the section to the east of where they had begun.

"Very well, we'll do Box G." He leant over the charts again to work out the co-ordinates needed to get the four submarines into position for Box G.

The evening light faded slowly into dusk. There is little darkness in these latitudes during the warmer months, even as early as May. Orchenkov received two more messages from Belinski. He had tried to pre-empt them with status reports. Clearly, Belinski was paying them no attention.

His Excellency Sir Humphrey Prescott, KCB, Her Majesty's Ambassador in Moscow, was in his office every morning at eight o'clock, regardless of whatever function he had been to the night before, and however late it had kept him. The morning of the eighteenth day of May was no exception. What was exceptional was the news the duty officer had waiting for him.

"Good morning, Sir Humphrey. Sir..."

"Morning, Bartlett. All quiet on the Eastern Front?"

"Sir, I have just had the Foreign Ministry on the phone. Vatutin presents his compliments and invites you to join him at his office, at nine o'clock precisely."

"Oh? Any idea what it's about?" He knew the question was useless. An invitation like that from the foreign secretary meant trouble of one sort or another, and Vatutin was not going to forewarn him. Actually, he got on with Vatutin quite well, or thought he did; it was difficult to be certain. They could both drink, and both had a sense of humour: it was a great help during the many sterile functions when they found themselves together, and made the day-to-day contact between the Embassy and the Foreign Ministry that much easier.

"No, sir, nothing untoward came through during the night."

"Good. Then we've nothing to worry about. Will you call Philip King for me? We'll be going there together."

"Very good, sir. I'll have your coffee sent in."

Philip King was the head of Chancery, who, in addition to running the Embassy's registration and passport section, was also effectively Prescott's second in command. Besides, he had a good, almost academic sense of protocol which had served him well, first in Hungary and now in Russia.

They stepped out of the Embassy entrance at eight forty-five precisely, to climb into the waiting Rolls. Sir Humphrey raised his eyebrows at the motorcycle escort waiting for them in the street, and as the Rolls emerged, the motorcycles fell in, two in front and two behind, to make sure that the road was clear of traffic. Sitting in the back, Sir Humphrey asked Philip if he had any inkling as to what the meeting was all about.

"No, sir. It's been absolutely quiet."

"Nothing in last night's diplomatic bag?"

"Nope, all routine, sir. I've no idea what it means."

"Well, I suppose we'll soon find out."

They were obviously expected at the Foreign Ministry, ushered through without preamble, and Vatutin did not keep them waiting, which was a good sign. When he met them, Vatutin was his usual affable self, chuckling as he offered them real Lyons coffee, asking how the new government was going to affect Sir Humphrey as ambassador and whether he was looking forward to going home, which would mean retiring.

At twenty minutes past nine, Vatutin came to the point. "Excellency, we have almost certain knowledge that one of your submarines, the *Saturn* to be precise, is in the Barents Sea on a mission of espionage."

Sir Humphrey's face showed nothing more than mild bafflement. Within himself, however, he was staggered at this news.

Vatutin continued. "Here in Moscow we are perplexed. We recognize and understand the great advances made by both you and your prime minister towards a meaningful detente. We cannot reconcile this with the presence of your submarine. Its presence is offensive, not just to both you and ourselves, but the very nature of its presence is offensive."

Sir Humphrey looked concerned, especially as he knew Vatutin had more to say.

"Our forces in the area now know where the *Saturn* is and are prepared to blow it out of the water, unless you give us your written assurance that this will never happen again, that British vessels will never again enter the Barents Sea without our own written authority." His eyes were still jovial, and in that moment Sir Humphrey knew for certain that his apparent joviality had always meant nothing. Vatutin checked his watch. "It is six-thirty in London. You have eight hours to give us that assurance."

The grey-haired British ambassador raised his eyebrows at Philip King, who simply shrugged his shoulders; there was nothing he could do or say to help. Sir Humphrey stammered, almost at a loss for words, "We don't . . . I don't know what to say. This is most unlike us. We will check with London, and I'll be back with you inside the eight hours."

Vatutin stood up and made a show of switching off the tape recorder. "Of course you don't know what to say. But please make sure you come back to us within the eight hours. There is nothing worse than needless loss of life."

There was nothing Sir Humphrey could usefully reply, except to say goodbye.

The news of the ambassador's meeting in Moscow was well known at both the Foreign Office and the Ministry of Defence before Big Ben had chimed eight o'clock. Arthur Wainscott was eating his breakfast in bed, flicking through the newspapers to see if there were any new caricatures of himself, when a copy of Sir Humphrey's telex was brought in. As he read it, his hearty appetite evaporated and he pushed the tray aside, wondering what the . . .

He picked up the telephone and dialled his private secretary. "Martin. Meeting here ten o'clock sharp. David Hogarth, Julian Randall, Sir Richard Hardy, Sir James Hythe, Douglas Oakley and Charles Vendon." The last two were the foreign secretary and the junior foreign secretary whose forte was eastern Europe.

Taylor was put out. "But you can't have it then, sir. You have the meeting with the Civil Service union leaders at nine forty-five."

"Can you suggest a better time, then?"

"Sir, you have a very full day until six o'clock. You have Question Time in the House of Commons, an hour's briefing before that, and then the telephone conference with the French and German . . ."

"Exactly, six o'clock is too late. Reschedule the union leaders, explain that there's an emergency meeting . . . that you can't say what it's about, but maybe if they were to come at six . . ."

"Not outside working hours, Prime Minister."

"Martin!"

"Yes, Prime Minister."

Sir James Hythe's depression had deepened still further when the Northwood switchboard operator finally located him and told him that Downing Street was on the line. "No," Martin Taylor had said. "You'll be seeing him in an hour's time so there's no point in interrupting him now."

Hardy had asked him what it was all about, and when Hythe told him, he too wished he could be in a better place. But unlike Sir James, his main fears were not for himself, but for the submarine and her crew. He felt that somehow he had allowed himself to be talked into an extension of the mission, and now he was dearly wishing he hadn't.

They had been held up by the traffic while crossing London and this made them two minutes late. Six days earlier they had stepped confidently from the staff car to request authorization for the Mission Order; this time they both felt distinctly bleak. The Cabinet ministers were already waiting for them in the prime minister's office, but not one of them had a smile. There were few pleasantries. Wainscott came straight to the point.

"Sir Richard, will you please inform us about the present status of the *Saturn* mission?"

"Yes, Prime Minister. *Saturn* left Faslane on schedule at zero six hundred hours. The frigates *Sirius* and *Phoebe* escorted her past the Russian ELINT vessel off Malin Head, and we were able to trace her progress up as far as the North Cape. There she went deep, at nine twenty-five yesterday, our time, to make her entrance to the Barents Sea as inconspicuous as possible." He faltered, shaking his head slightly. "At around midnight, United States Satellite Surveillance reported that four Russian submarines had abandoned their own exercise area, some six hundred miles to the north, and were making fast passage south to join the *Kharkov*, the subject of the mission. Both Sir James and myself have been in Northwood since then.

"At approximately eight-thirty this morning, we were able to receive Nimrod television coverage of the manoevres in that area. The position of the submarines, and the helicopter activity on and around the *Kharkov* as well as the firing of anti-submarine rockets, indicated a full submarine hunt. The Soviets warned the Nimrod to stand off and we instructed her to return to base."

Wainscott's jaw was set, his expression bitter and hard. "How do they know it's the *Saturn*?"

"They know it's *what*?" Sir James sat bolt upright. Hardy's eyes widened, his mouth open.

"Gentlemen, our ambassador in Moscow was this morning given a reprimand and an ultimatum: either we withdraw the *Saturn* and promise never to go past the North Cape again or they blow her out of the water. Apparently they know exactly where she is.''

Something clicked in Hardy's mind. ''When did the ambassador get this?''

''This morning, at nine-thirty their time.''

''They don't, you know. I mean know where she is. We saw the *Kharkov* at eight-thirty our time, that's two hours later, and it was very clear they still hadn't found her.''

''Oh? What makes you so sure?''

''Because we observed that the *Kharkov* was still conducting a search pattern, her helicopters were still aloft, both fore and aft. We saw her firing ASROCs. All these indications point to the fact that they have not yet found *Saturn*.''

The ghost of a smile crept over Hogarth's face. *Saturn* was not lost, the Russians had not found her. They were bluffing and they thought they could get away with it because they knew her name, and knew that knowing her name would hit the British prime minister right between the eyes. It had, too.

''Sir James?''

''I can't explain the leak. Full security precautions were taken; she was even loaded at night.''

The foreign secretary, Douglas Oakley, ventured into the discussion. ''If we were able to monitor her passage as far as the North Cape . . . How was that done?''

''With infra-red and magnetic anomaly detection.''

''Then can't the Russians do the same?''

''We don't think so. We have to use American Satellite Surveillance to do this; we just don't have the satellites and the technology. We know the Russians can do it to some extent, but nowhere near as effectively as the Americans. That is why we ordered *Saturn* to proceed at four hundred feet, within our detection range, but not theirs.'' Hythe knew this was weak, and hoped the lie didn't show.

Oakley let him off the hook. ''I think you're wrong. The American experience, and ours too, is that it's very difficult to prevent the Russians from buying, or otherwise acquiring, their technological expertise. I'm willing to bet that they also had her monitored from Scotland to the North Cape.''

''Very well, gentlemen.'' Wainscott was impatient. He

was not interested in a post-mortem. "The point is, what do we do now? They know it's *Saturn* and that's going to be a savage blow to detente. How do we get out of this situation? What are we going to do about this ultimatum?"

There was an uncomfortable shifting in seats, legs being uncrossed and crossed the other way round. Nobody seemed anxious to speak first.

Oakley sighed out loud, drawing attention to himself. "Well, what's the point? We keep whipping our tails trying to keep up with the superpowers, but we can't. So if we are never allowed in the Barents Sea again, except with their authorization, what does it matter? We rely on the Americans to defend us; they can still go up there if they want to. Somehow we've got to strengthen relations with Russia. They are closer to us, and speaking for a future that I hope will never happen, we don't want ever to be at risk of being sucked into a conflagration between Russia and America. They know it's our submarine, because they know it's *Saturn*. So why compound our crime with a lie? It could ruin all our objectives, objectives for which we have a clear mandate, just obtained at a stroke. We have no alternative; we've got to acknowledge her presence, apologize abjectly for some foolhardy naval captain or admiral, and promise never to go there again."

"Very well put, Douglas." Wainscott clearly approved. His endorsement shattered Hardy and Hythe, whose eyes met in total dismay. They turned to Hogarth and Randall, hoping perhaps to see strength in their quarter.

Hogarth was poker-faced. Though in favour of some rapprochement with the Soviet Union, he was not in favour of the outright unilateral throwing in of the sponge that Oakley wanted. But then, neither did he want to be associated too closely with the architects of a mission that had failed, and might later be construed to have been harebrained. Difficult. But he had to speak; Hardy and Hythe were not in a position to. They were, after all, only executives, appointed to carry out the orders of the Cabinet.

"With due respect, Prime Minister. Douglas, and I presume you too, Charles, may be giving away rather more than we are bargaining for. Our only winning card is that the Russians still have not found *Saturn*. If they can't, then they will know we have a very effective weapon. When the day comes and we talk disarmament, I want them to give up something for everything we give up. If we have nothing to give up, then there is no reason why they should pay us any attention at all. Since when did they ever listen to the Vatican? I can remember Stalin asking how many divisions the Pope had. They haven't changed. They are past masters at *realpolitik:* this is their way. I am talking about negotiating from strength. If we yield to this ultimatum, we will be seen as no more than a bully's sidekick, a sycophant, to be dispensed with the moment they no longer have a use for us. And then we would have no more control over our ultimate future, and no possible way of regaining control.''

Wainscott snorted. ''I'd find your argument a damned sight more convincing if it were as clear as Douglas's. No. I don't go along with lies, least of all when they know we are lying. Douglas, I leave it to you to arrange the necessary with Prescott.''

''Yes, sir.'' Oakley and Vendon stood up, reaching for their briefcases. The meeting was over.

''No!'' Astonished, the three of them faced Hogarth. ''No, I will not be bulldozed in this way, and if this is how you want to play it you can expect no Cabinet collective responsibility from me. . . .''

''We wouldn't ask for it.'' Wainscott was boiling. His comment meant resign or else.

''That's all very well, Prime Minister, but you are *primus inter pares*, first among equals. Not all the Cabinet is here and this ought to be a Cabinet decision, because it affects not just one submarine, but the whole of this country. And I know that half the Cabinet, and probably more than half the country, think as I do. And if we all resign, as I know we all would on this issue, then we can always support another party which does want a safe disarmament. What you are suggesting is lunacy.''

Astounded, but still in control of himself, Wainscott motioned to Oakley and Vendon to sit down again. Looking at his hands, but speaking to Hogarth, he said, ''You do realize what you're saying, don't you?''

''Yes. You cannot expect them to disarm without having

effective nuclear weapons yourself. *Saturn* is at present proving herself effective.''

''But *Saturn* isn't a nuclear weapon.''

''No, but she represents our nuclear capability.''

Wainscott thought for a moment, thought hard on the issues of jacking out at all costs, of using weapons withdrawal effectively, and above all, of his own majority and the possibility of his party disintegrating with the sacrifice of all their ideals. The others were waiting for him to speak, expectant. He sighed, lifted his head and focused on Hardy. ''Sir Richard, how quickly can you get *Saturn* out?''

It looked as though Hogarth had won. Wainscott was going for compromise, again. But not this way, Hardy thought, still worried. ''We have no means of contact with *Saturn*, Prime Minister. She's in communications blackout until the mission is completed. Any attempt at communication from us would expose her. It had to be done like this. Henderson's instructions were to abort this mission the moment he feels he has been detected.''

''Do you think he can?''

''It was one of the reasons why he was chosen. I should say that with *Saturn*'s depth and quietness he has a very good chance of not being found.''

''How good?''

''Say, fifty-fifty.''

''So there's a fifty per cent chance we are all right. And if he is detected?''

Hogarth broke in. ''At least if he is detected, *Saturn* may get blown up, in which case the Russians may never know whose submarine it was. If he comes to the surface the Russians will know that we do mean business. That is something they understand!''

''You're very sure of yourself.''

''Yes.'' As far as Hogarth was concerned, the case was open and shut.

''David, do you mind waiting outside with Julian, Sir Richard and Sir James? I want to have a word with Douglas and Charles alone.''

They did not have long to wait. Wainscott seemed older when he beckoned them in. Oakley and Vendon were standing with the broken expressions of bought men. Hogarth knew he had won even before he sat down.

"David, we agree. We will deny any knowledge of one of our submarines up there. As far as we are concerned, *Saturn* is on an exercise off Canada . . ."

"The Falklands, Prime Minister." Hardy had interrupted. "The Falklands is much better; everybody knows we have submarines down there but nobody knows quite where they are."

"Very well, then, the Falklands. Douglas, you will inform Sir Humphrey accordingly? Also ask them why they objected to our Nimrod."

"Particularly when they have their trawlers all around our coasts," Hogarth added.

Wainscott like it, and nodded. "Particularly when they have trawlers all around our coasts."

"Yes, sir."

The meeting was over.

Sir Humphrey Prescott telephoned through to Vatutin at three-thirty that afternoon, two hours before the deadline was due to expire. Vatutin was amazed at the reply, chuckling to hide his own disbelief. He was more than angry when he put the phone down; the comment about the Nimrod was downright cheeky, and it made his blood boil.

He telephoned President Kirov straightaway, and found himself summoned to the Kremlin; Rodichev too.

There were no pleasantries. As they were shown through his door Kirov asked Rodichev if they had found the submarine yet.

"No, but we are reasonably sure she is there. It is difficult water."

"You realize that we shall look stupid if we can't find her? That we cannot consider the Barents Sea as 'our' unless we prove that we can find her?"

Vatutin nodded, but Rodichev spoke. "We are painfully aware of both these facts." It was the right thing to say, though unfortunate that Rodichev's face did not look pained. Kirov found it slightly irritating.

"How sure are we that it really is the *Saturn*?"

"Comrade President, we can show you the satellite detection tapes and the recordings. We are as sure as we possibly can be.''

"Then we are certain that the British are bluffing. It is more than a bluff, it is a challenge. They have defied us. In doing so they have effectively given us permission to use that submarine for target practice." He thought for a moment, aloud.... "If you had reported to me that the submarine was American, we might not have sent that ultimatum . . . or perhaps we would." He addressed Vatutin. "Did the ambassador give any indication as to whose submarine it might be?"

"I tried that one. Obviously, even if he knew he couldn't say. He did hint, very obliquely I might add, that he didn't think it was a NATO submarine."

"Implying a French one?"

"I did say that the hint was oblique. Ambassadors are trained in that way."

"Rodichev?"

"All French submarines in the North Atlantic are accounted for. I don't think it can be French."

"Does that mean that not all French submarines are accounted for?"

"Most of them do their exercises in the Pacific. I would be very surprised if this one was French."

"Then it's British. And now we see who our friends really are." His eyes were fixed, pale blue chips that spelt retribution. "We must show that these people, who pretend to be our friends, are no more than spies and liars. It is clear, isn't it, that this submarine must not be allowed to escape?"

Rodichev inclined his head. "Quite clear."

"Then I think you should allow that Nimrod of theirs to take a really close look. There is, after all, nothing they can do except watch, and suffer the additional misery of seeing one of their submarines forced to the surface, or otherwise despatched." His eyes twinkled again. "Who knows, it might even make them into real friends of ours."

Vatutin thought this was enormously funny.

— CHAPTER 7 —

18th May, Afternoon/Evening

During the European afternoon, whilst Sir Humphrey Prescott was telephoning Vatutin, Washington was waking up to a brilliant sunshine and a fresh rain-washed sky. In the East Wing of the White House, the sun was streaming into the bedroom where President Patrick Mallory, forty-fourth president of the United States, was sitting up in bed drinking coffee. He was reading through a speech that had been written for him to deliver that evening at the annual dinner of the Institute of Bankers. His wife Carol was beside him, reading through her own correspondence, sighing at the number of requests from charities to attend their functions which she knew she must refuse simply because she had not got the time to fit them in.

Mallory spluttered. "Bullshit!"

"What's that, honey?"

"See here. It says, 'I therefore see our future direction, less and less to govern the world by force of arms, but by the force of a stable exchange rate and stable interest rate . . . ' We don't govern the world! It's bad enough governing fifty-two states."

Carol thought. "Try influence."

"I did."

"I mean, 'Less and less to influence the world' by force of whatever it was you said."

"Ah, I see what you mean. Yeah, makes some sense when you say 'influence.' "

The telephone chirruped. "Aw, already? Who wants to call me at this hour—" He flicked a hand through his shaggy, unkempt grey hair and picked up the phone. He was answered by the voice of Carl Zimmerman, his secretary of state.

"What is it, Carl?"

"We've got NATO problems."

"Not again. Do you have to tell me so early?"

"Afraid so. Forewarned is forearmed. I'm forearming you."

"I'm trying to get away from that word. What is it this time?"

"Soviets claim there's a British submarine in the Barents Sea. That's the one up by Murmansk. Claim they know its name too, the *Saturn*. They delivered an ultimatum to the Brits during the night: either Britain gets it out and promises never to go up there again, or the Soviets blow it up."

"And?"

"The Brits are denying responsibility. Should be passing the word right now, in Moscow."

"*Is* there a British submarine up there?"

"I don't know yet. I'll be calling Arn soon as I put the phone down." "Arn" was Dr. Arnold Winters, secretary of defense.

Mallory glanced at his watch. "OK. Find out if the British do have a submarine up there. And if they do, I'd like you and Arn with me, at the White House, nine o'clock. Can you make it?"

"Sure thing, Mr. President, and I'll call you anyway if the Russkies are up a gum tree."

The Russkies* were not. Mallory descended the sweeping staircase at nine o'clock to find both Zimmerman and Winters waiting for him. His heart stopped a beat when he saw them, but he continued his measured pace downwards.

"So there is a British submarine up there."

Winters nodded. "Morning, Mr. President. 'Fraid so."

Mallory reached the bottom of the stairs and shook hands with them both. "Well, coffee's hot, let's sit down and talk about it." He led them into the Oval Office.

Through the French windows they could see the wide

---

*"Russians" are those people of the USSR who live west of the Urals and are part of Europe. Correctly, Zimmerman should be referring to them as "Soviets," for Moscow is the capital of the Union of Soviet Socialist Republics. Their forces, because they are drawn from people of all these republics, and defend them, are Soviet forces.

expanse of lawn outside, silver-emerald with the night's rain and spring growth, looking clean and innocent. They did not open the windows, but chose seats beside them, round the coffee table where a tray was waiting.

Mallory poured the coffee. Whilst he did so, Winters rummaged through his briefcase, brought out two copies of the Mission Order and laid them beside the tray.

"Yes, Mr. President. *Saturn*'s there all right. And the Soviets are going after her with everything they've got."

Mallory fed saccharine tablets into his cup. "Everything?"

"Well," Winters counted on his fingers, "an anti-submarine carrier called the *Kharkov*, eighteen choppers and four nuclear submarines, and they're firing anti-submarine rockets. We're patched in through Satellite, and the RAF has a Nimrod over the area, so we've got some idea what's going on. And Admiral Fredenberger, he's Comsubatlant, has been in touch with the Pentagon through the night, so we've got it both ends, as it were."

Mallory sipped his coffee and then spoke softly. "Are they going to find her?"

"I wouldn't bet on it. The Brits have a top rate commander on *Saturn*. This submarine is super-quiet, and oh yes, she goes deep, mighty deep, deeper than any of our own submarines. But the Soviets have got ultra sonar, and we don't know exactly what or how good it is. Like I said, no bets."

"Ultra sonar. Do I recall . . . ?"

"You might. It came up last month, when we heard that the Soviets were re-equipping the *Kharkov*. It's the point of the whole mission: we're trying to find out what it does, what they're up to. Fredenberger, but more especially the British, are worried about it: when they found out by accident that the *Saturn* could reach three thousand feet, they sent her out *toute suite*."

"Uh-huh, and the Soviets were able to pick her up before she got there."

"No, no. They know her name. Somebody's told them, must have."

Mallory pulled a face. "So what are we supposed to do about it?"

Winters thought for a moment before replying. "There's nothing that I can see, except sit tight and wait. We've got a

Joint Staff group working out the options, and they'll be feeding the parameters into the computer. It's . . ."

"Good. Is there any way we can help the British? Short of sending our fleet up there, I mean. We'll need to play this thing as low-key as possible."

"They've got Western Satellite Control giving help with the surveillance. Beyond that, I don't see that there's much else we can do."

"Good. Make sure we give the British all the help we can, but nothing overt, not even an AWAC, get me? Now," he turned to Carl Zimmerman, "Carl, about Wainscott: what do you make of him?"

"Hard to say, he's still new to the job. He's shrewd, yes, but . . ."

Zimmerman trailed off, uncertain how to put his own misgivings into words.

"Go on."

"He got in on an anti-nuclear ticket. He's always considered himself closer to the Russians than any of his predecessors, but I smell a lot of giving and no getting."

"Pink?"

"With a capital 'P.' Lord alone knows how the Royal Navy got him to sanction this mission. I don't think he'll sanction any more, not with this little hoo-ha."

Mallory stood up to look out of the windows. "Is this man committed to NATO?"

Zimmerman shook his head in bafflement. "Goddamn, it's hard to say. He pays lip service to NATO but he wants the Pershings and Cruise Missiles out, or so he said in his electioneering. I don't care for his Foreign Secretary, Oakley: he thinks he can keep his conscience sweet by getting us to do the dirty, and every expensive, work. But Hogarth," he looked across to Winters, "your counterpart, he's OK. Seems to understand what the game's all about."

Mallory turned round to face them, closing the meeting. "OK, gentlemen, thank you for coming. We watch this space."

Since the shock of the first explosion, *Saturn* had slipped up to eight hundred feet and surrounded herself in a thin layer of warm water. They had heard other explosions, rumbling like summer thunder in the distance, and sonar had been reporting many more. It was clear from these reports that the *Kharkov* was looking for her, using a standard search box pattern. Moreover, Henderson could not slip out of his hiding place without exposing himself to Soviet sonar. He did not know he was in box "G," but then, neither did the Soviets.

At dusk they switched from white lighting to red throughout the submarine, and almost at once they heard the rumble of more missile explosions. Sykes noticed the coincidence. "Perhaps if we were to return to white lighting, sir, they might stop." It was true; all their uncomfortable experiences had taken place when the lighting was red.

Henderson smiled and shook his head. Before he could reply he heard the PA: "Captain, sir, Sonar . . ."

Ka-rumph! This time the missile had exploded much closer, causing *Saturn* to lurch. The red lighting flickered on and off, and they heard glass breaking in the wardroom pantry, accompanied by a muttered oath. *Saturn* had been shifted slightly from her position and Tate had to struggle briefly with the control column to steady her.

"Captain, sir, Sonar."

"Captain."

"Helicopter sonobuoy transmission bearing green one zero, possibly in contact."

"Shit!" Henderson instantly snapped back to life, recognizing the danger above him. "Port twenty. Take her down fast to two thousand five hundred feet."

Tate moved the control column forwards, turning up the revolutions with his other hand, his face grimly determined. Henderson's eyes moved from him to Sykes. "Hormones, we've got to shake 'em off."

"Sonar, Captain. Helicopter sonobuoy transmission bearing red six five."

"Dammit. Midships!"

Tate was adept at the helm, and weaving was something he had often practiced on exercise. But that had never been for real. Now he was feeling for the first time what it was like when it was, and found it curiously exciting.

And then before Henderson could give the next order, there was the split and crash of overhead thunder, jarring

Saturn viciously in the water. Sykes was stepping out of his seat when it happened, and it threw both him and Henderson off their feet. It is the unexpected that does the most damage, and neither was prepared. Henderson did not feel his head cracking the Navigational Plot: it hit him on exactly the same spot as his previous wound and knocked him out. Sykes bumped the back of his head against the periscope tube.

"Peep, peep peep peep peep peep," the reactor alarm sounded, shrilly piping itself through the control room. MacDonald's concerned voice reported from the manoeuvring room. "Reactor scram. Reactor scram. Switch off all non-essential services."

It was a very different kind of tension reigning on the bridge of the *Kharkov*, the kind that is born of frustration and fatigue. Both Orchenkov and Golitsyn had been on watch for fourteen hours, and it was beginning to tell. They watched the final salvo being launched, and knew it was hopeless. Golitsyn said so.

"Well, that's box 'G.' We can't carry on firing missiles at this rate: we'll have none left by morning and then where are we? We've had eight helicopters operating sonobuoys all day long, and not so much as a squeak . . ."

Orchenkov was drumming his fingers on the window. Somehow he knew *Saturn* was there, close to him. He couldn't say why, but it was there in his bones. How could he explain that to this highly professional captain who was always right? We don't have enough missiles; it isn't working. But dammit, I know. . . . "How many helicopters do we have? With sonobuoys?"

"Eighteen, Commodore."

"Then get them all up. Have them operate in threes; I want to search deeper—ninety metres, two hundred metres, even three hundred metres. They'll find her, I know they'll find her . . ."

"Three hundred metres? That's crazy, no submarine is . . ."

"Do as I say!" He glanced at Tyutchev, but Tyutchev gave him no help at all, not wanting to get involved in a conflict that was not just between two very different men, but a conflict that represented two very different disciplines: instinct versus modern technology.

"Do as I say! We won't fire any more missiles until we know where that submarine is."

Orchenkov took himself down to the flight deck. When he got there, three more helicopters had already been raised from the below decks, and he could hear the elevator humming with a fourth on board. The men were working with a silent efficiency, fueling, checking and preparing amidst the noise of wind and rotor engines, illuminated by floodlights from the top deck. He watched, grudgingly admiring Golitsyn for the well-oiled machine he had made of the *Kharkov*. There were no two ways about it: the ship was highly efficient.

Sometimes a fisherman knows he has put his bait in the right place. There is never an outward clue, but the feeling is strong, generating a taut expectancy. Orchenkov had this feeling now, even though he knew Golitsyn did not.

Helen Dawson was very much a career admiral's wife. She saw quite clearly that her husband moved in a man's world, but equally clearly saw and identified the one area where her husband was, by definition, incompetent. That was in handling servicemen's wives; in particular the wives of servicemen at sea, who did not always know when their husbands would be back.

Every second Wednesday evening she opened her house to all wives of servicemen on duty, officers and men, and for fifty pence they could have a glass of wine, unlimited coffee, and commiserate or rejoice in the absence of their husbands. It was not *de rigueur*, but as soon as their men were at sea, all were invited. For each evening Mrs. Dawson would plan a focal point: perhaps a short concert of light classical music, a cookery demonstration, a talk of flower arranging or the local Member of Parliament to describe his life as an MP. The "show" would never last more than half an hour, but gave the guests something new to talk about. If she felt it was going to be popular, she would use the wardroom at HMS *Neptune*. The numbers of those who turned up could vary anywhere between twenty and two hundred.

These soirees, for that is what they were, served several purposes. Firstly, they brought the wives together and were often a great source of comfort. Secondly, they showed that the top brass did care, and did something about it, and thirdly, Mrs. Dawson made a mental note of all the gossip she heard, in case it might bear some relevance to her husband. For his part, Harold Dawson did all he could to help, without being obtrusive, and would occasionally make himself discreetly available at the end of an evening, in case there was anything a wife needed to ask on an informal basis. All wives knew that there was very little they could ask an admiral that couldn't be better handled by the personnel officer, but there were some things, like, would he give out the end-of-term prizes at the local school, or open the church fete at Garelochhead, subjects which were all grist to the mill, and from which he did not wish to appear too distant.

On Wednesday, the 18th of May, the wives' evening featured Mrs. Patel and Mrs. Ranji giving a demonstration of Indian cooking. They also had a sales counter where wives could buy all the spices and ingredients which were not available locally. It was a great success: Indian food is not all mouth-burning hot, and the girls flocked to the sales stall afterwards, knowing they would be able to prepare something quite different from ship's fare when their husbands returned.

Mrs. Dawson did her best to say "hello" to as many wives as she could, and afterwards found that most of them were comparing notes about the different Indian restaurants in Garelochhead and Helensburgh. She caught sight of Penny Sykes standing on her own.

"Hello, Penny. You're looking nice this evening."

Penny lit up, the compliment also meaning it was not her fault she was standing on her own. "Thank you, Mrs. Dawson. It's really been a great success, hasn't it?"

"I think so. I had no idea their cooking could be so subtle. Are you going to have a go?"

"You bet; the hottest curry possible fairly takes Alan's breath away, stops him from talking so much." They laughed, but Mrs. Dawson was ever the perfect hostess.

"I didn't know Alan was a great talker. What does he talk about?"

"Just about everything and anything except submarines. A pity really, I'd really like to know what goes on when he's at sea, but he always clams up when I ask him; it's sort of forbidden territory."

"What turns him on, then?" Helen Dawson seemed genuinely interest.

"Oh, all sorts of things; he's really clever with his hands. Do you know he rewired all of our cottage, and put in the central heating himself? But I suppose gardening is his real love. It doesn't matter what the weather's like, he's always out there."

"Does he specialize?"

"Roses, old-fashioned roses. I must say I find them rather dull: all that work, right round the year, and they're only out for a week or so, and not very colorful at that. I keep asking him if we can have just a few of the brighter modern ones, but he won't have any of it." She paused. "If he's away much longer this time, then I doubt if he'll even see any of them in flower. I can already see the buds."

"How long has Alan been away now?"

Penny sighed wistfully. "Coming up for six weeks. I did see him briefly for a couple of evenings last week, but they were off again almost as soon as they came back in. I think it's really rotten."

"He's *Saturn*, isn't he? Commander Henderson's submarine."

"That's right. You are clever."

"Come to think of it, I didn't see Karen here this evening. Now she is a good cook. I'm surprised she missed it."

Penny's face showed frank puzzlement. "But didn't you hear? Her little boy's been really ill. He only came back home tonight."

"Well, couldn't she find a baby-sitter?"

Penny smiled with amazement. "No. You haven't heard. He had meningitis. They whipped him off to hospital, put him in intensive care. It was touch and go for a couple of days, but he's much better now. I don't mean *better* better:

he's still got another two weeks in bed, but he's on the mend and the ambulance brought him back this evening.''

"My God, the poor child. Poor Karen too, all on her own. When did all this happen?''

"About a week ago. We're so glad he's home again.''

Mrs. Dawson's face hardened a fraction. ''Did Commander Henderson know all this before he sailed?''

Penny frowned. ''I suppose he must have. Poor man, I . . .''

"Penny, do you mind excusing me for a moment? There's something . . .''

"Of course, and thank you for having me.''

"Bye, Penny, nice to see you here. Chin up, can't be too long now.''

She had spoken the last words in a hurry, tearing herself away and stepping quickly through the crowd of happily chattering womenfolk, a businesslike expression on her face which defied interruption.

She found her husband in his office, gently sipping whisky and smoking a large cigar, accompanied by two other captains. She knew them both, but nodded at them only briefly.

"Harold, can I have a word with you, please?''

The captains took their leave, not sure whether the subject was domestic or naval. Mrs. Dawson waited until they had gone. ''Harold, I've just heard, Commander Henderson . . .''

"Yes, James Henderson, *Saturn*'s Commanding Officer. Good man, that Henderson, he . . .''

His wife was impatient. ''Harold, will you listen to me! Henderson's son, Skip, has been in hospital with meningitis.''

"Meningitis? Isn't that something cows get?''

"Harold! No, it isn't, or I suppose they might, but you're thinking of mastitis. Meningitis is a killer disease in children. Skip has just spent several days in hospital in intensive care. According to Penny Sykes, Henderson must have known about it when he sailed. The least you can do right now is radio him that his son's better. But commanding officers, or anyone else for that matter, should never be allowed to sail when they have that sort of trouble at home.''

Dawson was quiet, pondering the implications of what his

wife had just said, remembering Henderson's angry words in the helicopter—"Just how long does a commander have to go on proving himself?"—and his own useless reply. He thought again of how well Henderson had proved himself recently, overcoming mental as well as physical strain. He was pleased that the marriage was a success, knowing that here was a good man, but one who needed stretching to his limits to get the best out of him. He had always prided himself on his ability to stretch a man, knowing he was often hated for it, but knowing also that in doing so he was moulding them into Titans. This stretching demanded a fine balance of judgement; he had not known that Henderson had been stretched by other forces, forces outside his control, and he knew very well that these could tip the man over, into instability.

The admiral's body began to shake uncontrollably, and with a vicious spasm he threw it off. "Thank you, dear." He reached for the telephone, and Mrs. Dawson knew it was a man's world again. She left.

Switchboard put him through, but it seemed a long time before she answered. "Karen Henderson."

"Karen, Admiral Dawson here. I've just heard about Skip. Is he all right?"

"Very much better now, thank you, Admiral. Is there any news of James?"

"No. He's on exercise and we can't contact him, though we should be hearing from him in forty-eight hours. When they do come through, I'll tell him Skip's on the mend. That suit you?"

"Oh, yes, Admiral, he'll be so relieved."

Those words told him the worst. "Karen, this should have been reported before he left."

He could feel her voice catching at the other end as she fought back the tears of relief, glad now to know that somebody else knew, and cared. "Admiral . . . I tried but he wouldn't let me. Said it was a very important exercise, that he had to go to London for the briefing . . . It was all happening so quickly that you wouldn't have time to find another man and brief him in the same way . . . that if he didn't go it would mess up his career with the Navy . . . it was very difficult, Admiral."

"He's a very brave man; one of the best, and you make me proud of him. He'll be back soon, and I'll see you then."

"Admiral, thank you for calling."

"Goodbye, Karen." He put the phone down. Damn, damn, damn, and damn again! He jabbed at the telephone receiver buttons. "Get me Admiral Sir Richard Hardy."

It took a long time. Dawson was surprised to find that the admiral was still at Northwood. "Admiral Sir Richard Hardy?"

"Yes."

"Harold Dawson here. Third Submarine Squadron, Faslane. Is there any news of *Saturn*?"

"Why?"

"Because I've had some disturbing news about something that may have an effect on her commanding officer, Henderson."

"Oh?"

"Well, it depends on how the mission is going."

He could hear Hardy sigh before replying. "Very well, Admiral, officially we know nothing, and presume all is in order. Unofficially, *Saturn* is in the shits."

"Good God. What's happened?"

"We suspect that the Soviets know she's there and they're trying to force her to surface." Dawson was silent, not sure now whether he should be passing the news on when Hardy obviously had enough on his mind, and if he did decide to, how to break it. But Hardy forestalled him. "Why do you ask?"

Dawson chose his words carefully, and spoke slowly. "Because Henderson might just be under undue pressure. I have only this minute heard that his son has meningitis. It's a killer disease for children, very painful, and Henderson left on this mission straight after his boy was taken to hospital. Previous to this he had spent five weeks at sea, returned early because of an unpleasant incident, had to suffer an inquiry, a briefing, and telling his crew that their leave was cancelled. I believe all this is too much for one man to handle."

There was a long silence at the other end before Hardy spoke again. "How does Henderson feel about his son?"

"Tiresome little brat, but then they all are at that age. Henderson worships him. Don't all fathers?"

"Yes, of course. . . . Thank you for calling, Harold. I'll see what we can do. I don't really think, though, that there *is* anything we can do. Do you?"

"No, but I thought you ought to know."

"Quite."

Dawson hung up, slumped back in his chair and relit his cigar. One thing was certain, there was nothing else he could do. So he tucked the issue away in the back of his mind, except for reminding himself to thank his wife for telling him so promptly.

Hardy was shattered. One of the main ingredients for the success of their original plan had been Henderson's prowess as a hunter-killer captain. Now he had learnt that this was no longer to be counted on.

Sir James looked at him with tired, red-rimmed eyes; they now knew that there were eighteen helicopters conducting a methodical search pattern to find *Saturn*. "What is it, Richard?"

Fredenberger looked up, too. Eyes with dark patches underneath, silently inquiring about the news which he knew must be bad. Hardy told them.

It was enough for Hythe; he got up, walked over to the telephone, and remained standing as he asked to be put through to Downing Street. It was ten-thirty in the evening, but he didn't care a jot.

"Prime Minister?"

"Sir James." Wainscott's voice was dry. Hythe knew he had been written off.

'Prime Minister, we've just received news that the captain of *Saturn* may not be mentally stable." He didn't care how he put it: if the prime minister had written him off, it didn't matter much either way.

"What are you saying?"

"Normally, Henderson would have been far and away the best man for the job. When we chose him he had already been through some considerable strain, but this didn't prejudice our decision to send him. On the contrary, he was performing remarkably well, justifying our own expectations. But now we have heard that a few hours before he sailed, his son was admitted to hospital with meningitis, a deadly and painful disease." He paused before adding, "Do you follow me?"

There was a longer pause from the prime minister. "Yes, I do. Thank you, Sir James, for your openness. How do you feel this will affect the mission?"

"I can't honestly say. All I can say is that it introduces an element of unpredictability, possibly also a feeling of resentment towards his employers. Unjustified, as he didn't inform us about his son, but perhaps there nonetheless."

"Mmmm. Thank you again, Sir James. Please keep in touch and keep me informed immediately of any developments. Good night."

Fredenberger smelt resignation in both Hythe and Hardy. For him it meant that the mission was about to enter its second phase: contingency plans. And that meant telephoning the Pentagon again. He excused himself.

Prime ministers have a busy timetable and Arthur Wainscott was no exception, though tonight was relatively quiet. His wife was able to watch the late-night film on television, and he was in his study, going through his despatch boxes, a pint of beer on his desk. Most of the business required simple initialling, but he knew it was not all like that, and he took care to read each document closely before authorizing it. Two or three pages had been taken out, and he placed them neatly on his left: he had a few more questions about these.

Hythe's telephone call had disturbed him for two reasons: firstly, because Hythe didn't seem to care any more. That meant Wainscott had lost his trust, implying that he would either have to go along with a hostile Naval Command or set about the messy business of replacing him. Secondly, he was more upset than he had realized by the news about *Saturn*. At first he had taken it with some equanimity, feeling that events would have to run their course and there was nothing he could do about it, except be ready for the worst. But now he found he could no longer concentrate on the papers in front of him. All the words beginning with a capital "S" made him think of *Saturn*. "H"'s stood for Henderson and "M"'s for Moscow. Finally he gave up, folded away the last of his papers, and reached for his beer. He drank deeply and stood up, stretching his legs.

If that submarine was going to be unpredictable, he thought, then the kindest thing he could do, both for the submarine and for the Soviets, would be to tell them so. Tell them they had a rogue submarine in their cherished Barents Sea. Why, he could even tell them he didn't know it had gone there, he had only just found out, and he was frightened for the Russians.

That would put it in their hands. They would understand his concern, and of course, it would dismantle the ultimatum.

Should he ring up Oakley? No, the man might try saying "I told you so"; he would agree anyway. Hogarth? No, again, he would try and talk him out of it. Besides, if he called one Cabinet member, he would have to call all of them, and he didn't have that much time.

He swallowed more beer, his mind racing. What could an unstable captain do? Why, he could provoke a major confrontation up there and that would be disastrous; best thing for all to tell Moscow, sort the thing out before it happens. Or he could sail straight into Murmansk, or whatever they call their naval base there, having given up. Again disastrous; pre-empt it therefore by calling Moscow. Or the Russians could blow up the submarine, taking fifty-five lives, because I hadn't the guts to call Kirov.

Kirov. Kirov, Kirov, Kirov, Kirov. What time is it in Moscow? Two forty five a.m. I've been told he works prodigious hours. I wonder . . .

Wainscott reached for the scarlet telephone, the "hot line," and ordered a scrambled call to be put through to President Kirov, as soon as possible, wake him up if necessary. His hand trembled slightly, and when he put the receiver down, waiting for the operator to tell him he was through, he saw that the handle was wet with sweat from his palm. He had never telephoned Kirov before, but examining all the aspects, he knew it was the right thing to do. He finished his beer, leant back in his chair, and waited.

It rang. Wainscott jumped even though he was expecting it, still not sure how he was going to express himself. "President Kirov?" He had expected an interpreter, but instead all he got was his own switchboard operator.

"I'm sorry, Prime Minister, this is most unusual, we've been told that President Kirov is presently unavailable. There is nobody in Moscow who wishes to accept the call."

"Oh." This was something he had not expected, and he knew it meant that he had upset them, presumably by his refusal to accept responsibility for *Saturn*. "Oh, then get me Sir Humphrey Prescott, the ambassador, straightaway if you would."

Waiting, the awesome truth came home to him that he had made an enemy of Russia. Perhaps not an enemy, but no longer a friend, and it would take years to build up the same *rapprochement* again. His stomach felt very hollow.

The red phone rang again and he had a freshly-woken ambassador on the line, trying not to sound sleepy.

"Prime Minister?"

"Sir Humphrey. It's about *Saturn*. I've got to speak to President Kirov personally. I've tried the hot line, but our switchboard can't get any sense out of them."

"Oh, dear. So you want me to see if I can clear the way. Well, there's nothing I can do now. It's as near as dammit three o'clock in the morning."

"Is there any way you can think of to get them to stop operations in the Barents Sea?"

"To what? Oh. Oh, dear. So we are in a . . . Prime Minister, we gave them your answer this afternoon. You will have had my report. Clearly they haven't accepted it. The best thing I can do is get through to Vatutin, first thing in the morning. That'd be around five-thirty your time. I'll wake you up."

"Do that, please."

Wainscott's telephone call did get through to President Kirov. He had just concluded an emergency meeting with his agriculture minister and a top pesticide scientist to try to safeguard the enormous harvest they had coming. An aide had buzzed him through, but he had no interest in taking the call. . . .

"No, why should I?" he said. "They've given me their answer, they can't have it both ways."

He was tired too.

* * *

The iodine smarted. Henderson came to, realizing that the back of his head was stinging, and somebody was making it hurt. He started, but lay back when he recognized Lt. Ashton, the submarine's medical officer, who was cleaning up and bandaging his head. He sat up, looked around, and saw that the attack computer screen was blank. And the explosions had stopped. And Sykes had a graze on his forehead.

Ashton was having difficulty in completing the bandage, trying to draw the knot over the side of Henderson's head whilst Henderson kept jerking about. "Christ, Number One, what happened?"

"The reactor scrammed, sir. The force of that last missile knocked out the number one busbar and the reactor scrammed."

MacDonald's voice broke in over the PA from aft. "Captain, manoeuvring room, sir."

"Captain."

"MacDonald, sir. I'm having trouble bringing the reactor critical again. The number one electrical busbar is totally inoperative. There was a leak in the secondary cooling system and water got in, completely blowing the busbar. The number two busbar was also slightly damaged. You'll have to run on electrical batteries for a while until I figure out some way of getting the reactor critical again."

"Dammit, Angus, we're at two thousand five hundred feet."

MacDonald's own frustration came through. "Well, it can't be helped. We're also checking out possible damage to the steam generator."

"Christ. How long's all this going to take?"

"Give us twenty minutes at least. We're on to it now."

Henderson felt faint and put his arm around the search periscope shaft. Ashton finished his bandage and stood back, looking to see if anyone else in the control room needed attention.

"I said we're on to it now, sir."

"OK, Angus. I must have power to manoeuvre. Get the reactor back on line as soon as you can."

"Aye, aye, sir."

Gingerly, Henderson felt the back of his head, biting his

lip as he felt a twinge of pain where it was more sensitive. He turned, and noticed the weapons electrical officer standing quietly beside him. "What is it, Robert?"

"Some of the sonar transducers on the starboard side are inoperative, sir. We are working on it now, but it would appear that most of the amplifiers are blown, sir. It could be a long job."

"OK, Robert, get on with it. . . . Robert?"

"Yes, sir?"

"Does that mean that we are 'blind' on our starboard side?"

"Virtually, sir. Yes."

"OK, Robert, do the best you can."

"Aye, aye, sir."

A punch-drunk fighter will go on and on and on. Henderson was starting to show similar symptoms as groggily, his head none too steady, he spoke to Sykes. "Number One."

"Yes, sir?"

"Order all tubes and weapons systems brought to the action state."

Sykes simply gaped at him, not sure what was in his mind, and even less sure he liked it. For basically he was a cautious man and it had not occurred to him that they could try anything other than to slip away. It was not the thought of action that made him apprehensive, but the consequences of what might happen if they decided to use any of their own weaponry. That frightened him. Unwittingly he pulled a finger to click a joint.

"Number One: I said bring all tubes and weapons systems to the action state."

Sykes hesitated a fraction longer before replying quickly, "Aye, aye, sir."

Henderson spun round, glowering with narrow eyes and raised eyebrows, the grogginess gone, replaced by a harder, and far more frightening, determination. "Dammit, Number One. The rules of engagement have just changed. We're going home. I'm taking *Saturn* home and nobody, nobody's going to stop me."

19th May

The weather conditions were perfect as Golitsyn and Orchenkov entered the third day of their submarine hunt. Both of them had been catnapping during the night; first Golitsyn, for four hours, and now Orchenkov was fast asleep in his bunk. The sea remained relatively peaceful. A light westerly breeze kept the surface free from fog, and the swell was not heavy enough to make the *Kharkov* uncomfortable.

A false dawn was opening up to the east: that peculiar time of day when the horizon lights up, but before the sun has risen, giving visibility but no colour, throwing the sea, sky and ship into shades of steel. From the bridge windows Golitsyn could see his helicopters, still strung out in all directions, operating in groups of three, attached to the sea by their long umbilical cords. The sight gave him immense satisfaction and the light on the horizon hinted at promise, giving him the premonition that this was going to be the day; that one way or another this British submarine business would be finally disposed of.

The radio chattered, as if in response to his thoughts, and suddenly he heard the excited voice breaking through the static. "Fishwatch Eleven. We have contact, we have a contact . . . Sod! . . .

". . . Fishwatch Eleven. We did have a contact, bearing red two three five."

Golitsyn spoke into the intercom, to the helmsmen below decks. "Port thirty, steer a reciprocal course." He held the microphone in his hand, bracing his feet on the deck as he felt the *Kharkov* slewing round. "Stop engines."

He hung up the mike and returned to the Helicopter Radio Command panel. "Fishwatch Eleven, confirm that contact."

"Fishwatch Eleven. Contact confirmed, bearing two three five."

"Was that contact the intruder submarine?"

"Most likely."

"Were you transmitting?"

"Yes, Captain."

"Then she knows you're there?"

"Almost certainly."

"Acknowledged, Fishwatch Eleven. Maintain your position. You will be having company, we shall be concentrating in your area." He switched off and dialled Orchenkov's sea cabin. The steward answered and Golitsyn barked down the phone. "Flag officer to the bridge, flag officer to the bridge."

He hurried back to the ship's intercom. "Both engines full astern." Seconds later he felt the *Kharkov* shuddering as the screws, thrown in reverse, bit water, and slowly the carrier came about until its bows pointed in the opposite direction. He ordered, "Stop engines," and the *Kharkov* slowly settled in her new position. Through the bridge window he could see two more Kamovs in the distance, hovering over the sea. High up in the sky he caught a glimpse of the RAF Nimrod, circling aimlessly about. He shrugged his shoulders and turned to the chart table, sticking numbered plastic pins into the positions where he wanted his helicopters.

Orchenkov clattered in. "What's happened?"

"You were right, Commodore. Contact here, but very brief." He showed him the shiny black pin on the chart, the only one of its kind.

"Aaaah." Orchenkov rubbed his hands before taking a mug of black coffee from the steward, the sleep having almost left him. He bent over the chart, nodding approvingly at the pin positions. "And our four Victors?"

"They are still in their old positions."

"Then bring them in. I want them here, here, here, and here. And I want them deeper now: three hundred metres. If you move these two Kamov groups here and here, you will see we have a very tight net."

Gradually, the new positions were translated into commands, and the commands executed. In threes, each group of helicopters left their old positions and settled down in their new ones, sending down their sonobuoys, looking like fat insects feeding off the sea. The sun rose, a huge saffron orb, quite clear, suffusing all with the light of hope, breathing colour and life into the machinery and men in and around the *Kharkov*.

Rubbing his chin, feeling the roughness of unshaved bristles, Orchenkov was thinking. "What bearing did you say? That contact?"

"Two three five degrees," Golitsyn replied. "This is the

second time that submarine has come and gone. Thermal or salinity layers, she seems to know exactly where to hide.''

''That is the man inside her, Captain. It's the man you must watch, not the machine. I wonder how he feels down there, knowing that we are on to him.''

''Their computers can calculate all escape possibilities, and give success probabilities. All he has to do is act on them.''

''No, Captain. If that were so, all we would have to do is bait their computer by leaving a false gap, maybe two false gaps, and then we could catch him with our Kamovs as he tried to slip through. I think you'll find that our man down there knows better. He will use his computers, yes, but he won't necessarily act on them.''

More coffee came in, together with sandwiches and a flask of brandy. For both men it was good to be alive, in command, feeling the excitement of the chase, knowing that something was about to happen.

''Fishwatch Four, contact bearing two four...''

''Fishwatch Three, we have a contact two four...''

''Fishwatch...''

''Ultra Sonar Department, contact two three nine...''

Excited reports came from all quarters as the three helicopters and the *Kharkov*'s own ultra sonar reported the contact simultaneously. Orchenkov stopped masticating, his mouth full of bread and cheese. Golitsyn turned down the radio, taking his message from the ultra sonar compartment.

''Report, Ultra Sonar.''

''Contact, Captain. *Saturn* now bearing two four zero, depth approximately two hundred and fifty metres, contact moving to port.''

Orchenkov shouted out, ''Then go, man, get it!''

Golitsyn was cooler. He glanced at the chart where the navigator was pencilling in the line, and flicked on one of the radio channels. ''Fishwatch Eight, do you read me?''

''Fishwatch Eight. We have contact, but... but that's strange.... This is a decoy.''

The butterflies were fluttering in Golitsyn's gut. ''Can you trace the original contact? The original contact?''

''No, Captain, only the decoy.''

Golitsyn hung up and called Ultra Sonar. ''Lieutenant...''

''Captain, that was a decoy missile. We are trying...''

"Then . . ."

"No, Captain. No trace of original contact." Golitsyn switched off in disgust. Orchenkov finished his mouthful and flushed it down with a finger of brandy.

They were quiet for a few seconds before Orchenkov spoke. "I told you he was clever. I'll bet he's controlled that decoy so we can never plot its point of origin."

"But at least it's told us one thing, Commodore. Now we know that he knows we're up here, looking for him. For the first time the hunt is really on. At last you have something to report to Belinski."

Orchenkov belched. "We still don't know exactly where he is. That's the first thing Belinski really wants to know."

The sun climbed high in the sky. Orchenkov widened his search box, positive that *Saturn* was still there. For his part, Golitsyn was developing some sort of respect for Orchenkov's combination of strategy and instinct. Despite Golitsyn's distaste for his revolting manners, his boorishness and his shouting, the two men were beginning to draw together, each realizing that the other had something to offer.

At ten fifty-five, the radio burst into life again, simultaneously with the intercom from the Ultra Sonar Department.

"Fishwatch Three, contact . . ."

"Sonar, Captain. Contact bearing zero four five, steady, depth three hundred metres. Approximate range twelve kilometres."

Golitsyn picked up the radio microphone. "Fishwatch Three, do you confirm, contact bearing zero four zero. . . ."

"We confirm, Captain. Contact. . . ."

Orchenkov snatched the microphone and yelled down it. "Then go, man, go! Hit that motherless fucker before he slips away again!"

"*Da*, Commodore." Within the Kamov helicopter the pilot pressed the scarlet button and prepared himself for the release of the weight that would send his machine upwards. The torpedo slipped away nose downwards and entered the water. Its propellers gripped instantly, thrusting it forwards, into the green. Complex electronics on its nose would pick up the noise from *Saturn* and guide it to her at fifty miles an hour. The pilot watched it enter, saw its silvery body beneath the water glisten from the sun, alter direction slightly, and slip out of sight. He spoke into his microphone.

"Torpedo launched, Commodore, and has acquisition."

The harsh *br-r-rp* of the telephone woke Arthur Wainscott at five-forty in the morning. He sat up rigidly, confused, and then remembered. Christ, Moscow! He fumbled for the receiver, straining to hear the voice issuing from it.

"Prime Minister?"

"Yes. That you, Sir Humphrey?"

"Morning. Bad news, I'm afraid. Vatutin's in his office but I can't get through to him. They were all very polite, but not interested. Eventually I was cut off. I think we'll just have to wait until this thing blows over. Otherwise try their embassy in London. If you have something important to say . . ."

"But it might be too late by then."

"Then there's nothing else you or we can do. Except pray."

He detected a certain sharpness in Sir Humphrey's voice. The sharpness meant reprimand and disappointment, for the loss of all the ground he had gained in the last two years. That meant another willing and important servant Wainscott was losing. "Thank you, Sir Humphrey. I'm sorry it's caused you all this trouble; I'll call the embassy."

He put the phone down, knowing that there was no possibility of further sleep. Perhaps he should make a visit to Northwood, see what was happening at first hand.

Neither Henderson nor any of the men on watch had slept: fatigue came upon them in waves, and they all had ways of dealing with it. Henderson had issued benzedrine tablets and these did indeed have some effect. The steward would bring in black coffee every hour on the hour, but the hour between cups was a long time. The men also had their own ways of keeping alert, which is not easy when they had to remain seated over their consoles. Alan Sykes would crack his knuckles from time to time, and wiggle his toes, which seemed to do the trick, though he felt himself having to do it more and more frequently.

Peter Howarth used his eyes, knowing that if he kept

them moving all the time he could fight his own drowsiness. But he was frightened too, and as his flickering eyes wandered around the control room, so his mind wandered also, and his fear grew, feeding on the long periods of inactivity, dreading what might come next. He had known all along that he was not very good in danger: he had known it from boyhood when he had funked so many tackles on the rugby pitch, and worse still, had to endure the hideous shame of having to face up to his teammates afterwards. Later, he had met it again on a skiing holiday, when he had broken a leg because of it.

So why had he chosen the Navy, where bravery and cool nerves were expected? He was only now starting to ask himself. Subconsciously, he knew it was the uniform: it made him look brave, and if he looked brave, perhaps he was brave. Perhaps it would at least hide his lack of bravery, so that his parents would think he was brave. His father had won the Military Cross in Malaya: he wondered if he had felt the same way when he was cutting his way through the jungle, knowing that ambushes came without warning. But in Cadet School Howarth soon learnt that this would not wash. But he dreaded the epithet "gutless" and, perversely, knew that that was why he had to stay.

He drew comfort from the men around him, in a sense feeding on them to supplement the courage he lacked. Dammit, why weren't they frightened too? If only one of them were to show just the slightest amount of fear, then he would know he was not alone. He could see Tate flexing his hands over the control column: no sign of fear or worry there; Sykes cracking his finger joints, but totally composed; and Henderson, deep in thought, mathematically calculating, and obviously heedless of any physical aspects of danger.

Howarth detached himself from them, suspecting that he alone was human because he alone felt fear. But if that was the case, why did he need them so, to give him the reassurance he so obviously lacked? An all-pervading drowsiness came over him; perhaps if he were to just close his eyes for a second . . . But no, that would never do. He reached for his dividers and pricked the back of his hand, sinking the sharp point deep in, and feeling the pain jolt him back into consciousness.

Henderson saw him do it but said nothing. He was aware of the fatigue element, knew they were all dipping into resources of stamina which could probably keep them on their feet for as much as seventy hours. After that fatigue would overcome them, blunting their reactions until finally they would be unable to manage. He desperately hoped the *Kharkov* would have moved away well before then, allowing him to make his escape.

Crooke's voice came through on the loudspeaker. "Captain, Sonar. Helicopter sonobuoy transmissions bearing red one five and red six five. Contact zero four on red four zero is closing, sir."

"Captain, roger." Henderson wiped his forehead with the back of his wrist and addressed Sykes. "There is only one way out now, Number One . . ."

Crooke interrupted, his sharp voice making the loudspeaker vibrate. "Captain, Sonar. High speed propeller noises bearing now red four two, twelve thousand yards and closing."

"Sonar, Captain. Confirm that."

"Confirmed. High speed propeller noises bearing now red four three, eleven thousand yards, closing. Torpedo, sir, torpedo."

"Captain, roger. Standby decoys one and two at ninety degree track."

Instantly the mood in the control room became electric, each man knowing that his fate was in the lap of the gods, knowing that the last missile explosion had impaired *Saturn*'s defences, considering their captain, wondering whether he was man or god.

Crooke's voice was steadier, cool now, and soft. "Ten thousand yards and closing . . . Eight thousand yards, bearing red four five, closing . . . Six thousand yards, red four seven, closing . . ."

Henderson was not mesmerised, he was calculating, wondering how effective the noise from his own decoy missile was going to be against an enemy torpedo he had never met before. He squeezed his microphone button. "Stand by. . . . Stand by decoys one and two. Fire one!"

Another speaker answered back, "One fired."

"Stand by two."

"Four thousand yards, closing."

"Fire two!"

"Two fired."

"Two thousand yards and closing. Both decoys running true." And then jubilation: "Torpedo locked onto the second decoy, sir. . . . Four thousand yards, opening. The torpedo has definitely locked on to the second decoy, sir."

"Reload decoy tubes." Henderson knew that this was only one torpedo. It signified that the rules of engagement had entered a third stage: no longer only weaving and depth-changing to avoid missiles and sonobuoy transmissions; torpedoes meant a merciless fight to the death. He looked across to Sykes, saw he was smiling and winked. "They really work, Alan."

"Do you think that was a real torpedo, sir, or a dummy to frighten us?"

Henderson grinned. "To find that out might be the sort of experiment you can only do once. I wouldn't like to try."

Crooke's voice came back on. "Decoy number two bearing red one three five, six thousand yards, range opening. . . . Captain, we have a contact on red one four zero, contact Zero Three."

"What! Confirm that, Sonar!"

"Sonar confirms. Christ, the decoy's expended itself. Yes, contact Zero Three bears red one four zero. The torpedo's latched on. Oh, Jesus . . ." His voice tailed away in disbelief.

Everybody in the control room stopped short, knowing full well what was about to happen. They looked to their captain, whose face betrayed nothing, brows slightly knit. Suddenly he shouted over the PA system: "Stand by for pressure-wave shock blast!"

Almost immediately there was the most monumental explosion. Not sharp, like the previous missile, but awesome in its power and strength. Seconds later the shock wave hit *Saturn*, throwing her up in the water, tossing her amidst the bellows of demons into a wild fourth dimension where time and space meant nothing.

— CHAPTER 8 —

19th May, Morning

Guided by sound, the pilotless torpedo streaked through the water at fifty miles an hour, rushing to accomplish its first and last journey. It struck the Soviet Victor Class nuclear submarine on her bows, detonating the seven hundred and fifty pounds of high explosive the torpedo carried in its nose: a sharp and vicious explosion, releasing a fierce heat that melted metal.

Almost immediately the Victor's aft end imploded, the pressure of the surrounding water squeezing the hull into a tight mesh of twisted metal, splitting the reactor compartment and releasing the contents of her reactor into the water. At the same time her own load of high explosive torpedoes, twenty-four of them, erupted, causing the cataclysmic upheaval that threw *Saturn* out of position.

Orchenkov and Golitsyn had been waiting an eternity for it to happen. So long that Orchenkov was convinced that the torpedo had misfired or failed to detonate, and had resigned himself to a continuation of the search which he had found frustrating, and, because it brought out the worst in everybody, somehow idiotic. Golitsyn reminded him that the torpedo had a travel time of twenty minutes, though the speed could vary, and he had meticulously noted the launching time in the log. Fourteen minutes can be an eternity: Dostoevsky once wrote that he had re-lived his whole life in the four minutes before being tied up in front of a firing squad. Neither Orchenkov nor Golitsyn used their time in the same way, and that made it seem longer.

They heard it first. Nothing dramatic, simply an underwater *crump*, a long distance off, only its tone hinting at the power released. Then the swelling in the water, the awesome upheaval which confirmed that the torpedo had struck

151

home, and, minutes later, the curious, silent eighteen-foot waves that spread out. The *Kharkov* rocked and wallowed.

The explosion silenced all activity on the bridge. The six men, Orchenkov, Golitsyn, Sverdlov, Tyutchev, the navigation officer and the signals yeoman all stood still, frozen like statues, each deep in his own emotions, each realizing and appreciating the finality of what they had done, and each feeling soiled as a result of it.

"*Do svidanya, Saturn, do svidanya.*" Goodbye, *Saturn*, goodbye. There were tears forming in the corners of Orchenkov's eyes. He wiped them away with the back of his sleeve. "But the stupid bastards shouldn't have been here in the first place!" He spun round aggressively to Golitsyn. "This is our water, ours! If we let these people get away with this sort of thing, then we would have no access of our own to the Atlantic. These stupid people should have thought of that. You do see, don't you?"

Golitsyn was embarrassed. He was saved from answering by the second signals yeoman entering the bridge and approaching him with a familiar bit of paper in his hand. He took it, glanced through it, and passed it over to Orchenkov. "Belinski."

Orchenkov read it through, turned and stared out of the bridge window, towards the area where the explosion had happened. He spoke carefully to the signalman, not looking to see if he was taking it down. "Send this message: 'To: First Admiral Belinski. From: Commodore Orchenkov, aboard the *Kharkov*. Para One:

'During planned anti-submarine exercise today have witnessed large underwater explosion in our area. Para Two:

'Have reason to believe that possible intrusion of our area by a foreign submarine has ended in disaster for the country involved. Para Three:

'Am investigating and conducting a search for debris in hope of identifying submarine concerned.' Message ends."

The signalman finished writing in his notebook and nodded at Orchenkov. Orchenkov nodded back his dismissal and turned to Golitsyn. "That should please Admiral Belinski."

Golitsyn shook his head. "We had no right to fire that torpedo, no right at all. Once we knew where that submarine was, and we did, it was a straightforward matter to force her up."

"Was it?" Orchenkov thumped the telegraph repeater in front of him. "She had a nasty habit of coming and going. Come now, my friend, a bird in the hand is worth more than two in the bush. We'd both be on patrol boats off Kamtchatka if she had got away. Besides, as I said, she had no business being there. We gave her every chance to come up . . ."

"Did we?"

"We gave her every chance to surface and she persisted in staying down. What else could she expect?"

Golitsyn held his tongue and Orchenkov could smell the rebellion. He thought hard for another tack, another way of changing his colleague's feelings. It came to him:

"You know, don't you, that you took that submarine out on your own? That you deployed the helicopters and arranged the search boxes? Do you realize that today you have achieved a major naval victory? That Moscow will be very pleased? People have been made Heroes of the Soviet Union for less than that."

Golitsyn simply stared at him, his features showing a mixture of disgust and pity at this blatant distortion.

Orchenkov snorted. Stupid little fart, he thought. He didn't say it, though, but instead: "Very well then, have it your own way. Let's start tidying up. Bring all but three of the Kamovs on board and have the Victors surface. Use them with the three remaining Kamovs to search for debris: any more and they'll get in each other's way. We want something, anything, to prove whose submarine that was."

"I don't think we'll find very much, not with that sort of explosion at that depth."

"You will be surprised, my friend. Maybe bits of panelling, bits of paper. A submarine cannot be torn apart like that without something coming to the surface."

Golitsyn shrugged his shoulders and picked up the intercom. "Ultra Sonar, Captain here. Switch to underwater telephone mode and order all Victors to surface. . . ."

Belinski was mightily relieved to get Orchenkov's message. Since his return from Moscow, he had been pacing his office, wondering why the *Kharkov* was having such difficulty when he already knew how effective the ultra sonar was. And he was in a dilemma: the *Kharkov* and the four

Victors should have been perfectly adequate to force an intruding submarine to the surface. The Northern Banner Fleet would have looked pretty feeble if he'd had to double those forces to get the task completed, especially as the *Kharkov* should have been able to do it on her own. So whilst he had other vessels at Polyarny and Severomorsk, he had not wanted to send them out.

And President Kirov had been badgering him, asking him why it was taking so long, and every time Belinski could only reply, "Any minute now, Comrade President, any minute now," and it hadn't happened. He knew very well the laws of cussedness which predicted satisfactory results only when he had sent out another anti-submarine carrier, and perhaps also a destroyer, and he knew how equally damaging that could be for President Kirov, politically, let alone himself.

Muttering prayers of thanks, he placed the message on his desk and pulled out the miniature icon he had kept so secretly in his breast pocket. He kissed the face of the Virgin Mary, blessing all the saints who had caused things to happen this way.

He called his radio officer and ordered the message to be relayed to President Kirov, Foreign Secretary Vatutin and, ten minutes later, Director of Intelligence Rodichev. After all, he was not going to have that man appointed as the messenger of good news.

Vatutin was with Kirov when the message arrived. They were discussing the British prime minister's attempt to get through during the night, as well as Sir Humphrey Prescott's approach in the morning. Both were convinced that they had done the right thing in refusing to talk. If they had accepted the call, which could only have been made because the British prime minister wanted to ask for something, they would have had to refuse his request. It would be kinder, easier for everybody if they didn't have to say "no." Besides, it gave them the advantage of timing and controlling the next *rapprochement*, for which they could make Britain sweat a little, feel a mite guilty, before realizing what good people the Soviets were.

When the telephone rang Kirov knew it could only be a message concerning the Barents Sea. That or a major emergency. He picked up the receiver and his eyes danced as he listened.

"*Horoshoa. Da, ochin rad.*" He replaced the receiver and paused, thoughtfully, before reaching for the brandy. Vatutin knew by his remark that it was good news. He waited expectantly.

"Vatutin, they got her."

"Ah . . . Sunk?"

"So I understand. Dramatically."

"*Otshudo.* They took their time."

"Didn't they? It makes me think. What time is it in London?"

Vatutin examined his Rolex. "Nine-fifteen. Why?"

"Supposing we asked our ambassador . . . Khlebnikov?"

"Khlebnikov, that's right."

"Khlebnikov. Supposing we ask him to telephone Mr. Wainscott and explain how sorry we were to learn he was trying to get through last night, that we were both completely tied up, and suggest to him that he, Mr. Wainscott, should tell him what it was all about, so that he could pass the message on to us. . . . After all, that is what ambassadors are for."

Vatutin frowned, thinking. Then his mouth broke into a wicked grin. He began to choke with laughter, real laughter, and tears rolled down his cheeks.

Kirov smiled too.

It was seven-thirty when Wainscott walked through the doors of the Operations Room at the Northwood bunker. He paused at the entrance, awed by the size of the screens, the breadth of the room, and the atmosphere that reigned in it. It was his first time there.

He saw three men beside the console at the same time as they recognized him. They stood up and Sir James Hythe came across to him.

"Good morning, Prime Minister. You remember Admiral Fredenberger?" He pointed to the American, who raised his arm in greeting.

"Yes, of course. Those were better times, when we last met, weren't they, Admiral? What's happening now?"

Hythe gestured towards the large screen. "The large red cross marks the *Kharkov*. Those little red crosses are her helicopters. You will see that they are in groups of threes. The Nimrod has reported that they are operating sonobuoys. As you can see, it is a conventional search pattern.''

''So they haven't found *Saturn* yet?''

Hardy spoke. ''No, we don't think so.''

''But you are worried, Sir Richard?''

''Those helicopters should have moved on by now. The *Kharkov* went about and stopped. It looks ominous.''

The prime minister studied the screen thoughtfully before asking, ''Where are their four nuclear submarines?''

''We don't know. They went deep about half an hour ago and now we've lost trace of them. That's something which is also worrying us.''

Wainscott turned to Hythe, bitterness distorting his face. ''Have you any idea what sort of diplomatic mess this has put us into?''

''There's no need to tell me. How did they react to the denial?''

''Nothing. I don't think they believed us for one minute.''

''Mmmm. Take a seat, Prime Minister, I'll see if we can't get the Nimrod to transmit live coverage of the area.''

Wainscott sat down dutifully whilst Hythe joined Hardy at the console, asking him in subdued tones to put them through.

Suddenly an enormous red blob appeared on the screen, expanding at an extraordinary rate. Wainscott saw it first. ''What's that?'' he called out, puzzled and nervous, drawing their attention to it.

Fredenberger answered for them. ''Goddamn, that must be an explosion of some sort. Kee-rist, just look at the size of it, Sir Richard!''

The Nimrod came through. ''This is Blue Peter One Six. We have just witnessed a large underwater explosion, approximately ten miles to the east of the *Kharkov*.'' The screen changed, flickering before settling on a picture of turbulent sea water, white and seething.

''Good grief!'' Wainscott looked to Hardy for confirmation. But Hardy was ash-white, his eyes unseeing. Wainscott persisted. ''What has just happened? Was that *Saturn*?''

There was a long pause before Hythe replied. ''We don't know, Prime Minister. If we watch we may find out.''

''How?''

Fredenberger began to explain. "If they carry on their search pattern . . ." and then the sudden realization hit him. "Hell, it doesn't matter what's happened, the shit's hit the fan either way."

The Nimrod captain was still reporting, though nobody was paying him much attention. "We are detecting a hell of a lot of radiation down there. . . ."

Hardy collected himself and took the microphone: "Blue Peter One Six. This is Northwood Control. Stay there. Your radiation and infra-red reports may help confirm identity of subject."

"Blue Peter One Six. Roger."

The telephone rang. Hardy answered it and called Fredenberger. "It's for you, Joe. Pentagon."

"Thank you, Sir Richard." He strode over and took the phone. The others scarcely noticed him, their eyes fixed on the screen, viewing the sea which was now settling down. The Nimrod cameraman zoomed in on the maelstrom of water, where dead fish were clearly visible floating with their silver bellies up.

Hardy was talking to the Nimrod, breaking away from the formality of radio communications jargon, talking with the pilot as though they were on the telephone, now asking him if there was any visible reaction on the *Kharkov*.

There was none. The ship remained still and the television cameraman panned the groups of helicopters, showing them all with their lines plunging into the water, as if totally oblivious to what had just happened.

One of the helicopters began winching up its sonobuoy. Then another, and another, until all but three of them were up and flying back to the *Kharkov*, gathering on her deck. The remaining three were proceeding to the position of the underwater explosion.

Wainscott spoke hoarsely to Hythe. "Is that what Fredenberger meant?"

"I'm afraid so, Prime Minister. It looks as though we may have lost *Saturn*."

Wainscott sighed. A long deep sigh that spelt bitterness, betrayal and sadness all in one. "Sir James, I want you and Sir Richard to report to me in my office in two hours' time. In the meantime, and until we know what we are going to do, the whole of this operation, and its results, are not to be discussed by anyone."

"Of course, sir, we understand. Eleven o'clock in your office, then."

The journey back to Downing Street took longer than usual. The rush hour was in full swing and rain slowed the traffic even further. Wainscott sat in the back of the brown Jaguar, trying to think out his next plan of action. The loss of *Saturn* need not be made public. It need not be announced in the House of Commons, at least not in the way it really happened. She would simply have failed to surface in the South Atlantic, wherever the water is deepest, and then nobody would be able to look for her. It would be a simple matter of letters of condolence to the relatives of the crew.

The one snag would be the Russians. They wouldn't believe him for a moment. How would he ever be able to gain respect from them when they knew what he had done, knew damn well he was lying? Hopeless. Even David Hogarth would agree that the worst had happened, and for the life of him, Wainscott couldn't see how Hogarth was going to turn this one to political advantage.

The Jaguar pulled up at the side entrance to Number Ten at nine-forty. Wainscott went straight to his office and cancelled all his appointments, asking Martin to set up a meeting at eleven o'clock with his foreign and defence ministers. Coffee was brought in. He poured himself a cup, sipped it meditatively, and tried to take stock of the situation.

The telephone rang and he picked up the receiver irritably. "I told you I wasn't to be disturbed."

"Sir, it's the Soviet ambassador. He's most insistent. Says he's sure you'll want to speak with him."

Wainscott froze, not having the faintest idea what to say. He had forgotten about his calls to Kirov and Sir Humphrey during the night. He wanted time, time to play this thing out correctly, not to have his hand forced. "Tell him I'm busy. Ask him what his business is and tell him I'll call him back, or better still, Oakley will. That's his job."

"Who? Me, sir?" the operator replied, totally baffled.

"Yes, you. You can do that, can't you?"

"Yes, sir."

He slammed the receiver down, cursing the Russians for choosing this particular moment to make their call. He poured more coffee, idly watching the rain outside.

The phone rang again.

"I said . . ."

"Prime Minister, Ambassador Khlebnikov is most insistent. Says he knows you will want to speak with him, can't understand why he's not been put through."

Oh, bloody hell, thought Wainscott. If I don't speak with him, then he'll construe it as a snub; and the Russians are the last people . . . "Very well, put him through." He waited, and then heard the unctuous, polished, but distinctly foreign voice:

"Prime Minister? Good morning, Prime Minister. Sergei Khlebnikov here. I have just spoken with Moscow. Apparently you tried to call President Kirov last night, and your ambassador Sir Humphrey tried to get through to Foreign Secretary Vatutin. They are both desolated to have heard they have missed you. They are presently deeply involved in urgent discussions with their Polish counterparts, and there is no possible way they can break off without seeming offensive. Perhaps if you were to tell me what it's all about, then maybe I can do something?"

His heart sank. What *do* I tell this man? He fumbled for words. "Ambassador . . . thank you for calling. Yes, I did try to reach President Kirov. Something had come up. But no, it's all right now. Please, will you send him my kindest regards and wish him all success with his meeting. We also have a soft spot for our Polish friends. I look forward to meeting him personally very soon."

"Yes, of course. But what was it about, Prime Minister? Or if you don't want to talk to me about it, and he did suggest that I approach you . . . well, would you like me to have him call you back?"

"No, thank you. It's quite all right now."

"Oh, come now, Prime Minister, surely you don't put a call through to our president at a quarter to three in the morning if you don't feel it's of vital importance?"

The bastard. He's patronizing me! Sod you all! But he held his temper. "No, it's quite all right. I'm sorry to have caused you all this trouble."

"That's perfectly all right, Prime Minister, no trouble at all. Goodbye."

Wainscott stumbled through to his own private lavatory. He retched violently, but only bile came out.

A burst tyre can send a car careering in the wrong direction and it requires great presence of mind, as well as skill, to set it right again.

Saturn was in a similar predicament: thrown off course by the massive onrush of water, she responded to neither rudder nor planes as Tate desperately tried to control her. She found herself lifted through one layer of water and deposited in another.

Given the noise, the shaking, the sudden increase and loss of gravity, it was a terrifying moment for the men on board. Henderson held grimly onto the periscope, mentally noting those who were thrown out of their seats, as well as the crashes from the pantry, the wardroom and other compartments where things had come adrift. Despite his bandaged head he was very much in command, waiting for the instant when *Saturn* came to rest, the moment when he would have to fight to regain control of the situation.

When she settled, *Saturn* righted herself from a list to starboard of fifteen degrees. The water around contained gases which were streaming to the surface, but making *Saturn* comparatively heavier, with nothing to bite into. Suddenly the bow tilted downwards, and Henderson knew what they were in for, they all knew it: an uncontrolled dive.

"Full astern! Starboard thirty!"

Tate called out the depth, feeling that this was something familiar, somewhere where they had been before. "Three thousand two hundred... Three thousand four hundred..." Dear Lord, not this, not when we've come so far! He watched helplessly as he saw the numbers on the gauge continue to increase, even though they were changing more slowly now.

"Three thousand six hundred."

The bulkhead panelling by the wardroom cracked with a loud report. It parted from the deckhead, suspended by one side only. But the pump jet blades were biting water as *Saturn* entered the still icy saltwater close to the sea bed, away from the foam and troubled waters higher up. The blades gripped, and within, the men felt *Saturn* respond.

"Stop engine!"

"Engine stopped."

"Five degrees bow up, half ahead."

"Five degrees bow up, half ahead."

"Two thousand eight hundred feet, Coxswain."

"Two thousand eight hundred feet. Aye, aye, sir."

Slowly, gingerly, *Saturn* made her way upwards. The sudden confrontation with a live torpedo being fired at them, the activity in firing their own decoy missiles, and the success in diverting the torpedo had generated adrenaline in a way the crew had never felt before. Even Sykes felt heedless to the danger they were in, enjoying a keenness, a vibrancy that throbbed through them all. Only Howarth was still, his jaw slack, his eyes vacant.

Elsewhere on *Saturn* there were men who did not know what was happening, who felt helpless in the maelstrom around them, and whose minds had short-circuited. Henderson was soon to find this out.

Tate spoke, expressing some of his own lightheadedness. "I think we're getting rather good at this."

And Sykes, who was more realistic: "God, sir, that was close."

"Too close, Number One." Henderson automatically reached for the microphone. "Sonar, report."

For once Lt. Crooke sounded rattled. "The sonar picture is confused, sir. Stand by." They could feel *Saturn* levelling off at two thousand eight hundred feet. "Captain, sir. Sonar."

"Captain."

"We can hear the Soviet nuke breaking up, sir." The water pressure was still mangling the Russian submarine, twisting her into a tight mass, working on her still as she lay on the sea bed.

"Captain. Roger. Report all contacts as soon as you can."

"Aye, aye, sir."

Saturn was safe. Henderson's second most immediate priority was the crew: "Casualty report, Number One."

"Stand by, sir." Sykes started speaking to the navigational pilot, and then back to Tate. Henderson wanted the status of his sonar capability, and also his own weaponry. There was a lot to do, and quickly.

Sykes interrupted him. "Captain, sir."

"Yes, Number One?"

"Casualty report, sir. Leading Seaman Willis is dead. The force of the shock broke the harness on one of the torpedoes. It rolled off the cradle and fell on him."

"Christ! What else?"

"Two broken limbs, sir. In all, nine cases have been reported, but seven of these are minor injuries. And er, sir, three other men have had to be restrained. It was too much for them."

Henderson did not reply; his lips thinned grimly and Sykes knew there was a change coming over him—a change which worried Sykes, because it was a change that made him no longer the hunted, but the hunter, feeling a vindictiveness towards the men on the surface who had put him into this impossible position, a resolution to drive through them and to hell with the consequences. He faced Sykes, his eyes alight.

"Number One, there's a madman up there who's got us boxed in. He doesn't want us surfaced, but sunk. I promised to bring *Saturn* home and I damned well will, and there's only one way we're going to do it."

Sykes cocked a nervous eye at him. "You are more than determined, aren't you, sir?"

"Determined." He had heard that before, but where? Home. Scotland, images of Karen with her innocent but shameless laughing eyes, her long blonde hair, flashed before him. *She* had said he was determined, too. He thought of Skip, of that horrendous night, and his broken promise to take him to the beach. And he didn't even know if he had recovered. . . .

"Captain, sir?" It was Sykes, with an odd expression on his face.

Henderson pulled himself together. "Determined? Of course I'm bloody well determined!"

Orchenkov could see that Golitsyn was worried. Not just from the feeling of having soiled his career but something worse, something that affected his own professionalism. He was fidgety and there was sweat under his eyebrows. Twice he had personally been down to the ultra sonar compartment, each time returning greyer than when he left. Orchenkov saw him hang up the microphone after talking with one of the helicopters, and Golitsyn's face told him that something deep inside the man had just cracked.

Orchenkov could already guess the reason, for he could also see the three submarine fins, seven miles out, and it was coming home to him why there weren't four, and he didn't like it.

Golitsyn started to speak, a deep intake of breath without looking at his superior officer. Orchenkov knew what he was going to say and answered first, his voice rasping.

"Are you sure, Captain? Are you positively sure?"

Golitsyn's jaw was working. "Quite sure, Commodore. It is now forty-five minutes since the other three surfaced. The *Vitebsk* does not come up. She does not answer our signals."

"Maybe she's too deep?"

"No, Commodore. That was Fishwatch Eleven. They have found some debris . . ." He wiped his forehead with his hand and sat down, choking back the sobs that wanted to come out.

Orchenkov gazed out of the bridge window, towards the helicopters, the three submarines, the rubber speed boats that were mooching around them, but seeing none of this. Orchenkov had known war as a cadet, he was familiar with the fortunes of war, the unpredictability of events, and the need to use them as best one could to one's own advantage. He was not a man who gave up, ever.

He sympathized with Golitsyn, put a hand on his shoulder and spoke to him softly. "We are not finished yet, Captain. Send another message to Belinski, cancelling the first message. Tell him that we have reason to believe that the British submarine has deliberately and unwarrantedly fired on and destroyed the *Vitebsk*. As a result of this we are ordering our remaining Victors to submerge and continue the search in a triangular pattern."

Golitsyn started, rejecting the paternal overtones. The proposition went contrary to all the tenets of his naval academy training. "But Commodore, we fired first. Shouldn't we . . ."

"Did we? How do you know?" Orchenkov exploded, shaking everyone else on the bridge. "Tyutchev! All we know is that we've lost a submarine, a nuclear one at that. Did we fire at our own submarine?''

Tyutchev was thrown; this was not why he was on the bridge, to answer questions like this. He found himself being helplessly drawn into complicity, into something which had nothing to do with his job or his position.

"Eh, Commissar?" Orchenkov persisted.

And Tyutchev did not like being called "commissar."

"No, of course not."

"Then the British did!" Orchenkov shouted triumphantly at Golitsyn. "Send that message; the responsibility is mine!"

Hythe, Hardy and Fredenberger had retired from the Operations Room to Fredenberger's office. There they began an unofficial post-mortem on the failure of their mission. They all saw that its failure involved much more than the loss of *Saturn* disastrous as it was. The Barents Sea was becoming increasingly difficult to penetrate; *Saturn*'s failure, even though the odds had been loaded against her, spelt out a clear warning: the Barents Sea was now Soviet territory and foreigners were not welcome.

Norway was going to need a lot of help in maintaining her sovereignty over Spitzbergen and Bear Island, particularly since there were more Russians than Norwegians on these islands.

How had the Soviets been able to do it? Clearly their prior knowledge was a help, but the key seemed to lie in their ultra sonar. It didn't matter if their own submarines had a maximum operating depth of only about eight hundred feet. If their anti-submarine carrier had the capability of sussing out submarines some distance away and two and a half thousand feet below sea level, then ultra sonar was the key to protecting that piece of water. Eventually, *any* piece of water if they could preserve the carrier from air attack.

The two Britons and the American admiral all remembered playing "Battleships" as kids. The submarine represented only one square, and even though a player might have lost the rest of his fleet, that one square could still win him the game. But now the rules were changing, and all navy vessels were going to have the same number of squares. As Fredenberger so aptly explained, it put them into "a whole new ball game."

They were interrupted by a call from the Operations Room: the Nimrod was still up there, and had something to report. All three of them rushed out of the office.

Hardy went straight to the communications console and took the microphone. "Blue Peter One Six, this is Northwood Control. Report, over."

"Northwood Control, this is Blue Peter One Six. Further to our last report, we have been maintaining surveillance around the area of the explosion. Three of the Soviet nuclear submarines have surfaced. The *Kharkov* has picked up speed and her helicopters are taking off again."

"Roger, Blue Peter One Six. Give us television coverage."

"Roger, Northwood."

The screen lit up, flickered, and cleared to show the now familiar picture of the *Kharkov*. As they had just heard, the helicopters were taking off again, in groups of three, and the exercise also looked familiar.

Fredenberger interrupted. "Richard, we want Navstat to see what those submarines are doing." They all gazed at the Navstat screen with the red crosses superimposed. Sure enough, the submarines were moving apart, each in different directions, their markers representing the points of an ever-growing equilateral triangle. One by one, they faded out.

"I thought so. They've gone deep again." Fredenberger was half-anxious, half-jubilant. "*Saturn*'s alive, gentlemen!"

"Thank God." Hythe stood up, not knowing how he should feel, and walked over to the telephone. He picked it up and asked for Downing Street, for the prime minister.

"Yes, Sir James?" The voice was weary.

"Prime Minister, I have fresh news for you. It now looks very likely that that was a Soviet submarine we saw blown up. We don't know how or why. They have now continued to search for *Saturn*: she is still very much alive."

Wainscott was quick to grasp the implications. "You realize they will accuse us of sinking it?"

"But we don't have a submarine there, Prime Minister."

"Blast you, Hythe, they think we do."

"*Saturn* should have slipped away by now. In all that ruckus she had plenty of time to move."

"Christ, I hope so. I want her surfacing in Port Stanley. Yesterday, if it were possible. It's the only thing that can get us off the hook."

"Quite. By the way, we might be a little late at your office. Admiral Fredenberger's on the telephone to the Pentagon and we'll be leaving as soon as he's finished." He hung up, turned to Fredenberger, and noted the very serious expression on his face as he talked.

Fredenberger put the phone down thoughtfully before facing him. "That explosion was monitored by Pentagon Satellite Control as well. I have just spoken with President Mallory, and because we suspect it was a Soviet submarine that blew up, he has ordered a primary NATO alert. He's speaking to Mr. Wainscott now." He swung round to Hardy, addressing him formally. "In accordance with NATO procedures, I have to order all British forces seconded to the NATO structure on to a Primary Alert."

Hardy and Hythe were dumbstruck. Silently they picked up their raincoats and briefcases. The screen was still on, showing the *Kharkov* and the six groups of three helicopters.

Wainscott cradled the phone gently after speaking with the American president. How a stable situation could have careered so wildly out of control in forty-eight hours was beyond him. There was no possibility now of phoning back the Russians: he had closed that option when speaking with Khlebnikov. Primary Alert meant all leave cancelled, soldiers confined to barracks, the issue of ammunition, packing kitbags, fueling Hercules transports, arming missiles. Heavens, there was going to be a lot of questions. And presumably the Warsaw Pact forces were doing the same.

And Mallory hadn't been too kind, either. Clearly if there were going to be a confrontation, he didn't want a European power to have caused it. So there was somebody else who was going to be difficult to deal with.

And he had this damned meeting in fifteen minutes.

Ugh.

— CHAPTER 9 —

19th May, Midday

"Captain, Sonar."

"Captain."

"Contact Zero Two bears red one two two, range eight miles. Contact Zero Four bears green one zero four, range nine miles. Contact Zero One, the *Kharkov*, bears green zero two, sir, almost dead ahead, range twelve miles."

"Thank you, Sonar. Anything on Contact Zero Five?"

"No, sir. She may be masked by the *Kharkov*."

"Thank you, Sonar." Henderson was about to click his microphone into place, but changed his mind. Instead he glanced at the clock and called Robert Bayliss, his weapons electrical officer, and Angus MacDonald to the control room. Whilst waiting, he glanced over the Navigational Plot where Howarth had marked in the *Kharkov* and the two submarines they knew about.

Howarth leant back so Henderson could get a better view, at the same time raising his eyebrows, worried. They both understood the pattern: two submarines stationary, their bows facing each other, their sonar straining to pick up any foreign noise. And the *Kharkov* poised to come slowly between them, using her own ultra sonar, ready to deliver the *coup de grace* as soon as she detected *Saturn*. Henderson stood up and beckoned to Sykes. "Come here a sec, will you, Number one?"

Sykes stepped over. He recognized the situation instantly and, in the moment of recognition, knew how his captain was going to play it. They had four options: the first was to do nothing; to lie low and deep, and hope to remain undetected. This involved the risk of detection by the *Kharkov* when she transmitted, and if she did find *Saturn* there would be no hope of escape. The second option was to try to run east, using all her speed to outrun them, but this would take them out of the Barents Depression, into shallower waters where the helicopters would find them. The third option was to try to slip round one of the Victors, but that was equally risky; they were too close already.

Which left the fourth option, the bold option: to steer straight for the *Kharkov*, to pass under her, and somehow evade the remaining Victor that the *Kharkov* was now masking: it was easier to evade one submarine than two. MacDonald and Bayliss came into the control room.

Henderson spoke. "We don't have much time, but I see it this way. If we run for the *Kharkov*, then neither she nor her Victors will be able to use their homing torpedoes, because all of them generate more noise than we do down here. That means ASROCs. I think, even if we are detected, that we have a far better chance of evading ASROCs than homing torpedoes."

The four men nodded. ASROCs were bad enough, but it is not always possible to evade homing torpedoes with decoys, especially if a spread of three or four is fired.

"To avoid damage by ASROCs we may need to use speed and we may need to use force. Do you understand me?"

They nodded again, thoughtfully.

"Good. Robert: the starboard transducer amplifiers?"

"Some are already working now. That's how we picked up Contact Zero Four. Give us three more minutes and you'll have as good as we're going to get on this trip."

"Three more minutes is about as much as you're going to get. We don't have much time. And if we want to go active?"

"No problem, sir."

"Good. Oh, and Robert, before you go, are the Stingfish missiles ready?"

"Yes, sir, and armed."

"Thank you. Angus?"

MacDonald was grimly confident. "The number one busbar is still out, but the number two is fine. I can give you the power if you want to transmit on sonar."

"Good. And speed? I'm going to want every available revolution you can give me, even if you have to go through the emergency seals. Are you with me?"

"Aye, aye, sir. We'll give you everything we have."

"Thanks, Angus." Henderson clapped him on the shoulder. "You'd better be off and ready. We'll be going in any minute now."

Sykes hesitated before returning to his place by the Systems Console. "What about Contact Zero Five?"

"She'll be waiting for us on the other side of the *Kharkov*. We'll have to make damned sure we're ready when we detect her."

"Mmmm." He returned to the Systems Console, more preoccupied with what was going to happen when they passed the *Kharkov* than with the gauges in front of him.

Bayliss's voice came through the loudspeaker. "Captain, sir. Fore Ends."

"Captain."

"One, two, three, four and five tubes are loaded with Mark Fifty-Twos. Firing Control in local, sir. Decoy tubes one and two are reloaded."

"Roger, Fore Ends. Sonar, Captain. Report contacts."

"*Kharkov* bears red zero four, range eighteen thousand yards, speed ten knots and closing. Contact Zero Two on red one four zero. Contact Zero Four bears green one two six."

"Roger, Sonar." He replaced the microphone calmly, but his mind was racing: the *Kharkov* had started to move. "Number One, we're going in. Now!"

"Aye, aye, sir."

"Coxswain, steer two five two, revolutions for eighteen knots."

"Aye, aye, sir."

"Sonar, call out the ranges on Contact Zero One as she closes."

"Aye, aye, sir." They could feel *Saturn*'s speed increasing and sense a new purpose in her, feeling but not seeing the acceleration in the water. *Saturn* was primed, and she was running.

Sonar reported. "Sixteen thousand yards, sir, and closing."

Henderson bent over the attack computer screen in front of him, and checked that the *Kharkov* was still on her bearing. With a combined speed of over thirty knots, he calculated twenty minutes before he was due to pass under her.

That was too long. Everything depended on if and when

Saturn was detected. He turned to Tate. "Full ahead, Coxswain."

"Aye, aye, sir."

Henderson closed his eyes, checking back on his own calculations, wondering how fast *Saturn* really could go and knowing that this could be the clincher for his escape. His thoughts were interrupted by Tate. "Twenty-five knots, sir, increasing."

"That's better. Come on, Angus, surely we can do better than that." He glanced over to Tate's console, trying to read the speed log from where he stood. Tate sensed his curiosity and gave it to him. "Twenty-seven, sir." Henderson nodded, also noting that they were still at two thousand eight hundred feet.

"Twelve thousand yards, closing."

"Twenty-eight knots, sir. . . ."

"Captain, sir. Sonar. We are cavitating badly." Even as Lt. Crooke was reporting, Henderson could hear the rattle coming from above, somewhere on the fin, billowing into a crescendo and shattering their hopes.

"Dammit! Revolutions for eighteen knots, Coxswain." Tate was only too ready to punch in the new speed. Silently Henderson boiled, livid that his plan should have been thwarted by something so unexpected. He swore, realizing now that the previous explosion must have damaged the aluminum plating on the fin. It meant he could no longer count on his speed, that he must have given his position away, and worst of all, that he had lost the element of surprise.

Saturn slowed, the rattle faded out, but it still seemed far too long before Sonar reported:

"Captain, sir. Sonar. Cavitation has ceased. Range now ten thousand yards and closing. Sir! Helicopter sonobuoy transmission red three two, possibly in contact, range six miles."

"Roger, Sonar."

Bloody hell, that's really torn it. He called to Sykes over his shoulder. "Sorry, Number One, they're sure to have picked us up with that racket. It'll be ASROCs from now on in."

They waited for the explosions which they knew must come, but which seemed an eternity in coming. "Eight thousand yards and cl—"

Crump! Crump, crump, crump, crump. The explosions

were forward of them and Henderson realized that by
reducing their speed he had caused them to miscalculate.
"Coxswain! Full ahead, maximum revolutions."

"Aye, aye, sir." Tate looked back at Henderson, worry
and fear on his face, knowing that the violent clatter would
start again, giving their position away for a second time.
But one look from Henderson told him he meant it. Tate
punched in the keys for maximum revolutions, and in
seconds the vicious rattle started again.

Sonar came through the clatter, barely audible. "Those
explosions, sir, it looks as though they've got our depth."

"Roger, Sonar."

"Thirty-two knots, increasing."

Crump. More thunder, but this time well aft and Henderson's
face broke into a wide grin, knowing he had confused them.
"Revolutions for twenty knots, Coxswain, five hundred
feet, using twelve degrees bow up."

"Aye, aye, sir." Tate was grinning too; this was real
helmsmanship and he understood the game. They felt *Saturn*
surge, reaching upwards, and at the same time freeing
herself from those dreadful vibrations.

"Four thousand yards, closing."

Another pattern of explosions erupted from underneath
them. They sensed the turbulent, violent water heaving and
pushing *Saturn* further upwards. Then there were explosions
all around and they felt *Saturn* being buffeted by the impact.
Alarms began sounding on the Systems Console, adding to
the pandemonium. Sykes switched them off, making a mental
note of the red lights that remained, flashing on and off.

Sonar's voice came through the din. "Two thousand
yards, closing."

"Stand by, Decoy Number One. Sixty degree track...
Fire Decoy!"

"Decoy fired. . . . Track good."

"Coxswain, starboard twenty."

"Aye, aye, sir."

Saturn leant into the turn, banking like an aeroplane and
keeping up her momentum, leaving the *Kharkov* and the
noise of her ASROCs to port.

"One thousand yards, closing."

"Port twenty."

Tate reversed the helm, and again they banked into another turn. Suddenly there were no more explosions.

Sonar's voice on the loudspeaker traveled through the silence. "Contact passing overhead."

"Midships, Coxswain, two thousand five hundred feet, ten degrees bow down."

"Sonar. Contact Zero Five bears green zero eight, sir, range fourteen thousand yards."

"Roger, Sonar." He hung up the microphone and sighed with the satisfaction of knowing he had been right, before saying aloud, "Aaah, long stop!" The cricketers amongst his men knew what he meant.

Presently there was the thunder of more anti-submarine rockets, but this time much higher up: they already had a thousand feet to cushion the shock. Almost as soon as it had begun, the thunder stopped.

"Range two thousand yards and opening. Sir! Active sonar transmissions from Contact Zero Five."

All eyes in the control room turned to Henderson. His eyes glinted. "Steady as she goes, Coxswain. They're transmitting too early."

Orchenkov had personally taken over the search. His uncanny sixth sense put *Saturn* in a block of water to the east. He stationed the *Vladimir* and the *Voronetz* eighteen kilometres ahead to block the front exit and he proposed cruising up to a point between them, using the ultra sonar to detect any attempt by *Saturn* to escape. He expected to find her somewhere in the middle, skulking in the deep, and hoped to sink her as she made her dash for freedom. He sent his helicopters, the Kamovs, outside the triangle in case he had, after all, misjudged *Saturn*'s position. Golitsyn stood by the radio controls, active as his chief executive, ready to co-ordinate the response to the first signs of detection.

For his part, Orchenkov was angry and trying not to show it. Of course things were bound to go wrong from time to time, but the idea of giving up, getting dispirited in the way that Golitsyn had, was total anathema. One submarine against three Victors, an anti-submarine carrier and eighteen helicopters, why, the odds were ridiculous, and they should have mopped her up long ago. Certainly there was no reason to get dispirited. And as for Golitsyn's stupid Sunday school morality, that should have been excised from the military with the Revolution. Ridiculous! You use every event as best you can.

When the *Kharkov* began her sweep he took another cigar from his breast pocket, bit the end off, and carefully began lighting it. The phosphor from his match, combined with the clean, fresh grey smoke, soothed him a little, as he started the next long wait, mentally preparing himself for the unexpected reappearance of the intruder submarine.

Golitsyn's feelings were mixed. The loss of their own submarine had come as a bitter blow. He was convinced it was due to Orchenkov's impetuous command to that helicopter pilot. But there was something funny there too: the helicopter's sonar recording did indeed show an alien submarine. There could be no blame laid with him. He was aware that all the odds lay in their favour, but that didn't mean subtlety should be cast aside. And this oafish lump had no finesse at all, no finesse and no morals whatsoever. It made Orchenkov a dangerous man. Especially as he was angry now. And that revolting cigar smoke; there seemed to be bits of ash all over the bridge.

Both Ultra Sonar and the helicopter alerted the bridge as soon as *Saturn*'s rattle came through, giving away her bearing and depth. Both factors astounded the two commanding officers, who gazed at each other in stunned disbelief. Eight hundred and sixty metres deep! And running towards them!

Golitsyn was quick to react, getting Weapons Control to adjust the detonating depth on the rockets, co-ordinating the speed of *Saturn* with their reaction. They watched from the bridge windows as the first salvo was fired.

But as the hunt progressed a new problem arose: it seemed that though the ultra sonar had latched on, the Weapons Department was never quick enough to react to *Saturn*'s changes in depth and speed. Nor was there any hope of firing torpedoes in this confined space: they were more likely to latch on to one of their own submarines rather than this silent intruder.

"Tell me, Captain. Have you ever fished for trout? With a fly?"

Nonplussed, Golitsyn looked back at him: the idea of this

ox, fly fishing, was too much for his imagination. "No, Commodore. I can't say I have. Why?"

"Don't laugh, my friend. When I was a boy I used to. In the Urals."

"Sir, I don't think this is the time to talk about fly fishing."

"Oh, but it is. You see, you stand in the middle of the river, wearing great big waders, and the water up to your knees. The bottom is slippery and the water is fast, so you have to be careful not to lose your balance. You cast upstream, so the fish can't hear or feel the disturbance you make in the water, and you cast for a fish you can see rising: you know where it is." He paused, drawing on his cigar, and watched another salvo of missiles being launched. "It is very exciting. But sometimes, sometimes you meet an educated fish. He takes the fly and fights like hell for a second or two, so you give him line. Then he swims straight at you, and he'll go between your legs."

Orchenkov paused again, flicking ash onto the deck. "I think we've got one of these now."

Golitsyn swallowed. "So what do we do?"

"That fish is usually lost. We carry on trying with our missiles, but if we get him it'll be pure luck. No, this is what the *Vologda* is there for. Have you informed her captain?"

"Yes, Commodore. I've also warned him about firing too close. We make more noise than that submarine."

"Good. That submarine will try to use us as a shield, for as long as she can, to stop torpedoes coming her way. But sooner or later she's going to have to leave. That is when we use the gaff."

"The gaff?"

"I mean the *Vologda;* her torpedoes will do what we can't."

They stood waiting, listening to the voices on the radio intercoms, hearing the rockets being launched, feeling the slow throb of the *Kharkov*'s engines. Golitsyn was confused at the paradox in this man, an oaf who likes fly fishing. Probably likes painting too, and the ballet.

Ultra Sonar called through. "Contact, Captain. Contact . . . No! . . . That's a decoy. Original contact has turned to starboard, bearing red four five, two hundred metres, rising.''

''Inform Weapons.''

''We are on a common line, Captain.''

''Good.'' He turned back to the bridge window. Helplessly, he watched another batch of anti-submarine missiles being delivered in the wrong place.

Orchenkov spat. ''Cheeky little sod, isn't he? But don't worry, my friend, the *Vologda* will sort him out.'' He was also staring through the bridge window, knowing that only a few hundred metres in front of him, to the left, there was a giant fish in its last death run. Or was it? A ghastly thought suddenly struck him. ''I hope she hasn't got any more nasty tricks up her sleeve.''

The intercom loudspeaker was chattering. ''Contact now turned to port, on course to pass directly underneath us.'' The voice was agitated, and Golitsyn made a mental note to speak with the lieutenant about that afterwards.

''Thank you, Lieutenant,'' he acknowledged coldly. He looked back at Orchenkov. ''No, it's not us he's after, but it may confuse the *Vologda*'s sonar. She'll lose her if she's not careful.''

''Then contact her.''

''She's too deep.''

''Underwater telephone? There can't be any harm in it; that submarine knows where we are.''

''I'll try.'' Golitsyn stepped back to the intercom and called Ultra Sonar. Afterwards he busied himself in checking with the Kamovs, putting them on stand-by to move quickly if necessary.

Orchenkov stared uneasily through the window, suddenly afraid that they might after all be losing the submarine, fearing the redoubtable Belinski, who was going to have some awkward questions anyway for him when he returned. Well, he thought, Golitsyn could try the hot seat. If a captain can't defend himself, then he's no business being a captain. And he didn't think Golitsyn would be able to defend himself, not after he, Orchenkov, had presented the facts.

But that submarine piqued him. He was no longer so sure that their plan was fail-safe. This British captain, who came and went so unpredictably, seemed to be running circles around them, teasing them, provoking them. It made him angry.

But *Saturn* was neither teasing nor provoking. She wanted out. And Henderson knew that Contact Zero Five was there to stop her.

He was also keenly aware that time was running out. They had been on action stations for nearly sixty hours. Around the control room he had noticed the men fighting their fatigue, and knew they had only eight or ten hours left before they would simply collapse. Sykes's finger-cracking irritated him, possibly because he felt those fingers should be perpetually hovering over the keys on his console. He knew Howarth had been in a funk for half the time, and was wondering if he should have been replaced. But a sixth sense told him not to, though he could not explain why.

The success of their run to the *Kharkov* had restimulated the adrenaline: the men were back onto peak efficiency, but he also knew they had few reserves left and he was not sure how much longer he could count on their speed of response. He gave a command:

"Stand by decoys."

Howarth replied, "Decoys ready."

Another long wait. Henderson knew Zero Five would wait until he was well clear of the *Kharkov*. Minutes passed, punctuated only by Lt. Crooke calling out the ranges of the *Kharkov* and Contact Zero Five.

"Contact Zero One range eight thousand yards and ope . . . Contact Zero Five has transmitted again, bearing green zero seven. Computer confirms in contact."

"Roger, Sonar." Henderson was cool, his voice defying any of his men to lose their own self-control. Correct timing alone would see this through.

"Contact Zero Five has fired two torpedoes. Computer predicts . . . impact fifty-five seconds."

"Roger, Sonar. . . . Confirm sonar locked on to Zero Five."

"Confirmed, sir."

They knew timing was the thing. But it didn't stop the electric atmosphere which had built up invisibly around them in the control room.

"Torpedoes six thousand yards."

"Set a forty-five degree track."

Howarth answered. "Set."

Men sitting at their stations, taut and silent. Slowly, Sykes drew his fingers out, and cracked the knuckles one by one.

"Stop it, Sykes!" Instantly Henderson regretted the outburst and turned his head away. Sykes bit his lip, deeply, and gave an involuntary shudder.

"Torpedoes four thousand yards."

Tate moved, arching back his head, beseeching his captain with frightened eyes. Then Sykes looked up, the same questions forming on his face.

"Torpedoes two thousand yards."

"Fire one."

"Decoy one fired."

"Fire two."

"Decoy two fired."

"Sonar!"

"Both decoys running true, sir. Torpedoes one . . . and two latched on, sir. Torpedoes two thousand yards and opening."

The tension eased. Clammy hands opened, handkerchiefs were brought out, spectacles cleaned. But Henderson didn't move: he still had the microphone in his hand.

"Stand by One Tube."

"One Tube ready, bow doors open."

"Shoot."

"Set."

"Fire!"

"One Tube fired." Howarth looked up, horror-struck at what had just been done, but Henderson gave him no time for guilt.

"Shut the bow tube doors."

"Bow tube doors shut."

Henderson stared around at the officers and men in the control room, challenging anyone to question his last action. Nobody dared, realizing that there had been no alternative.

"Soviet torpedoes four thousand yards and still latched on to decoys, track good. Our own torpedo . . . fifty seconds to impact, track good."

"Roger, Sonar."

Fifty seconds. Seconds when the Soviets might try their

own decoys. It was the first offensive weapon used by *Saturn*, designed to clear a path as well as intimidate.

"Sonar, Captain. Fifteen seconds to impact, track good . . . Five seconds to impact . . ."

They heard the explosion, similar to the first, but much more distant.

A subdued Lt. Crooke reported over the intercom, "Impact. Target destroyed."

Nobody spoke. Contact Zero Five had represented a dark and sinister force, set on their destruction and death, but instead they had destroyed her. But almost immediately their relief was confused by wider implications: they had sunk a Soviet submarine, this time deliberately, and they dreaded the possible reaction from above. But then, did they have a choice? Contact Zero Five was not simply blocking their way home, she was there to sink them, no matter what they did, and every man in the control room knew that the way was now clear to make good their escape. There was nobody left to stop them.

Henderson was still calculating, wondering what he would do if he were captain on Contact Zero One, left with only two submarines, his pride at stake, his fleet threatened and his mission still unaccomplished. . . . He was interrupted by Sykes, whose tired voice whispered hoarsely through.

"I know you're a determined man, sir, but just how much further are you prepared to go to get us out of this?"

"Determined" again. Memories flashed through his mind, memories of a crackling fireplace, Karen urgent beneath him, her tongue seeking his, the flat of her stomach pressed against his own. . . . And he wanted her, he wanted to be home, away, out of this terrifying ordeal which seemed to have no end. . . .

"Sorry I spoke, sir."

Henderson realized that Sykes needed an answer, and he remembered his Mission Order.

"Number One, I have my orders: all the bloody way, and I'll use all the means I have at my disposal."

Hardy and Hythe did not reach No. 10 Downing Street until fourteen minutes past eleven. They bustled through the side entrance, anxious not to alert the press that there might be some sort of crisis brewing. Martin Taylor led them straight through to the prime minister's office, pausing only to relieve them of their raincoats and umbrellas.

Wainscott seemed even more drawn than when he had left them earlier that morning at Northwood: they were not to know that he had already endured the Soviet ambassador on the telephone. But one glance at the ministers, Hogarth, Randall, Oakley and Vendon, told Hardy and Hythe all they needed to know. They had been arguing again, and the atmosphere was still tainted with the venom.

Nobody had a civil greeting for them, nor a word of sympathy, and Wainscott silently showed them the two empty places. The telephone rang as they were sitting down. Wainscott plucked up the receiver testily, angry that there should be yet another interruption when they were going to need all their wits focused on the present issue.

"Yes? . . . Fredenberger? Yes, you'd better put him on. . . . Hello, Admiral. . . . A what? Another one? My God. . . . Yes. . . . Yes. I quite see. . . . Yes, go ahead." He replaced the receiver slowly, and the six men gathered around had a brief premonition of what had happened before he spoke to them.

"There has been another underwater explosion in the same area. Admiral Fredenberger has informed the Pentagon. He says we can expect to hear from President Mallory in a few minutes."

There was a brief, appalled silence, before Oakley spoke. "I'll bet we will! Doesn't this just prove my point? We should never have gone there in the first place. It's quite indefensible."

"No, it's not indefensible." Soberly, Hogarth responded, choosing each word carefully. "As I have said before, if you want to achieve anything . . ."

"Then blow up two Russians submarines. Because that's what you've done. None of this would have happened if you hadn't sent *Saturn* up there."

Wearily, Hogarth shook his head, pursing his lips. "You won't understand, will you, you don't want to understand. We did not send *Saturn* up there to blow up submarines. Quite the contrary, she was to get out as soon as there was any sign of danger. Turn it round: your friends, the Russians, want blood, our blood, and that is why they are not letting *Saturn* go. What is dangerous is that they've got hurt doing it. Wounded animals don't behave like healthy ones.''

"Then we should have accepted responsibility for her. That way they wouldn't have wanted any blood at all.''

Hogarth sighed. "With that ultimatum? What sort of friends do you think they are?''

Oakley feigned exasperation. Vendon decided to take his side. "He didn't say they were friends. We just happen to live rather close to them, and we both feel we should try to get on together, rather than snarling at each other like cats before a fight.''

"I couldn't agree more. But it's very difficult not to when we are surrounded by Russian 'trawlers' that aren't trawlers, when our factory floors are being infiltrated with trouble makers, and MI5 is continually telling us that half the Russian Embassy staff here have no diplomatic function at all.''

Drawn into the argument, Vendon persisted. "But that's just the point. Aren't we doing the same? We supported Solidarity in Poland, for heaven's sake, and what was *Saturn* doing up there in the first place?''

"So you think that if we didn't have any *Saturn* missions we wouldn't have any trawlers?''

"Now we're getting somewhere!" Oakley homed in, adamant. "If we didn't have any nuclear capability on our shores then they wouldn't have any interest in us in the first place.''

Desperate, Hogarth raised his eyes to the ceiling. He was about to reply when Wainscott demanded order.

"Gentlemen, please! The American president will shortly be on the phone. How are we going to deal with him?''

"What's he going to want?" Hogarth asked.

"I should imagine he's ordering a red alert. If we sink two Russian submarines, then surely that's war.'' He looked around. "Isn't it?''

Finally it came home to them. They sat there, stunned, terrified and almost certain that Wainscott was right.

The fear reinforced Oakley's determination. "God forbid, but surely this is something we can stop now, before it's too late? Why don't you call President Kirov?''

"I tried that last night.'' Disconsolately, Wainscott stood up and sighed. "I tried that last night and he wouldn't speak with me. I tried our ambassador, Sir Humphrey Prescott, and he had no joy either. To make things worse, their ambassador, Khlebnikov, rang me this morning to find out what it was all about. Thinking that *Saturn* had been sunk, I told him it was all right, that nothing had happened. There is no way we can contact the Russians now. That avenue is closed.''

''Why the hell didn't you . . . Oh, never mind.'' Hogarth was furious at this direct attempt without any form of consultation, but he had to let this pass for the moment. ''Couldn't we ask the Americans to try?''

''Maybe. But they are NATO and so are we. It puts them in an impossible position, of having to apologize for a weak upstart ally over whom they have no effective control.'' He turned to Oakley. ''The Americans don't think like we do. They are confident and strong; at least they think they are. So why should they eat humble pie for our sakes?''

''To save them from a nuclear holocaust.'' Oakley was quite definite, quite certain that this needn't happen. ''Nobody in their right mind wants that, not even Russia.''

''That is why I said 'maybe.' Heaven knows what Mallory would promise Kirov behind our backs, but one thing is certain: we would be the ones to be making sacrifices.'' He switched his attention to Hogarth. ''I think you understand what that might mean.''

Hogarth pulled a face and shifted uncomfortably in his chair. The red telephone rang and Wainscott moved to pick it up.

''Yes? Yes, it is. Yes, Mr. President. . . . Oh, are they? We were afraid that might be the case. . . .'' Wainscott closed his eyes, trying to evaluate the implications of every word the president was saying. ''What do you mean you can't? We can't either. . . . Perhaps an intermediary, the Swiss or the Finns. Yes, please, Mr. President. . . . Yes, I'll call you back as soon as anything happens. Goodbye, and thanks.''

Wainscott replaced the receiver and faced the group around him. ''That's it. The president has ordered a Red Alert. It appears from radio traffic in Russia that the Soviet Union is doing the same. The Americans can't get through to them either. It's as though they've retreated into a shell, and they're frightened too.''

''Does that mean we're to be on a Red Alert as well?''

Hogarth was still anxious to play down the incident as low as possible, desperately anxious. Being Minister for Defence he would have to answer the questions in the House of Commons.

"All of NATO is on Red Alert. That includes us. Fredenberger has already called the Primary Alert."

They sat awhile, all of them thinking hard. Hogarth was the first on his feet. "I think I had better get back to my office: things are going to be busy."

The meeting broke up and they all departed in silence. Neither Hardy nor Hythe had said anything, and for a moment they wondered why they had been called there in the first place—that is, until they realized how much things had changed in the one hour since they had left Northwood.

Wainscott closed the door after them and returned to his desk. He sat musing, not thinking of anything in particular, idly twiddling his gold Cross biro. Even that had been made in America. The telephone rang and he picked it up.

"Press Office. Prime Minister?"

"Yes."

"It seems the press have got wind of something. They claim there's a Primary Alert on. I know nothing. What do I tell them?"

"Nothing. Slap a 'D' notice on it. For the moment, anyway."

"And the foreign press? They're all here, too."

"Tell them nothing. It's business as usual."

"With a 'D' notice?"

"No, it *isn't*, dammit. Look, keep them quiet. Any way you can think of. Tell them there'll be a full report later, perhaps this evening, if not tomorrow when we call a press conference. That should keep them happy."

"I hope so, Prime Minister. You know what the press are like when they start shouting, 'The public has a right to know.' "

"Then let them sweat."

Kirov called a meeting with his chiefs of staff. Of course they were ready for war. Weren't they always? But Kirov knew better, and he knew his marshals knew better. What frightened him was a pre-emptive strike: if NATO believed that Russia would retaliate for the loss of her submarines, then it might be tempting for them to strike first.

He knew there was no way he could get through to the British. Khlebnikov had told him so. Perhaps President Mallory. But what could he say to a man like that? Stop your mobilization, please, I promise we won't do anything?

He knew he would never be believed.

— CHAPTER 10 —

19th May, Afternoon

The explosion that ripped through the sea was identical to the first one. The six men on the bridge of the *Kharkov* stood silently, as before, but numbed. For the explosion had not come from where it should have come from, and they were frightened.

Orchenkov frightened for his own losses, fury rising within him for the failure of the *Vologda* to destroy her target. That one submarine could make such fools out of him and his command proved incompetence: he feared the ridicule more than failure. Golitsyn frightened of the British submarine as well as her commander, realizing that together they represented an awesome power, a queen on a chess board against his own knights, castles and bishops. The conviction was gelling inside him that this prey was too dangerous to handle. Sverdlov, Tyutchev, and the navigation officer all frightened in the same way as Golitsyn—like little boys fishing for mackerel finding that they had an eight-foot conger eel on their hook and were too frightened to try to cut the line.

The *Kharkov* dipped in the shock waves, triggering Golitsyn to speak. He thought he could read Orchenkov's mind, and it was now his turn to be comforting.

"Commodore, we must let this fish get away. We would be crazy to continue: he has sunk two of our submarines and we are nowhere nearer to bringing him under control."

Tears of anger, frustration and impotence caused Orchenkov's red-rimmed eyes to shine glassily. His jaw worked and he spoke in a whisper. "This is ridiculous. We are the Soviet Navy, the most powerful navy in the world, and we let one lousy British submarine do . . . *this*?" His eyes widened in amazement and disbelief. "It's not possible, it's just not possible, Captain."

"I don't think it is a lousy submarine. I think it is a very special, and very powerful one. . . . I would suggest we go home, lick our wounds, and come back stronger to fight another day."

The idea was unthinkable. Orchenkov was shocked, shocked to imagine it could even be considered. He glanced at the other men on the bridge, but none of them would meet his eye. "Go home? Fight another day? But this submarine is here! Now! Do you seriously mean to let him get away, after all this? Do you realize that this means failing in our mission? Worse, failing because we would be deserting in the face of the enemy!" His face became apoplectic, and he latched on to the unfortunate Tyutchev. "Tyutchev! That is treason! Isn't what this man says treason?"

And Tyutchev cursed the day he joined the Party, cursed the mentors who had taught him to look out for reactionism, deviationism, negativeness, who had taught him about morale, how to build it, how to control it, but who had never taught him how to choose or react between good, loyal, patriotic Soviet citizens who thought so differently. And he was frightened. The submarine frightened him, and Orchenkov, flag officer of the Northern Banner Fleet, frightened him. He fought for words, diplomatic words. "What the captain is suggesting is a retreat . . ."

"Desertion!"

"Retreat. If you remember the great battle of Volgograd, victory was only secured because our troops decided to withdraw, reinforce themselves, and attack when they were ready. I do not believe the captain has shown cowardice, on the contrary . . ."

"Running is cowardice."

"Commodore, my position here is as political representative of the Politburo. It is my duty to ensure that morale remains high and that commanding officers behave in a loyal manner, consistent with the aims of our government, which happens to be a Communist government. I see this as a tactical issue, one for which you are both trained, and which you must resolve between yourselves.'' He finished defiantly, but knowing that in securing his own position, he had given Orchenkov the edge: he was the commanding officer, and to disobey him would be mutiny. Golitsyn understood this clearly. So did Orchenkov.

''Then we continue, Captain! Bring the *Kharkov* round, so we can use our ultra sonar. That submarine is running for home now, and judging by her speed we can outrun her. I want the Kamovs up too, all of them. We won't use the Victors: we don't need them and it's too risky anyway. We shall do this thing on our own, and we shall do it well.''

Resigned, but still determined to do a professional job, Golitsyn gave the order. ''Full ahead. Starboard . . . thirty, steer two six zero.''

A moody silence descended on the two officers, broken by a signals yeoman who stepped through with another flimsy. He looked around the bridge anxiously, smelling the atmosphere, not sure whether to disturb Orchenkov, who was fully engrossed at the chart table. Golitsyn saw his anxiety, took the message and dismissed him.

He unfolded it, and permitted himself a tight smile when he read the message:

```
URGENT        TOP PRIORITY
TO            KHARKOV, FLAG OFFICER AND CAPTAIN
FROM          CINC NORTHERN BANNER FLEET
CEASE ALL ANTI-SUBMARINE OPERATIONS FORTHWITH AND
RETURN TO BASE. IMMEDIATELY.

END
```

His eyes narrowed and he put on a grim expression as he approached Orchenkov. Then he realized that this signalled the end and failure of their mission, that there would be no hero's welcome awaiting their return to Polyarny, that he would almost certainly be replaced on the *Kharkov*. His expression changed from mock to real. He tapped Orchenkov on the shoulder.

Orchenkov took the message casually, read it, and then reread it, his face confused, like the gladiator who saw his arm lopped off, not feeling it, but knowing it meant certain death. But there was a way out, his way, and he was appalled that his commander could have thought otherwise. "Cowards!" he shouted. They were cowards at Severomarsk. We do not give up. True Russians never give up. Savagely he tore up the message, stepped out onto the bridge wing and defiantly threw the pieces into the air. They were gone in a second, whipped away by the wind.

Orchenkov closed the door. "Captain, we never saw that message, did we? We continue the search and we destroy this Britisher. Right?"

Nonplussed, Golitsyn stammered for words. "Commodore. . . . No. . . . No, Commodore. I cannot support this." He turned to Tyutchev, drawing him into the confrontation. "I want it to go on record that I cannot support your actions. This submarine is dangerous. I shall send the signal myself to the First Admiral. . . ."

"Go and do it then! But remember, if we come back without a submarine, then it's trawlers off Kamchatka for you! As for me, I'm not going to let my career be spoiled by one impudent, flea-bitten . . . are the Kamovs out?"

Sverdlov replied. "Twelve in position, Commodore. The other six are being refuelled."

"Well, hurry up, then. This isn't a Sunday afternoon picnic. . . ."

Howarth found he was no longer frightened: something to do with firing a lethal weapon in self-defence, and being successful, had proved to him that the most frightening thing about fear was fear itself, not the cause. And fear had gone. It was like being instantly cured from a lifelong disease. For the first time in his life he felt whole, complete, and equal to the men around him. His hand still shook, but from pure exhilaration; his face took on colour, but it was the colour that comes with self-confidence. He now understood why servicemen were excited by the possibility of action.

He tried not to grin, aware of the serious expressions on the faces of those around him, and equally aware that they were not out of danger yet, but the danger no longer bothered him: he had won his most important battle, and he felt they were invincible.

Sykes felt differently, still smarting from his captain's reprimand, and apprehensive about his attitude. It would have been different if this was wartime action, but it was not. They were, after all, simply on an information-gathering mission, and he felt sure he would have handled it differently, though not sure how. Certainly he would not be conducting the escape with so much aggression, and perhaps it was this that was worrying him.

As the minutes elapsed, though, he began to feel more at ease: it seemed as though they might just make it after all.

Henderson had sensed the change in Howarth, and now understood that this was why he had kept him in the control room. He was also aware of the incipient antagonism in his Number One, an antagonism which was born more from innate caution than failure to see the need for boldness to get out of a tight situation. And he might just have done it.

He surveyed the faces in the control room, noting that apart from Peter Howarth they were all still tense, mentally counting the minutes.

"OK, gentlemen, one all round."

Gratefully the men in the control room on *Saturn* reached for their cigarettes and lighters. The *Kharkov* was twelve thousand yards away, seven miles or so, and each minute was putting her further behind, making them safer still. Perhaps they were going to make it, perhaps they were finally on their way home.

Though nobody could be certain. Nerves were still taut; they would be until they were well past the North Cape, with a hundred miles between them and the *Kharkov*. Then they would be able to relax.

The men were jittery because they were still not sure whether they were free from danger, but now other fears were creeping in: they feared retribution, not knowing if, where, when and how it might come, but knowing that they were the cause, should that retribution be inflicted on another NATO submarine instead of *Saturn*. It would mean a difficult homecoming, and the men on *Saturn* were relieved that they would not have to answer the questions their captain would have to face. They smoked their cigarettes quickly, in short, urgent puffs, heating the smoke and softening the stems, aggressively stubbing them out in dirty ashtrays. They knew it would be a good eight hours before they could feel comfortable again.

Their worst fears were confirmed when Sonar came through on the loudspeaker. "Captain, sir, Sonar. Helicopter transmission bearing red two zero, possibly in contact."

"Roger, Sonar." Oh, God, why won't they give up?

"Captain, sir, the *Kharkov*'s going about, bearing green one seven two, range fourteen thousand yards."

"Contacts Zero Two and Zero Four?"

"Nothing." I'm not surprised, Henderson thought. The realization was coming to him that if the *Kharkov* was not going to let him go, he was going to have to do something about her. Jesus, I've shown her we mean business, why doesn't she just go away? She knows we're on our way out. And I don't like helicopters; they sting. . . .

"Captain, sir, Sonar. Second helicopter sonobuoy transmissions bearing green three zero, possibly in contact."

"Captain, roger." Oh, you bastards, you stupid bastards, well, now you've bought it! "Coxswain! Slow ahead, periscope depth!"

"Aye, aye, sir." Tate reacted smoothly. The others held their breath, sensing the climax of their past three days, willing the climax to happen, pining for the relief of knowing they were safe to go home.

Sonar continued reporting the helicopter transmissions. They knew they were detected, understood they would have to act fast if they were to stave off their final Nemesis.

"Two hundred feet . . . One hundred and fifty feet . . ." Tate was as confident as his captain. "One hundred feet . . ."

"Up attack, 'scope!"

They felt *Saturn* level off. "Sixty-four feet, sir."

Aggressively, Henderson manhandled the periscope. "First helicopter bears that."

Howarth replied, almost sang, "Red two two, on."

"Second helicopter bears . . ."

"Green three four on."

Savagely he jerked the periscope back again. "*Kharkov* bears that."

"Red six three, on. Attack computer tracking."

"Roger, down 'scope."

Howarth spoke up. "Attack computer has acquisition, sir."

"Roger. Raise the Stingfish mast."

Sykes flicked the switch on the Systems Console. They heard the whizz and click, confirming that the mast was raised.

"Up 'scope." Henderson settled the eyepiece on the bearing of the first helicopter. "First target bears that."

"Red two eight on."

"Shoot."

"Set."

"Fire."

"One fired, sir, on track."

But Henderson had already swung the periscope round. "Second target bears that."

"Green three four on."

"Shoot."

"Set."

"Fire!"

"Two fired, sir, on track."

"Down Stingfish mast. Down attack 'scope. Reload the Stingfish launcher."

"Aye, aye, sir." They heard the *clunk* as the Stingfish mast retracted. The Stingfish are small and very nasty missiles. Each weighs about a hundred and fifty pounds, of which only fifty pounds is Amatol G 1 high explosive. The damage they can do is out of all proportion to their size. The missiles themselves are solid-fuel-powered, and pre-programmed for active radar homing. Once set and launched, they cannot miss: they travel too fast for decoys and counter-fire. They are hydraulically loaded into the launcher, and it only takes a few seconds to have them ready and armed.

Howarth reported, "Stingfish launcher reloaded, sir."

"Roger. Raise the mast. Up attack 'scope." The eyepiece was already in position before Henderson could see. "The *Kharkov* bears that."

"Red one seven zero. Attack computer has acquisition."

"Fire!"

"One fired."

"Fire two!"

"Two fired. Both on track."

"Down mast, down attack 'scope. Full ahead, Coxswain, five degrees bow down, nine hundred feet."

"Aye, aye, sir."

They heard nothing.

Orchenkov saw himself as fighting alone against two foes: a gutless crew behind him and a powerful enemy in front. His eyes glazed, shining with an obsession that was bordering on insanity. He held his fists close to his sides, tightly clenched, listening to the commands going on around him, ready to explode if any one of them was likely to frustrate his objectives. He was unapproachable.

The men around him were cowed and on edge. They knew Orchenkov was angry with their lack of support, frenzied with his and their impotence in dealing with the British submarine. They understood very well that he would be quick to choose his friends and enemies if he won, and equally that they were all doomed if he lost.

The tight atmosphere was shattered by the rattle of the loudspeaker. "Captain. Fishwatch Eight. We have her. Range twelve thousand nine hundred metres, bearing from you two four two degrees. Captain! She's rising!"

Golitsyn jabbed at the microphone button. "Does anyone else confirm that?"

"Captain, Fishwatch Three. We confirm that position, and, yes, she's rising."

"Depth?"

"One fifty metres."

His worried eyes found Orchenkov's, stubborn and relentless. "What do you want to do? Sink her or see if we can take her?"

Orchenkov hesitated and bit his lip. Every instinct and emotion said "Sink her!" but he knew he was disobeying orders. True redemption would only come if he could capture the submarine intact. There must be a lot of technology in that submarine, technology they needed, and she would be a prize of war. Besides, he would dearly like to meet that captain, if only to . . .

"One hundred metres."

Reason triumphed. "Let her come! Tell them to keep

their tabs on her, get Ultra Sonar to lock in. I want her surrounded by transmissions.''

"Seventy-five metres."

"Captain, this I want to see!"

Golitsyn gave the command, "Full ahead. Steer two four two," and picked up the microphone to summon the other Kamovs.

"Fifty metres. She must be surfacing!"

A new admiration lightened Golitsyn's face as he studied his flag officer. Dear mother, have I underestimated this man? And I sent that message to Belinski. Oh sodding hell, it's impossible to get anything right. I just hope . . . no, she can't be going to attack us, she doesn't need to surface to attack us.

He lifted his binoculars up to his face and saw that Orchenkov had done the same. Both were hoping to see a periscope, though fully aware that if they did, it would be a triumph of hope over expectations.

The radio crackled. "We see a periscope, Captain, and a missile mast . . ."

They heard a sharp crack on the radio, and simultaneously they both brought their binoculars round. They saw the ball of fire, its size and power jolting them. Anxiously they swung round to the other Kamov, just in time to see it explode in the same way.

Orchenkov blazed with fury. "I'll get him! I'll get that motherless . . . I'll get him for that! Do you see, Captain? That is what happens when you show mercy. Get those Kamovs there, all of them. Make sure they're armed, sink him before he gets us all."

"No!"

"Yes, do as I say! That is an order!"

They stood glowering at each other, eyes locked in deadly conflict, each one summoning up every last ounce of will-power to overcome the other, to impose his own will. Golitsyn was the first to break away. Helplessly he turned to Tyutchev.

"Commander?" he said softly.

"Yes, Captain. Do it now."

Orchenkov had raised his binoculars, scanning the sea in front, watching the first helicopters moving in to replace the two that had disappeared.

"Commodore!" But Orchenkov did not hear him, or didn't appear to. The binoculars remained glued to his face. "Commodore! Under the Naval Articles, section twelve, subsection fifty-three, concerning the incapability of a commanding officer . . ."

Orchenkov was still looking through the bridge window, but now he was laughing. His stomach heaved.

". . . this section states quite clearly that a subordinate may relieve his commanding officer under the following circumst—"

Now Orchenkov bellowed out: "Tovarich! You are too late, we are all too late. . . ."

The flash and boom destroyed the bridge in a fraction of a second. Almost simultaneously another explosion devastated the rest of the central superstructure. The towering pillar of black smoke could be seen for miles around.

Sir James Hythe opened the door to the Operations Room gently, as if it were the entrance to an intensive care ward in a hospital. He held it wide for Hardy to pass through.

The big screen was blank, the lights were dimmed, and there was an air of finality about the place, as though the film was over, the curtains drawn to, and the audience departed.

Admiral Fredenberger was sitting on his own by a communications console, lost in thought and quite alone with himself. He looked washed out, withdrawn.

Hythe called him. "Joe! What's happened? We heard about the nuke, the second one."

Fredenberger came to and rubbed his eyes. "Yeah. And all hell's broken loose since that happened. That's history now."

Hardy stopped on the way down to him, in mid-stride. "Then what has been going on?"

"Your prime minister's on his way over right now. The *Kharkov* had another go at *Saturn*, and *Saturn* hit back."

"And?"

"Knocked out two choppers and blew up half the bridge superstructure on the *Kharkov*."

"Jesus! *Saturn* did that?" Hardy was aghast.

"She sure as hell did. We picked her up on both infra-red and magnetic anomaly. No doubt about it. She came to periscope depth and bang! bang! bang! bang! That commander of yours, Henderson, he must be one hell of a guy.

"We're all on Red Alert and Washington's as jittery as hell: the covers are off the buttons and they're holding their breaths. All US Navy forces are standing to, as well as the troops in Central Europe. They all know what to do and they're ready. Trouble is, there's guys around who don't want to wait to see if the Soviets are going to do anything. They reckon it's coming anyway, so why wait?"

"Because it might not happen." Hythe slumped into a seat beside the console.

"Yeah, but what are the odds? If the Russians did that to us you'd have half of Congress up on their chairs and shouting Pearl Harbor.

"And you know something? We're the authors of this cockup. Christ, all we wanted were a few decent recordings and we'd know how good that ultra sonar thing of theirs is. But no, we reckoned if we could prove to them it didn't work they would forget it. Hell, I don't know how you two sucked me into this one, I really don't." His eyes wandered over them, sourly. "As the man said, if we've got you two people for friends, we sure as hell don't need an enemy."

"So you told the prime minister?"

"Yup, he knows. He's on his way over right now. You'd just left when I called." He pointed to the screen. "They're setting it up for Central Europe. I don't know what the trade-off's going to be before they're happy."

They sensed the door opening, and looked behind them to see the prime minister and Hogarth peering in. The three of them stood up.

Wainscott pointed his finger at Hythe. "You!"

"Sir?"

"Yes, you! You and your stupid, hare-brained machinations! Do you realize what you've just done? Do you realize what sort of a position we are in now? What has happened is tantamount to a declaration of war, without so much as consulting Parliament, let alone our own forces. The First World War started from a damned sight less."

Hythe sucked his breath in. Hardy shifted uncomfortably. Wainscott continued, "I have to speak in the Commons, straight after prayers. It'll be no use rambling about routine missions that have gone wrong; as far as they're concerned there are no routine missions in that part of the globe.''

Feeling that he had the mastery over the two men, Wainscott ranted on. ''They will expect heads to roll. Your two will be the first. When I authorized this mission, Sir James, you said you'd be pleased to put your head on the block if things went wrong. I believe those were your words. In the circumstances that's just what we're going to do, and we'll clean out the Naval Command from top to bottom, and make sure this sort of thing can never happen again.''

Hythe's forehead was knit in deep concentration. He bit his lower lip before replying. ''I wouldn't do that if I were you, Prime Minister.''

Wainscott exploded. ''Why not?''

''Because you signed that Mission Order, and I have the original, or rather my solicitor has it. In any case I have a photocopy. You, who are supposed to decide how this country is to be run, cannot blame your executives if things go wrong. After all, we are simply carrying out your orders.''

Stupefied, Wainscott could only gape. He fought for words. ''You . . . you . . . bastard!'' The words rolled out and Hythe knew how much he meant it. ''You dirty . . . I'll have you out of there before . . .''

''On what grounds, Prime Minister?'' Water off a duck's back: Hythe was cool.

''On the grounds that neither he nor I can work with you,'' Hogarth replied. ''One way or another we'll have to shat on.'' Between the two, Hogarth was the more frightening.

For an instant Fredenberger was really enjoying the fight. His eyes glinted between them, relishing the punch and counterpunch. Hardy stood silently, knowing he ought to help Sir James, but also knowing that he couldn't. He was amazed by his foresight, even if it was selfish.

But Wainscott was broken. He saw himself as some puny being trapped in a massive vortex, unable to climb out or alter the forces that were driving him under. He took his handkerchief and wiped the saliva that had escaped from the corner of his mouth. He spoke to Hogarth. ''Then, for heaven's sake, what *do* I tell the House?''

Soothingly, Hythe stepped in. ''Tell them the truth, Prime Minister. Tell them that one of our submarines was peacefully going about its own business in international waters when it was unexpectedly attacked by Soviet forces. That is true, isn't it? And you can tell them that our submarine fired back in self-defence, after numerous missiles had been thrown at it, because it was boxed in and had no other means of escape. That is also quite true, isn't it?''

Wainscott was only partially mollified. ''*Are* they international waters?''

''*Saturn* was a lot more than twelve miles from the coast.''

''But didn't you say that the Russians had designated this as a highly sensitive area?''

''Well, yes. But it was unilaterally designated that way. I don't recall us ever having agreed to it.''

''Then they could claim we have no business in the South Atlantic?''

''That is a hostile area, Prime Minister, even though there are no actual hostilities. It is quite different. They have trawlers twelve miles off our coastline and we can't touch them. What makes *Saturn* any different?''

''She was spying.''

''Yes, but peaceful spying, the same as those trawlers.''

Hogarth had his tongue in his cheek, seeing the viability of this new approach, seeing that it could indeed be used. Suddenly he found himself very favorably impressed with Hythe's mental resources as well as his capacity for self-preservation. They were all quiet for a second before Wainscott spoke again.

''Meanwhile we are still on Red Alert. Has anything else happened?''

Fredenberger called from behind. ''No, sir. That last we saw was the *Kharkov* stationary with her main superstructure on fire. Their two remaining nukes have surfaced. We assume *Saturn* has escaped.''

''Christ, I hope so. When's she due back now?''

''Seventy-two hours. She should be reporting off the coast of Norway, though. Give her twenty-four hours to get there.''

''Mmm, then there's nothing I can do here?''

''Not unless you want us to show you the NATO forces deployment.''

Wainscott shuddered. ''No. I think I had better be back at Number Ten.''

* * *

Downing Street is literally only three minutes' walk from the Houses of Parliament. The Parliamentary day in the House of Commons starts at two-thirty in the afternoon, with prayers, followed by ten minutes of Question Time.

The Prime Minister's brown Jaguar drew up alongside Number Ten at twenty-five minutes past one, with Wainscott and Hogarth sitting in the back. Wainscott's heart sank even further when he saw the police cordons and the hundreds of reporters and photographers waiting for him with notebooks, flash and video cameras at the ready. Presumably the news of the alerts had leaked, which meant he would certainly have to be in the House for Question Time. Questions for which he had no answers, except to try Hythe's rather facile evasions, and if MPs were going to ask him what he intended to do about the situation, he had no answers to those questions at all.

He reacted petulantly to the surge and clamour of the reporters around him, brushing them off with "no comment" until one journalist pressed him too far. Wainscott snarled at him, telling him in no uncertain terms that the Press had no right to interfere with the Prime Minister's duties either. Thankfully the door was open before he reached it. Wainscott and Hogarth dived in, shaking their coats off as though they had just reached sanctuary from the most terrible blizzard outside. Hogarth, though, had not had to endure quite the same welter of questions and taunts, and he was much more composed.

Martin Taylor rushed up to greet them. "Prime Minister, I'm so glad you're back. The switchboard is jammed. We've had calls from the president of France, and the prime ministers of Germany, Norway and Sweden." He consulted his notebook. "Also Field Marshal Filton, Air Marshal Conway, the Leader of the Opposition, and oh yes, Buckingham Palace." He turned over the page and began again. "The Cabinet Sec—"

"Not now, Martin, later. We're going into my office and I don't want to be disturbed. That is vital, do you understand?"

"Yes, Prime Minister." Hurt and confused, Taylor stepped aside to let them through. "Oh, and Martin, get me Oakley, will you? I want him here, now."

The foreign secretary lived next door. It was no problem. In five minutes the three of them were seated, and Wainscott was feeling aggressive.

"Bloody NATO! That's one of the things we're going to have to sort out in our first year. Do you realize that's twice, this morning, that Mallory has ordered an Alert. He ordered them. He never bothered to consult me, simply told me, without so much as a 'by your leave.' Bloody cheek; *Saturn* is our submarine, this is our business, we can sort it out our own way, but he puts his bloody great foot in it by ordering Alerts."

"Arthur, no." Hogarth was again finding himself exasperated.

"*Saturn* was on a NATO mission. She was briefed by a NATO admiral. . . ."

"She has a British captain and a British crew. She was built in Britain and paid for by Britain, and I signed the Mission Order. . . ."

"She is part of the NATO force and she has put all the NATO countries, collectively, at risk."

"Then there shouldn't be a NATO!"

Hogarth slumped. He was outnumbered and being outmanoeuvred by arguments that he knew were spurious. Then he caught a glimpse of Oakley, looking pious and prim, and his hackles rose. He was damned if he was going to be beaten.

"Prime Minister, I know it sounds childish, but I'm going through it again. Have you any idea of the enormous size and power of the Russian and Warsaw Pact military machines? Have you any idea how puny we, in Britain, look in comparison? Without NATO they could pick off each European country, one by one, like cherries off a tree, with total impunity. Was it a democratic process that made Poland communist after the War? Was it a democratic process that threw Masaryk out of the window in Czechoslovakia in 1948, or invaded Czechoslovakia in 1968 and sent Dubcek packing?

"NATO was designed to stop this and has been very successful. It's been said before, and I'll say it again, if we don't hang together, we'll hang separately, and we'll hang most horribly. So this cannot be solely a British issue. If you think about it, it's not just a NATO issue either, the whole free world is at stake.

"Because, make no mistake about it, the Soviet Union will be doing something, they have to, and it's not going to be very nice."

Wainscott was hardly listening. He had heard it all before and he didn't like being lectured. "No, David, you're making me angry. They know it's our submarine, they'll react against us. We can deal with it, we must."

"How? If you do nothing you're admitting responsibility."

"Which we should have done in the first place."

"No! They still don't know it's our submarine. Supposing they react against the United States, for maximum effect?"

"That's what I mean about not being part of NATO."

"No again! NATO sticks together, that's what we're in it for. These people are our friends, we trust them."

Wainscott held his head in his hands. "Oh my God, David, what do we do? What do we do?"

— CHAPTER 11 —

Washington, 19th May, 3:30 a.m.

The telephone chirruped softly in the night. Curled up beside his wife, President Patrick Mallory was breathing easily, rhythmically, before he opened his eyes and the rhythm stopped. The telephone chirruped again, insistently. With a minimum of fuss, so as not to awaken the First Lady, Mallory sat up and brought the one-piece set quickly to his ear.

"Mallory."

"Mr. President, Arn here. I was afraid I might wake you, but this may be important. You remember this *Saturn* thing that came up this morning?"

"Uh huh."

"Well, there's been a big bang up there in the Barents Sea. Something's gone up. Satellite tells us there's a lot of radiation about. Pentagon's just woke me up, so I'm going over there, see what it's all about. Thought I ought to tell you, that's all.''

Fuzzily, Mallory shook his head, trying to recall what had been said about *Saturn* during the day. ''This happened in *Saturn*'s area? Any idea what went up?''

''No, Mr. President. *Saturn* could well have been in the area, but we've no idea what actually went up.''

''OK. Tell me as soon as you know, will you? Thanks for the call.''

''Sure thing. I hope I haven't spoiled your sleep. Good night.''

''Night, Arn, thanks.''

Mallory put the phone down and lay on his back, thinking, before an uneasy sleep overtook him.

Twenty minutes later the phone rang again. Mallory cursed mildly as he turned over to reach for it.

''Mr. President?''

''Arn. What's the news?''

''Looks like the Soviets are winding up the operation: the choppers are returning to the carrier, submarines surfacing, that sort of thing. In which case it could be that that British nuke's not coming home.''

''Oh.'' Mallory thought for a moment. ''Problem solved, then?''

''Sadly. Could be that the Soviets have got something with that ultra sonar thing of theirs. In which case it is 'sadly.' Feel bad about the submarine, though, may've been the best we had.''

''Sure, but that can wait until the morning, can't it?''

''Sure thing, Mr. President, sorry to be troubling you.''

''Don't mention it, Arn.''

He replaced the phone and shuffled down inside the bedclothes. Carol stirred beside him. ''What is it, honey?''

''Nothing, Hon, nothing that can't wait 'til the morning. Go back to sleep.''

Carol sighed and slipped back to her dreams. Mallory squirmed for a moment, before he dropped off, too.

But they were not due for an easy night. At five-thirty the telephone burst into life again, bringing him quickly out of a dreamless sleep.

''Mallory.''

"Arn here, Mr. President." Mallory sat up, catching the edge in Winters's voice. "Er, they're continuing their search up there, in the Barents Sea. Choppers're strung out again, but we were only able to detect three submarines diving. Mr. President, if that was a *Soviet* nuke that went up . . . and if it was *Saturn* that did it, I don't think the Soviets are going to be any too pleased."

"Goddamn right they won't."

"So I feel that, as a precaution, we should order a Primary Alert for all NATO forces. . . ."

"Now hold it right there. We don't want to overreact." Mallory had swung his legs out of bed.

"Mr. President, if a NATO nuclear submarine has taken out a Soviet one, and if the Soviets know that's what happened or even think so . . . well, that's a warlike act. And I'm suggesting this merely as a precaution."

"Oh, shit! OK then, you order the Alert. I'll get hold of Wainscott right now, see if I can find out what the hell's going on over there."

Mallory did not like American soldiers, as part of NATO, being put on Primary Alert because of some ineptness on the part of one of his allies. Moreover, he found Wainscott totally lost, unable to think constructively, and not having a clue as to what he should be doing. So he was a little sharp with him, though he didn't feel any better for it.

He also called Carl Zimmerman and charged him with informing the rest of the leaders of the NATO member nations.

Feeling nervous, Mallory got up, washed and, halfway through shaving, called the White House duty officer. He ordered him to convene a meeting of the National Security Council, as soon as possible, downstairs in the Oval Office. And he wanted his chiefs of staff waiting in the ante-room: they were going to be needed for military advice.

The United States National Security Council consists of the president, the vice president, the secretary of state, the secretary of defense, and the director of emergency operations. In the past American presidents had varied enormously in how they used the Council, but Mallory was a firm believer in it: five heads were better than one, and in a crisis, more would be cumbersome. His vice president was Sam Freeman, a cultured negro from Atlanta, and his director of emergency planning was Ralph Carstairs, an able administrator who had worked his way up through the Defense Department before taking on the job, at Mallory's request.

Mallory was doing up his tie when the telephone rang again. This time he snatched it up, beginning to feel hassled and wondering if he would ever get dressed.

"Yeah?"

"Mr. President, Arn here. Yes, I'll be over shortly. Look, there's been another massive explosion up there. . . ."

"What! Whose?"

"We don't know. About the same size as the last one. Also there's one hell of a lot of radio traffic going on in Russia, and so far as we can tell, most of it's military command traffic. . . ."

"What are they saying?"

"We don't know. It's all in code."

"Oh, shit!" Mallory used the expletive to vent his feelings. He then saw his wife's concerned expression. A breakfast tray had been brought in, and she was in the middle of pouring coffee. Some of it had spilt. He glanced at his watch. "When can you be here?"

"It's still early. Fifteen, maybe twenty minutes."

"OK. Look, I want you to put out a Red Alert. Yes, the works, and then get your ass over here as fast as you can."

"Right, Mr. President."

He slammed the phone down, feeling a flutter in his chest that spelt nerves. Carol passed him a slice of toast and jam, but he couldn't thank her before the phone rang again. Carl Zimmerman had been trying to raise the Soviet Embassy in Washington, as well as the American ambassador in Moscow. There was no answer from the Soviet Embassy, and his own ambassador had nothing to tell him. It was a good twenty minutes before the telephone stopped ringing, and only then was Mallory able to put a second call through to Arthur Wainscott in London.

When that was over, and feeling even more irritated, he put on his jacket, gave his worried wife a peck on the cheek, and hurried out of the room, towards the noise of people downstairs.

There were possibly a dozen men waiting for him, and their chatter stopped the moment he appeared, leaving an uncertain silence. Nobody wanted to wish the president ''good morning,'' partly because it might sound frivolous and partly because there was nothing good about it anyway.

Mallory caught the mood, and felt the need to reassure them.

''Good morning, gentlemen. This is a day for Valium, isn't it? Thank you for coming.'' Nobody laughed, but he sensed their faces softening a little, and he knew his feeble joke had helped.

He acknowledged his chiefs of staff and told them to wait while he showed the four Security Council members into the Oval Office. The others were members of the White House Staff, and they disappeared to their own offices.

The telephone was ringing even as he entered the Oval Office. Mallory swore obscenely at the interruption, furious that he was unable to get down to business when time was so short. He grabbed the receiver and shouted down it.

''Yes?''

And as he listened, the colour drained from his face, leaving his eyes dark and hollow, his cheeks drawn. The men stood silently waiting like statues in the dawn, straining to catch what was being said at the other end. Softly, Mallory cradled the receiver and faced his Council.

''Gentlemen, take a seat. There's coffee on the side.'' Nobody move, so Mallory continued. ''That was the Pentagon. Fredenberger's just phoned me direct. That son of a bitch on *Saturn* has just hit the *Kharkov* and knocked out two ASW helicopters as well. Fredenberger tells me that *Saturn* hit the *Kharkov*'s bridge. . . . Gentlemen,'' he whispered, ''we are in trouble.''

There was no reply. Each man was shaken and, as the shock wore off, began thinking, retreating into his own thoughts. Mallory walked over to the side-table where coffee had been laid out, helped himself, and sat down. The others followed suit.

Mallory stirred his coffee noisily, and when they were all seated, put his spoon down and called the meeting to order. ''Arn, what would you do if the Russians did that to us?''

The old-fashioned clock on the mantelpiece was ticking, and the ticking seemed to get louder with every second that Winters delayed his reply. They all felt there wasn't much time.

Winters appeared unperturbed. ''Wrong question, Mr.

President. The Soviets don't think like we do. And we've got a few minutes to talk this one out. All Soviet forces are on maximum alert, but nobody over there is going to act on his own initiative. Everything goes back to Moscow. Moscow will want to know what happened. Then Moscow will think, and then Moscow will act. At this moment in time I should imagine they will be trying to find out exactly what happened up there.''

Mallory's voice was still soft, but exasperation was creeping in. ''They know damn well what happened up there. They lost . . .''

''They don't know how or why they lost them. Those forces should have been ample, in their minds, to take *Saturn* out. They didn't, and Moscow will want to know why.''

''And then?''

''And then, or meanwhile: they've lost a lot of face; they'll want to get that back.''

Zimmerman spoke up. ''I'd like to stress that point. They'll want to save face for three powerful reasons: to convince their own people they are strong, to convince the Warsaw Pact countries they are strong and to show the outside world, especially China, that they are strong. Most important of all these will be convincing their own people.''

''So?''

''So they'll most probably overreact.''

''Ah,'' said Mallory, ''now we're coming to it. And what sort of overreaction do you think that will be? We already know they're on maximum alert, what next?''

Winters replied. ''I had a word this morning with the planning officer on the team from Joint Staff we put on to it yesterday. He reckons they'll want ten for one. There were about two hundred men on each of those Victors and probably another two hundred have lost their lives on the *Kharkov*. So we can expect a retaliatory strike involving six thousand men or so, and a lot of military hardware.''

''Six thousand, huh?'' Mallory nodded his head, suspecting this sort of an answer, but equally shaken by its impact. ''Sounds like an aircraft carrier. And what do they suppose we're going to do about it? Lie down and take it, trying not to flinch? Turn the other cheek like we're told in Sunday school? I think we all know that our people, our public, won't take it. And Congress won't take it. They'll demand action, and get it, even if it means hounding me out of here. And I dread the consequences.''

"It won't necessarily be our aircraft carrier." Freeman's soft southern drawl stayed the unease. "Why should it be? After all, it's a British submarine that's caused all the trouble.''

"Don't count on it," replied Mallory. "As far as they're concerned, *Saturn* is a NATO submarine. They'll try and hit NATO where it hurts, because they're looking for effect, tangible, visible effect that's going to stun the world. So it could well be one of ours. Even if it isn't, NATO is NATO, and we would be obliged to assist the country that has been attacked, otherwise the pact crumbles, and the Soviets will have achieved more in two weeks than they've done in twenty years. Isn't that right?''

The four men nodded.

"So how are we going to play it when they do whatever it is they're going to do? It may come today, accompanied by a torrent of propaganda which, because it will contain some elements of truth, will be very difficult to deny. Gentlemen, I need answers, and quick!''

Their apprehension deepened as, one by one, they came back from their thoughts and turned to Dr. Winters. Mallory sensed too that he was the only one who could reply. "Arn?''

"Mr. President, there are three options. Firstly, as you yourself mentioned, is to do nothing. That's always an option. But in doing nothing you will be seen as unwilling or unable to defend the United States and/or her allies. We know our forces have the ability, so there would be immense pressure to force you out and install somebody who will react. What I'm saying is that it will be very difficult to make the 'do nothing' option stick.

"The second option is a tactical limited response, restricted to conventional weapons. What sort of response? An eye for an eye, a tooth for a tooth? That would only provoke them into a third response, and willy-nilly we'll find ourselves being sucked into a war, and one where there will be no winners, only losers.

"The third option, and we have people on the other side of the Potomac who are pushing for it right now, is to pre-empt them. Because if whatever we do in response is going to lead to war, then as I say, it's a war we can't win. But if we hit them first, and hit them really hard, with everything we've got, then there's a chance we might get away with it. The one thing we cannot do is allow ourselves to drift into a war.''

With that Mallory exploded. ''Dammit, Arn, we're looking for a way out. We don't want a war, the Russians don't want a war, nobody wants a war. There must be some other alternative.''

''Well, if that's the case, why don't you try talking to the man?''

''Who? Kirov?''

''Sure.''

''Well, what the hell am I supposed to say to him? 'Please don't try and strike back. They didn't mean it, so sorry, I promise they won't do it again'? He can't let it rest at that, no way. Just like us, his own people won't let him.''

A sinister thought began to creep into Winters's mind, a thought he found so compelling that he felt obliged to speak out. ''Mr. President, I don't believe the Soviets can make a clean retaliatory response.''

''What do you mean?''

''Well, you suggested an aircraft carrier, which I think is most unlikely. But supposing it is to be an aircraft carrier. All our forces are on Red Alert. There's no way they can attack an aircraft carrier, without that aircraft carrier fighting back. American or British, I can't see any captain and crew not defending themselves.''

''So supposing they try something else. Move into West Berlin, for instance. Again, very messy. Block the Straits of Hormuz. . . .''

''No,'' Zimmerman was quick to interrupt. ''They'd make more enemies than friends that way. It's self-defeating.''

''Yes, of course. But that's the point I'm making: what sort of a retaliatory response can they make that *won't* get messy?''

''Supposing,'' Zimmerman was speculating, ''supposing they launched one, just one ICBM against some outlying base. Say, Ascension Island, because it's British.''

Winters shook his head. ''No, not an ICBM. They know that if they launch one of those, we will know from the moment it goes up, even if we don't know its destination. They know we will have to respond before it lands. No, not an ICBM. My betting is that they'll try to engineer a situation that'll really piss us off, but a situation we can do nothing about.''

Mallory growled. ''You mean they'll try and provoke us into doing something?''

''Maybe. The point I'm making is that their response alone can lead to a war, irrespective of what we decide.'' He stopped, thinking, before adding pointedly, ''I wonder if the Soviets have thought of that?''

''Ah,'' interjected Freeman, suddenly inspired. ''If they have thought of all this, and I'm sure they must have, then supposing they claimed something from us diplomatically?''

''Nope, I'm sorry, Sam, it can't work. Remember, the Brits never admitted it was their submarine, so there's no way the diplomats can even start negotiating. Besides, Russia has to act quickly, within twenty-four hours at the most. She has no time for diplomats.'' Zimmerman shrugged his shoulders in apology.

The room fell silent again as each of the men brooded on his own thoughts and fears, not knowing how they were going to extract themselves from a predicament which had been brought on them by another nation, and because that nation was an ally, involved them totally.

At length Mallory spoke. ''Gentlemen, as I see it, the predictions are that the Soviet Union will react because she has to. Even though she will have no intention of starting a war, the odds are overwhelming that this reaction will cause one. Therefore we cannot afford to wait for something to happen, we must act first. . . .''

Freeman looked up, aghast. ''Christ, you don't mean. . . ?''

''No, no, nothing like that.'' Mallory smiled. ''Somehow we've got to draw the teeth out of the situation. What I'm saying is that it's up to us to act first to restore the status quo. There is no other alternative.'' His eyes fell on Winters. ''Arn, you're right. First we buy time, and I'll do this by calling President Kirov. What time is it in Moscow?''

Winters glanced at his watch. It said eight forty-five. He added another eight hours before replying, ''Sixteen forty-five.''

''Four forty-five in the afternoon, good.'' He reached for

the red telephone, and asked to be put through, person to person, to Kirov, the president of the Soviet Union.

The White House has its own team of Russian interpreters, and Mallory knew that they kept English interpreters in the Kremlin for precisely this sort of contingency. Whilst he waited, the ghost of a grim smile formed on his lips, reflecting his certainty that he had found a way to defuse the situation, and that he knew the words he would have to use when Kirov came on the line.

He could hear his own interpreter speaking, a pause and then speaking again. Finally the words were in English:

"I have President Kirov for you now, Mr. President."

"President Kirov?"

"*Da*. President Mallory?"

"*Da*, I mean yes. President Kirov, we believe we know what happened in the Barents Sea today." He heard the words being put into Russian, and Kirov's reply.

"*Da*."

Mallory continued. "Mr. President, we suspect you may be planning some form of response, possibly military." He waited as the interpreter took over. The soft Russian consonants were almost musical, lulling him as he heard his sentence being translated. Suddenly they stopped and the line was silent.

"Yes, Mr. President? President Kirov is waiting." It was the interpreter.

"We feel we understand the position as much as you do. I must tell you that we do not condone what may have happened in the Barents Sea, and if anything, we are more distressed about it than you are." The interpreter took over, and Mallory waited patiently for him to finish. He had a shrewd idea that Kirov understood English anyway.

"President Kirov, if you will give me twenty-four hours, I believe I can provide a solution which will be acceptable to both of us."

This time the silence at the other end was so long that Mallory thought he had been cut off. Then he heard voices in Russian, and knew for sure that Kirov was consulting his advisors. They spoke in muted tones, but sounded urgent nonetheless. Eventually they stopped and he heard Kirov's hoarse voice, rasping down the phone.

"Horoshoa. Dradshatshetiry shaca." Good, twenty-four hours.

"Thank you, Mr. President. Within twenty-four hours I shall call you back. Goodbye."

Mallory heard Kirov's muffled *"do svidanya,"* and he knew he had won the reprieve, even before the interpreter began his task. Inside, he was overjoyed.

But the men around him were still silent, clearly relieved at the respite, but uncertain where to go next. Winters said so.

"Well done, Mr. President, you've given us the initiative. Now what are we going to do with it?"

In answer Mallory picked up the Military Command telephone and spoke to his operator. "Get me Admiral Joseph Fredenberger, COMSUBATLANT, at NATO Operations centre in London."

Frowning, Zimmerman stood up and walked towards him. "Mr. President, shouldn't you be calling Wainscott first, after all, it's his . . ."

"Screw Wainscott! I don't want to talk to the man. He's cost us enough already and he hasn't done diddley-shit to help. Fredenberger can tell him."

The west coast of Spitzbergen, with its wild, rugged coastline, its crashing seas and freezing, screaming winds, was the most easterly point Captain Chuck Benson had to traverse in his patrol of the Icelandic Gap. Chuck Benson was captain of the US submarine *Rosemont*, a "Los Angeles" class nuclear-powered hunter-killer submarine.

It had been a dull tour. They had spent five weeks moving from "A" to "B," monitoring the passage of other vessels, including Soviet submarines, and passing their positions back to US Navy Headquarters. From the day they left Philadelphia, they had been looking forward to going home, hoping their next voyage would involve them in an exercise with other vessels.

But finally something had come up. Off Spitzbergen, Benson received a message that was cryptic to say the least. It simply stated:

TO: USS ROSEMONT
FROM: CHIEF OF NAVAL OPERATIONS

PROCEED AT MAXIMUM SPEED TO POSITION 69'23 NORTH, 23'15 WEST, AND AWAIT FURTHER ORDERS.

Which he did. Mystery tours like this were nothing new to him: he would normally reach his position and find he was detailed to rendezvous with another US Navy vessel, or, if they were lucky, take part in some impromptu naval exercise. Except that this message had come from the chief of Naval Operations, the man in the Pentagon who directed all American Fleet movements, and he was surprised at the seniority, wondering why he alone should have been picked out for such individual attention.

Scratching his fuzzy crew-cut head, he opened a can of non-alcoholic root beer, and gave the order. And with thirty-five thousand shaft horsepower behind him, made remarkably good time, leaving Bear Island to port, and arriving at his new position in just seven hours. There, he came up to periscope depth, raised his radio mast, and awaited the next message, burning with curiosity to see what it was all about.

He did not have to wait long before the radio officer brought him the second message, and this one shook him.

TO: USS ROSEMONT
FROM: CHIEF OF NAVAL OPERATIONS
YOU ARE TO SEARCH LOCATE AND DESTROY NUCLEAR
SUBMARINE EXPECTED TO TRANSIT YOUR AREA 0100 TO
0200 HOURS.

And that was something he did not like, no sir. If Chuck Benson was going to start blowing submarines out of the water, he wanted to know whose they were, and why the orders had been given. Was this a Soviet nuke? If so, was this World War Three? And if it was somebody else's, what was it doing up there, and why the orders? Hell, he should have had a proper briefing for a mission like this, not just two short radio messages. That is, unless they were at war, and if they were, his radio operator would have told him. Hell, if there was a war on there'd have been Soviet nukes all over the place, and he'd have been told, so what the hell was going on? He called the radio shack.

"That last message you gave me. Have it verified.":

"Aye, aye, sir."

He opened another can of root beer and lit a cigarette whilst he waited, brooding over the terse instructions that had come without any explanation at all.

"Cap'n, sir, Radio Room."

"Cap'n."

"We have the reply."

"Bring it up."

The radio operator arrived with his signal pad, and tore off the top sheet. Benson took it from him, and read:

TO: USS ROSEMONT
FROM: PRESIDENT OF THE UNITED STATES
ACT AS ORDERED.

"Phewee!" He turned to his chief executive officer, Philip Sanders. "Hey, Phil, take a gander at these, will you?"

Sanders leant back, stretching out his arm to take the two messages. Impassively he read them both through, his face quite still. Eventually he shivered and passed them back.

"Orders is orders. You got 'em, we do 'em. Wonder what sort of a nuke she is."

"We'll find out."

They waited. Steadily the square green digits on the control room clock passed zero one hundred. Benson became morose, snapping his commands at the men around him, reading and re-reading the sweat-soiled messages in his hand. He drank coffee, chain-smoked, and his morbidity infected the crew, so that though they executed his commands quickly enough, there was a fractious tone in their replies: if Chuck Benson didn't like what they were going to have to do, they didn't like it either.

The minutes crept by, agonizingly slowly, until at last they reached zero two hundred hours. Phil Sanders sighed as he swung round on his seat and faced his captain. "Guess that's it, sir."

"No it isn't. The man said 'expected.' I'll give it another hours, and then radio again."

"Aye, aye, sir." Sanders turned back to his console and

began paring his nails. He didn't like the orders, and he didn't like the waiting. It was becoming a very long watch.

At two thirty-six the intercom crackled into life.

"Cap'n, sir, Sonar. We have a contact, bearing one seven zero. . . . Classified nuclear submarine. Computer trace shows she's British."

"Roger, Sonar." Chuck Benson became even more unsure of himself, but shit, he had the two messages, and the orders came from the president himself, so what the hell could he do but . . .

His voice was weary and sullen as he turned to Sanders.

"OK, Exec., sound Action Stations, start the attack computer."

Saturn was hurt. The maximum speed she could safely manage was twelve knots. Henderson could not increase this speed, for fear that the damage to the fin would cause her to cavitate again and betray her passage through waters that could still be hostile. Though they had escaped the *Kharkov*'s area a good eight hours previously, the watch remained closed up with the crew at action stations. The men were beginning to breathe more easily now, suspecting that at last they were out of the net which had once been closed so tightly around them.

It was like surfacing from a bad dream. The noise of depth charges had ceased, the reports from sonar were continually negative, proving that they were alone in the deep, and Henderson's commands had become routine again. And like the sleeper who wakens from a nightmare, realizing that it was, after all, only a dream, their nerves were still on edge and their fear was still very real.

At one o'clock in the morning, Henderson gave the order to clear stern arcs. Sonar reported no contacts, and two minutes later, Bayliss, the weapons electrical officer, entered the control room. He asked Henderson for permission to carry out work on the sonar transducer amplifiers: the repairs they had done previously were not permanent, and he wanted the time to fix them properly. He estimated that two hours should be enough, and then they would have maximum sonar cover to help them transit through the busy Norwegian Sea with its trawlers and freighters.

Thoughtfully, Henderson stepped aside to check his position on the Navigational Plot. They had left the Barents Depression, and the depth beneath *Saturn*'s keel was diminishing. On the other hand they were two hundred miles west of the position where they had fired at the *Kharkov*. Since then, Sonar had not detected a single sonobuoy transmission, nor anything that sounded remotely like a submarine or warlike vessel. Theoretically, the sea should be empty, certainly for the next two hours, and if the Soviets were looking for him, it was highly unlikely that they would find *Saturn* now. So Henderson gave his permission and Bayliss acknowledged gratefully.

Without sonar, *Saturn* was blind. It was a weird and uncomfortable sensation, a calculated risk, but Henderson understood that sonar repairs had to be done somewhat between here and home, and here was certainly the best place to do them. Added to this, Henderson knew that unless he ordered some of the men on watch to stand down from action stations, there was nothing he could do to prevent them from falling asleep at their positions. He studied the crew around him, noting their drawn faces, the worn black smudges around reddened eyes, and the stubble beards that now darkened their cheeks, making them parodies of the crisp team of officers and men they had been when they had set sail only four days previously. They were sagging: now that they felt themselves away from immediate danger, the adrenaline that had kept them going for so long had vanished, leaving them prey to the devastating fatigue that was creeping over them, threatening their collapse. He knew they would be unable to respond to another challenge.

"Number One."

"Sir?" Sykes looked at him bleakly.

"Stand down those who are least able to remain on watch. Let them get some rest."

"Aye, aye, sir." There was a depth of understanding in Sykes's reply.

"I'm going to my cabin. You take the con. Call me in two hours, or as soon as the repairs are completed."

"Aye, aye, sir."

Henderson withdrew to his cabin, peeled off his shoes and

gently massaged his swollen feet. Finally he lay on his back and closed his eyes.

Howarth stumbled to his own bunk beside the wardroom, and collapsed in it fully dressed. For a brief moment he thought of home in Sussex, his mother, full of concern and attention, always adoring him, and his father, whose piercing eyes always seemed to see through him, and he knew he would meet those eyes when they next met, and they would enjoy each other's company. Sleep flooded over him.

Sykes remained at the Systems Console, but without sonar, and with course, engine speed and depth set, there was little to occupy him. The steward brought him coffee, and for the first time during the voyage he allowed his mind to wander. Penny was talking to him, showing him all the things in the garden that had grown whilst he was away, leading him on to the rose beds where he hoped he would be able to see the first buds on *Rosa Penelope*, which apart from its name, he loved for its crinkly pale lemon flowers and its fine scent. He found himself looking forward to being home again, and as he sipped from the plastic mug, felt a craving for real coffee from real china cups.

Henderson found that the sleep he needed so much would not come. Instead he found his mind wandering, becoming hyperactive as he thought through the events of the past sixty hours, from finding himself boxed in, from the shock of the first ASROC attacks, to the first moment they had been fired on by a torpedo and realized that somebody on the surface wanted *Saturn* sunk. Could he have played it differently? Had there been an alternative means of escape? No, their main search had been to the west of him. Then had he been too hasty in firing his Stingfish missiles at the *Kharkov*? No again, they were not going to let him go. He had had no alternative but to stop them, otherwise it would have meant certain death for *Saturn* and her crew.

What were London thinking? That strange man Hythe, and Fredenberger whom he wasn't so sure he trusted, what would they think now? Was this what they had planned? Had they concealed something from him in the Intelligence briefing? Now it seemed evident that they had, for the

Soviets were waiting, determined to force him to the surface, or, as it appeared, determined to sink him. There was all the difference between that and simply being detected.

As a result of which he had been forced to do things, yes, forced, which . . . dear God, Russia! The Soviets weren't going to take this lying down. Bloody hell, their General Staff must have exploded when they heard the news. They'll do something, Jesus, they'll have to. I wonder . . . Christ no, but they were, they were definitely waiting for us. Was *Saturn* sent up there to provoke something? Was Fredenberger a hawk, anxious to provoke Russia into starting the final showdown? Was that why he didn't like him?

No. That's ridiculous. Fredenberger was very anxious that they did just the opposite. Then why all the provisions and this full warload? If you're given a full warload, then you must be expected to use it in certain circumstances, so was this one of them? Had they planned for this? Or somebody else, Hardy perhaps? No, that's again ridiculous, that man was as honest and straightforward as the day is long. Then the prime minister, Wainscott? He signed the Mission Order, he knew what was going on, but dammit, the man was an out-and-out pacifist. Perhaps Hythe then, but for what possible motive?

The Soviets were going to want reprisals, savage ones, Henderson realized. He couldn't see them sitting back, not after the pasting *Saturn* had given them. Christ, their admirals and generals would be smarting. They'd hit back all right, but where?

He didn't think he and his crew were going to be loved when they got back to Faslane, not by anyone, but hell, what options did they have?

Faslane. His thoughts turned to Karen, with her laughing blue eyes, her long fair wispy hair, and Skip, running crazily along the beach, holding a crab tightly in front of him, running towards him, shouting with excitement. . . .

And then there was nothing.

Twelve miles to the west, the United States submarine *Rosemont* came up to periscope depth and raised her radio mast. The message she transmitted was very short and simple. It read:

TO: CHIEF OF NAVAL OPERATIONS
FROM: USS ROSEMONT

MISSION ACCOMPLISHED.

— EPILOGUE —

Murmansk, 18th June

It was quite warm. The ever-present arctic sun had heated up the sea and earth, giving a comfortable seventy-two degrees in the shade. The men in the dry dock were working in their shirtsleeves, cheerful and efficient. They knew it could equally well rain the next day, with the temperature dropping to the low forties. It often happened that way. For the present all was well: they had plenty of work to do, and the flies were not yet a nuisance.

Few of the workers paid any attention to the six-man delegation picking its way through the dockyard. They had seen high-ranking officials before. Whilst what they said and did might affect the yard management, it would never affect them: they were too far removed in the yard's personnel structure. So they hammered and welded and clanked and drilled, their noise combining with the size of the structure around them to make the men in the delegation seem insignificant.

Viktor Nikolev paused by the basin that held the *Kharkov*, gesticulating at her black, torn and twisted superstructure. "They still haven't told me what to do with her yet. We put her here because we wanted to remove the ultra sonar nacelle. If they do want her repaired, well, we can do it, but I don't see the point. Far better to have her towed to the steelworks; they can use scrap over there. By all accounts she was a sloppy ship at sea, and I believe the architects at Nikolayev South have developed a far more positive design for an anti-submarine carrier. I must say, though, we certainly weren't expecting to have her back so soon. It is you, Admiral, who decides what we're to do with her?"

"Eh?" Belinski started, not having heard a word of what the shipyard director had been saying, instead mesmerized by the tangled and twisted iron girders which at one time had been part of the ship's bridge.

"I said, Comrade Admiral, is it you who decides what happens to this? She should be scrapped, you know. At all events, she can't stay in this dock forever. That's valuable workspace she's occupying."

"Oh, yes. I mean no. It is a difficult decision. There are some people who would like her repaired and then transferred to the Baltic Fleet. Besides, the Baltic's much more stable, unlike the Barents Sea, don't get such a big swell there. She'll be fine there."

"Just as you say, Admiral, but somebody's got to tell me. Now, if you'll all follow me . . ." He strode off, knowing that they had to have someone to lead them, and making sure that no time was being wasted in idle dawdling. They crossed through rows of packing cases until they reached another basin. Here, the long hull of a submarine was supported in a cradle by numerous wooden cross beams. Men were already working on her bows with laser cutters. Nikolev waited impatiently for the men to gather round. He took Belinski by the arm, but watched the others while he spoke, including them in the conversation.

"This one must be very special to you, Admiral. You remember the *Vladimir*?" The others smiled. Vladimir was not only a large town between Moscow and Gorky, it was also Belinski's first name. "As you can see, it's a tricky job. Should be another two months before she's ready. That's with working three shifts. So far she's coming along nicely. I hope it's going to be worth the effort."

Professor Uvarov put on as brave a face as he could. "I think you will find that with the alterations we've made . . ." He looked around nervously. "I think she'll operate effectively."

"A good word, Professor." Rodichev's tone was distinctly chilling. "For your sake I hope she does."

Belinski paid no attention to the remarks. Instead, bafflement was clouding his face as he studied the *Vladimir*. Eventually he spoke. "One thing concerns me: why are you putting it in a submarine and not another- anti-submarine carrier? I would have thought that with the added advantage of helicopters to deal with the target while it is still out of range . . ."

"Yes, point taken," Uvarov replied. "But it is a question of dimensionality. A ship can only move forwards or backwards, and is restricted on speed when operating ultra sonar, and the helicopters can only search where they are directed. A submarine does not have these restrictions, and of course operates beneath the surface, which is where our prey is. We will be able to detect another submarine long before it can detect us. We can integrate our torpedoes with the ultra sonar so that they will home in only on a hostile sound signature, and not be misled by decoys. So you will see the advantages of placing ultra sonar in a submarine rather than a surface vessel."

Belinski scratched the back of his head. He didn't like the idea of the Northern Banner Fleet being reduced to a handful of submarines to do the job of surface vessels. "You're sure all this is going to work?"

"No. As I explained last time, we need trials. We need to test the whole thing out. But please, Admiral, not on real live hostile targets. That's not testing, that's using . . ." He stopped, cowed by Belinski's chilling glance.

Nikolev permitted himself a smile, but wiped it off when he saw the other serious faces. Rodichev stepped aside, taking Kirienko, the KGB colonel, by the arm. "Colonel, has the security been tightened up in the yard now, for this sort of development?"

"Yes, it has, Comrade Director. Those Karelians were the only ones. We've been through the whole workforce with a fine tooth comb. There will be no more security leaks. I think it most unfortunate that Captain Kaledin was caught out the way he was. We have now tightened up the whole recruiting procedure and all workers will be vetted on an annual basis. I am sure that nothing like that will happen again."

Belinski overheard them. He called over to Rodichev. "And that yard in England, Comrade, Kender's I think you said, are we able to get better information on them now?"

Rodichev grimaced. "Yes, the information is better. By the way, it's Kendall's, and they are in Scotland, not

England. The difference is quite important. Kendall are a private company, and their workers are dedicated capitalists, not one of them is enlightened, which makes it particularly difficult for us. However, they also have their disaffected elements. There are people there who would like Scotland to become an independent nation. Admittedly they are reactionaries, their prime motive being greed for the oil which England steals from them, and sells at an enormous profit to the rest of the world. These people do not know it is us they are helping, but we now know the yard is preparing another submarine, identical to the last." He turned back to Uvarov. "So ultra sonar had better be ready to deal with the threat."

Uvarov understood the challenge. "Two months, Director, two months and the *Vladimir* will be ready for trials."

Belinski nodded. Rodichev was satisfied. He drew his tie up neatly and pulled down his cuffs. "Then I think that's about all, then. Does anybody else have questions?"

Nobody did. They all followed Nikolev towards the main gates.

Belinski caught up with Rodichev in the car park, beside his shiny black Zil. "How are things in Britain these days?"

Rodichev seemed surprised. "Why, Admiral, haven't you been reading your newspapers? There's an election going on. They're voting today."

"Ah." Belinski opened the car door for him. They could hear a siren wailing from back in the yard. "They're strange, these western democracies, always elections, most unstable. You never know where you are. They should try a democracy like ours." He indicated the grey hordes of workers swarming neatly through the gates. "See, it works."